Dangerous Decisions

Evie Jacobs

DANGEROUS DECISIONS

CHAPTER 1

Taking a day off from work would be difficult.

A week would be painful.

But a *month*? Brutal.

Angie Liu's gaze swept over her tiny office. Each morning when she stepped into the lobby of the George Bush Center for Intelligence, her skin prickled with anticipation. This forced leave of absence was going to suck the life out of her.

Four whole weeks. Sleeping late, wearing pajamas all day, staring at the TV like the living dead. Her mouth went dry. No, thank you.

Movement beyond the glass wall of her office caught her eye. Henry, the only other Asian American analyst in the department, leaned around the doorjamb and stuck his head inside the room. "See you Monday, Ange."

"Nope." She shook her head. "I'm banished for the next month. Won't be back until after the holidays."

"Right." A smirk played on his lips. "Man, what I wouldn't give for a month off, especially this time of year. I could never accrue that much PTO."

Of course he couldn't. He had a life. A family. They did things. Like a one-week vacation at Disney World last March.

Standing, she grabbed the box of gourmet candy canes a colleague had given her and took it around the desk. "Do you think your girls would like these?"

"Absolutely. They're fans of anything with sugar." He took the carton and looked inside. "I might snag the cherry for myself."

"Go for it."

Henry held up the candy. "Happy holidays."

"Give my best to the family."

He rapped his knuckles on the door frame, gave her the finger gun, and disappeared down the hall.

The ticking of the second hand pulled her eyes to the wall clock. Quarter-to-five on a Friday. Any minute now, colleagues would pour from their offices, eager to start the weekend. Sometimes she wished she could be more like everyone else. But any chance at a normal life fled when she was fourteen years old.

She returned to her desk and plopped into her chair. The kaleidoscope pattern surged and swelled across her monitor, a perfect representation of what she expected from this forced holiday. Her life for the next month was a screensaver. Repetitive. Compulsory. Endless.

A soft knock on the open door drew her attention. Gary, her supervisor and the closest thing to a friend she'd had in years, stood at the threshold. He was also the reason she'd been forced into six hundred seventy-two hours of paid leave.

He stepped into the room. His cologne—a fresh scent of citrus with a touch of musk—wafted in with him. "It's nearly five. You should get out of here." He hummed and mimicked a hula dance.

When she didn't answer, he fell into the chair across from her.

Instinctively, her right hand reached for the manila folder on the corner of her desk. A classic subconscious defense mechanism. She regretted the motion the moment her fingers made contact. Gary's gaze fell to her hand. God. She hated being so transparent.

He pursed his lips. "You need to let it go."

She pushed her tongue into her cheek and shook her head. If only it were that easy. "How? It's my fault."

He leaned back and laced his hands behind his head. They'd had this conversation before. Many times. "Informants get burned. Sometimes they get killed. It's an unfortunate part of the job. And this one might have been an accident."

"It wasn't, and you know it." She wedged her thumb under the clip of a pen, remembering the moment she learned the plane had been found at the bottom of the Caribbean. "He was different."

Gary tugged on his purposely windswept hair and scrubbed a hand over his jaw. "The only thing different is you made it personal."

"He deserved better." She tried to control the quaver in her voice. In her mind's eye, she pictured Rick Hughes, with his graying temples, weathered skin, and kind eyes. She didn't tend to interact with assets but had been drawn to Rick and his corny dad jokes from the moment they met. The agency psychologist would have plenty to say about that.

Gary leaned forward, forcing her to meet his eyes. "He was a criminal. Working with us kept him out of jail. Don't get sentimental and start thinking he had some unselfish motive. He needed us as much as we needed him."

"Except his crimes were years ago. For the last two decades, he'd been a model citizen."

"A model citizen living under an assumed identity."

"To protect himself and his kids." No matter how many times they had this conversation, she couldn't shake that useless feeling. She'd failed Rick. To everyone else, he'd been just another confidential informant. Only Angie remembered he was a human being. "We have to find out what happened."

"You liked the man. His death hurt. I get it. But there's nothing else for us to do."

"How about investigating? Isn't that our job?"

"Our allegiance is to the Constitution, not to an individual citizen. You know that."

Her head throbbed. They could go in circles all day. "Don't you have a happy hour to get to?"

Though past forty and graying, Gary was single and still garnered a ridiculous amount of female attention. On a typical Friday night out, women flocked to him like tourists to the Lincoln Memorial.

He pulled on the knot of his Space Invaders tie. "No concrete plans. Thought maybe you'd join me." He hadn't invited her to happy hour for a long time. Certainly not since he became the Task Force Commander.

"Thanks, but I've got yoga at the gym. It's almost impossible to get a spot with this instructor."

"Really? The gym on a Friday night?" He cocked his head, his gaze scrutinizing. "Angie, you need to get a life."

"My life is fine." She prepared herself for a rebuttal about her sad, lonely existence but got only a loud huff.

He reached forward to rearrange the Ironman 70.3 coffee cup she used as a pencil holder and her Ruth Bader Ginsberg bobblehead. He tapped the toy, sending RBG's head into a happy shake.

"I'd hoped to tell you this after you had a couple, but since you're not going to cooperate—"

She stiffened. What other craptastic news could he pile onto this already shitty day?

"It's official. We got word today that the DEA is dropping the investigation in Jamaica. That means the inquiry into Rick's death is over. As far as they're concerned, he was a smuggler flying a plane filled with cocaine. The fact that he worked for them is irrelevant. It's done."

Angie chewed on her lip. A year had passed since Rick's plane ended up at the bottom of the Caribbean. In truth, she shouldn't be surprised the DEA ended the investigation. It was mostly for show anyway, but tanking the entire operation didn't make sense. "Are you sure?"

He nodded. "The decision is final."

So not only was she being told to drop it, but the DEA was done with it as well. She felt like a balloon about to pop. "But what about his family? They're supposed to believe he was a crook?"

"The DEA recruited him. It's their call." He pressed his hands into the arms of the chair. "There's nothing else for you to do."

Was he right? Should she let it go? "I know the arrangement. Doesn't make it okay."

He leaned forward, and dammit, he looked sincere. "If I had the authority to let you investigate, I would, but this one's above my pay grade."

"I can talk to Claudia." Surely the department chief could be made to see reason.

Gary shook his head and stood. "She's signed off on it too. When you get back, you'll have a new assignment." He shoved his hands into his pants pockets. "I'll see you four weeks from Monday."

Angie watched him leave, her frantic heart pounding into her throat. They'd destroyed a man's life. And for what?

Rick Hughes was the second person to die on her watch. The first had taught her that loving meant losing. The second? That she couldn't keep anyone safe.

CHAPTER 2

"**O**h my God, I won!" The woman three stools down clapped and shrieked and covered her mouth with her hands. The slot machine wailed, and the little beacon at the top flashed a blinding red light.

Angie shook her head and sighed. She wasn't sure which was worse. Her month-long exile or spending any of it in a casino balanced on the edge of a swamp. Right now, the spur-of-the-moment trip to Miami didn't seem like the bright idea she'd thought it was yesterday in her office.

Her current predicament sauntered to the middle of the aisle, positioning himself between the Wheel of Fortune and the Mega Bucks slot machines. He plucked the Florida Marlins cap from his head and rubbed sweaty hair from his brow with the back of his hand. The smell of stale beer wafted off him as he replaced the cap and offered a smarmy grin.

Angie rolled her eyes upward, wishing a grappling hook would drop from the ceiling and carry her away. All she'd wanted was a simple distraction, something to take her mind off the impulsive decision to disobey orders. Twenty dollars or thirty minutes of video poker—whichever came first. Then, up to her room for an early bedtime.

Gary had forced her into this vacation. So what if she chose to spend it working on a case? That was her business. As were the consequences if she was caught. A reprimand for sure, but more likely, she'd be demoted, might even lose her security clearance. Or worse—her job.

Now this jerk stood in front of her with a chubby arm stretched out like a blockade. A boot to the groin wasn't an option. She glanced at the domed video camera monitoring the floor. She could see the headline: *CIA Officer Incapacitates Fat Redneck in Florida Casino.* Definitely out of the question. She was already headed for Gary's shit list if he found out what she had planned, especially since he'd explicitly told her to let it go.

Impulse control had been one of the action items on her last evaluation. Of course, if she cared about performance metrics, she wouldn't be anywhere near the Key Largo airline owned by the offspring of a deceased asset, and she certainly wouldn't be conducting an unauthorized investigation.

"Come on, baby. One drink. I promise I'll make it worth your while." The weasel licked his lips and waggled his eyebrows. If anyone deserved an elbow to the face, it was this guy.

She eyed a half-empty glass of amber liquid abandoned beside one of the machines. Tossing it at him would feel incredible—for about three seconds—but not worth the complications that would follow. "While I appreciate your offer, I need to get going." She tried to scoot past him without touching the pale white stomach poking out from beneath the bottom of a floral print shirt.

"Hey now." He leaned in, his pungent breath warm and wet. "At least give me a chance."

Sometimes you had to put a dipshit in his place. She opened her mouth to do just that, but her eyes snagged on six-plus feet of lean muscle striding their way. Rigid posture. Close-cropped dark-brown hair.

Great. Just what she needed. Captain America barreling through the cruise ship set, swooping in to save the day.

Damsel in distress was not a role she could fake with any conviction.

She gripped the sweaty arm of the loudmouth still blocking her exit. "You need to leave." She added a lilt of urgency to her voice. "Now."

"Why? Wh— what's happening?" He started to turn.

"My husband is coming." Her would-be savior stalked their way. "He looks angry."

The guy tugged his shirt over his belly and gripped the back of a chair for balance. "That's your husband?"

She nodded.

The man had an athletic build and broad shoulders. His stomach and pecs flexed beneath his plain gray tee. Taking in that scowl, combined with the brows drawn together and narrowed eyes, angry husband seemed entirely plausible. He wore black cargo pants and a pair of all-black skateboard shoes.

"Nemo," Cargo Pants growled, his deep, resonant voice cutting through the relentless hum of the casino. "What do you think you're doing?"

Angie tried to send her defender a message with her eyes. *Please, play along.* "Oh, honey, I'm so glad you're here. I was coming to meet you when this gentleman offered to buy me a drink and wouldn't take no for an answer."

His left eyebrow quirked. "Is that so?" He turned his attention to the other man. "Didn't make enough of a menace of yourself at the poker table?"

"Look, guy," Nemo stammered. "It's been a bad day. I thought spending time with a pretty lady would help. I didn't know she was with you. I swear."

Angie moved to her rescuer's side. He draped an arm across her shoulders.

"Consider yourself informed." He straightened to his full height.

Nemo took a step back and lost a dirty flip-flop when he collided with one of the stools in front of a poker machine. He pushed the shoe back onto his foot and scurried away. Angie snorted. God help the next poor, unsuspecting woman who landed on his radar.

The man removed his arm, taking the pleasant warmth he radiated with it.

"Thanks for following my lead." The fluttering of her pulse was unexpected. She tilted her head to study him. A total stranger, but somehow, she'd known she could trust him. And he hadn't disappointed her.

The furrowed brow disappeared. He smiled, a twinkle lighting up his brown eyes. "Something tells me you didn't actually need my help."

"Less violent than my other options." She shifted her purse from her right shoulder to her left. "So, you know that guy?"

"Not really." He gave a bemused shake of his head. "He sat next to me for a while during the poker tournament. Kind of an ass."

"You're telling me. Is his name really Nemo?"

"Nah, that's what we called him at the table. He's a fish."

Was she supposed to know what that meant?

"Poker slang. It means he's a shitty player."

"Clever." She rubbed moist hands on the back pockets of her jeans.

"I should mosey back to the game." He glanced at his watch. "Don't want them to start without me."

She stuck out her now-dry palm. "I'm Angie."

"Nate." He grasped her hand in a firm grip and gave it a brisk shake. "I'll probably be out of this thing before too long. Will you be around?"

"I was just heading to the blackjack table when the clownfish got in my way." *Blackjack?* Where had that come from?

"I'll look for you." He rocked back onto his heels. "If that's okay."

Gary's words about needing a life echoed in her head. "Sure. Why not?"

Patience. The cardinal rule of poker. Nate Hughes had honed his ability to wait for good starting hands and build his stack slowly. At the moment, patience was the last thing he felt. How could he think about Texas Hold 'Em when his gaze kept straying toward the blackjack tables?

Angie. Something about her commanded attention. He'd felt like a complete dumbass when he realized the last thing she needed—probably wanted—was a man to blow in and save the day. And yet, he couldn't regret the decision to intercede. Not after pulling her close and inhaling the most delightful fragrance—fresh cut grass mixed with a hint of citrus.

He blinked his attention back to the game where the recycled air of the casino blended with cheap perfume, stale cigarette smoke, and sweat.

He'd given two days of his life to this tournament. Winning came with a modest pot, but the real incentive was entry into the state championships. Nate had come close to qualifying three times, but only once did he earn an entry. Then his dad's plane disappeared, and his life turned upside down. The tournament came and went. He'd not even noticed.

This weekend offered a chance to try again.

Another round started. He tapped a chip against the soft green surface and rubbed his thumb back and forth against the disk's raised outer ring.

With his other hand, he slid the cards closer and flicked up the edge. An ace and a queen. Best hand of the night. Throwing down a hefty bet would narrow the competition. He pushed a stack of chips toward the center of the table. The player to his left folded. Nate rubbed his fingertips against the cottony tabletop.

Two more players threw their cards into the muck, but an old guy in a cowboy hat called his bet. The dealer laid out a series of cards. When the third card landed, Nate held in the whoosh of air that wanted to explode from his lungs. An ace.

Cowboy Hat checked. Nate counted out an even bigger stack of chips and pushed it forward. The man peered at his cards and called. The fourth card went down. Another ace.

Three of a kind.

His hands trembled, but he forced himself to still. The woman across the table—one of the other four remaining players—caught his eye and winked.

Down went the final card—the river card.

Another round of bets and he flipped his cards over and glanced across the table.

"Well, yee-haw," said the cowboy.

Nate glanced at the other player's cards.

Shit. What were the chances? Exact same hand except for Nate's queen, the other guy had a king. One damn card.

Nate tipped his head. "Nicely played."

Since the tournament kickoff yesterday morning, he'd played competently, winning hand after hand. But in truth, he'd been a mess, barely able to concentrate.

Luck certainly wasn't with him tonight. He needed a miracle. Otherwise, he'd be done in a few more hands.

Strange, but he didn't feel all that upset. A cute, bow-shaped mouth and a pair of dark, passionate eyes preoccupied him instead. But it was more than that. There'd been something about the way she managed the situation with Nemo, her willingness to play pretend wife, and the satisfaction on her face when Nemo scampered away.

Another hand came and went. The woman across the table raked the tokens to her chest.

"You always this lucky?" The guy to Nate's left asked as she stacked her newly acquired chips.

She smirked like a well-fed feline. "Lucky you suck."

Playful player banter, one of the most enjoyable aspects of the game, had taken a dark turn when Nemo was still at the table. Things got bad when another player christened him after the cartoon fish and launched into the theme from *Jaws*. Everyone laughed. Nate included.

The guy probably never thought he'd make it this far and didn't know how to handle it. The teasing pushed him over the edge. Nate could have stepped in—and maybe he should have—but it was hard to feel sorry for him now, knowing he accosted Angie after leaving the game.

Still, Nate hated sitting back and watching others suffer.

That helpless feeling was part of what had brought him to the casino on the edge of the Everglades—the desperate need for control. Yet, looking toward the blackjack tables, a new kind of determination bloomed in his chest.

The dealer button landed at Nate's position, reminding him there was a game going on. He pushed forward fifty in chips and peeked at the two cards in front of him—a seven of spades and two of diamonds. *Ugh*. He should fold...

To hell with it. He pushed another stack of chips to the center of the table. Blackjack suddenly seemed a lot more attractive.

CHAPTER 3

"You're in the hot seat tonight," the dealer said, placing a card in front of Angie.

"Shhh. Don't jinx it." She laughed.

After dealing two cards to each of the four players, the dealer laid her second card face up. Six of hearts. Angie considered her own hand. A seven of clubs and a four of diamonds. She tapped her finger, and the dealer gave her a queen. She waved her hand over the cards, then waited for the other players to take their turns.

The dealer dealt herself a jack and flipped over her bottom card. Another royal. "Twenty-one takes it." She pushed a little stack of chips in front of Angie's betting box.

Table games were a rare indulgence. For one thing, the minimum bet was almost always more than Angie was willing to lose. For another, she preferred the solitude of machines and found comfort hiding among the slot zombies.

But for some reason, the word *blackjack* had rushed from her mouth. And now, here she was, listening to the hum of the shuffle machine and waiting for the next hand.

Much to Angie's surprise, what had started as a way to kill time had turned into a satisfying evening. It had been one winning hand after another. Just over an hour of play and her luck had never been better. But her unexpected good fortune brought with it a familiar apprehension, a reminder that happiness was short-lived.

Two aces landed on the table. Looking at the other players, she felt a twinge of guilt. She split and added a second bet. The dealer gave her two more cards.

Holy crap.

Blackjack on one hand, a dealer bust on the other. Another small stack of chips landed in her betting circle. She pulled the chips closer and glanced up. Her fake husband stood on the other side of the table, staring back at her.

Her breath caught, and a pleasant warmth swelled in her chest at the sight of him. More than enough enticement to leave the game. She pushed a token to the dealer and nodded to the other players.

His face softened, the tight lines relaxing into an easy grin as she approached. God, he was handsome. His hard body and expressive chestnut-colored eyes were part of the appeal, but it was his gaze that really pulled her in. She'd heard of smiles reaching someone's eyes but had never seen it for herself. Until now.

She gave herself an inward shake. She hadn't come to Miami to meet a guy. She'd come to set things right.

Then again, it wasn't a crime to have a bit of fun. Tomorrow she could be boring, old Angie. Tonight, she might decide to live a little.

"Want to walk to the cage so I can cash these in?" She held up her chips.

He motioned her forward. "Lead the way."

They passed row after row of gaming machines. Lights flashed and bells clanged as the electronic slot machines worked to mimic the one-armed bandits of yesteryear.

Nate rubbed his hand along his jaw. "I don't get it."

"Don't get what?"

"Slots. I don't get the appeal. I like games that require skill."

Interesting. "Video poker is my game, but I get the allure of slots. A routine. Repetition. Not having to think. It's an escape. Also, when you win, the reward is immediate."

He tilted his head to the side, giving her comment serious consideration. "Okay, I'll give you that. But it still seems so passive. You're at the mercy of the machine."

So, he likes being in control. Probably keeps a tight leash on his emotions too. She shook her head. Profiling him wouldn't lead anywhere good.

Nate slowed as they approached the motorbike displayed on a platform and surrounded by screens of Texas Hold 'Em.

"Do you ride?" she asked.

He shook his head. "You?"

"I've got a little cruiser in storage, but it's been a while since I've taken her out." It had been at least two years since she'd ridden her bike. Why had she neglected the things she enjoyed? Probably the same reason she avoided attachments. "How'd the tournament go?"

He stuck his hands in his pockets and shrugged. "About how I expected. I had a few decent hands, but not enough to overcome the hole I got myself into."

"I'm sorry."

"It's all good. I wasn't really into it."

They reached the cashier and stepped into the queue.

"I know you said you're not much of a gambler, but you seem to know what you're doing."

She couldn't help but smile. Little did he know, gambling had once been a regular pastime. "Just because I don't usually gamble doesn't mean I've never been in a casino."

His eyebrow went up. Just like earlier, when he'd saved her from Nemo. "Do tell."

She laughed, remembering the hours of wasted time. "My college roommate was a math whiz fascinated with odds and probability. We traveled to Atlantic City a few times and even found an underground casino just off campus. I had to do something while she tried to break the bank."

He quirked his mouth into a smile of genuine interest. "You obviously learned a thing or two."

"She's a professional blackjack player now. Runs a company in Vegas that teaches players how to beat the odds."

A new clerk appeared and motioned her forward. She set the chips on the desk and waited for the man to count out the money. Satisfaction washed over her as he handed over the cash. A net win. Not bad.

"How about a drink?" Nate said when she turned back. "There's a martini bar around the corner."

"I'm sorry to say my martini days are behind me." The ghost of sharp, metallic vermouth and too-strong gin made her grimace. "But I'm sure they make other drinks. Let's give it a try."

The bar was small but almost empty. Nate pulled out her chair and waited for her to sit. She nearly swooned. Not a drop of alcohol yet, and her legs had gone weak.

A bartender who looked like he could be in middle school approached to get their orders—a vodka cranberry and Scotch on the rocks.

"Yikes. He's young," Nate said. "Or am I getting old?"

Angie laughed. "I thought the same thing." The stool swiveled under her weight, allowing her to avoid his gaze. She pretended to inspect the menu. "How old is old?"

"Thirty-seven. Rolling into middle age, or so my sister tells me."

The bartender placed their drinks on the bar. Angie picked hers up and took a sip.

"Gosh. That is old." She kept her face neutral.

His mouth fell open. She didn't even try to suppress her belly laugh and nudged him lightly on the shoulder. "That was too easy."

With an elbow on the bar, Nate swirled the ice and the thick amber liquid around the tumbler. She watched the gooey legs of the drink cling to the glass. He narrowed his eyes and studied her. "You're no college kid yourself."

"No, but I'm a baby compared to you." A complete lie.

"Come on. Spill."

Dammit. She'd started this. She wasn't vain about aging, but that didn't mean she wanted to admit to being a still-single woman in her mid-thirties. Good thing she'd prepared to evade such questions. "I'm the product of two prime numbers."

His groan was loud and exaggerated. "I thought your room-mate was the math whiz."

"My age is the same as the number of states at the beginning of the Civil War."

The shake of his head reminded her of the exasperated expression her father wore when she'd spun some ridiculous tale to justify bad behavior.

"The atomic number of selenium?"

"Fuck. I give up."

"Thirty-four." She finished her drink and ordered another.

He grinned again, and her stomach did a celebratory flip. Never had she met a man whose smile made her want to run a victory lap.

She studied his strong profile, imagining what the stubble on his jaw would feel like under her fingertips.

Vodka cranberry number two slid down her throat. Nate took another sip of scotch. Man, he nursed that thing. Whereas she'd shown herself to be more of a guzzler.

An overwhelming sense of joy flooded her chest. Her cheeks warmed. Oh boy. She needed food. Two rather weak drinks and already a little tipsy. Once she put something in her stomach, she'd be in much better shape.

"Where's a decent place to eat around here?"

He scratched his cheek. "You mean outside the casino? Only place in walking distance is the gas station across the street."

"Those sandwiches in triangle containers? No thanks, I'll pass."

"Aren't you hoity-toity?" He grinned, and her insides did another cartwheel. "Do you like Cuban coffee? If so, that's your place."

She pulled a face. "Sorry, not for me. Too sweet."

"I'm sure the buffet is still open. Don't know about the other restaurants."

Her stomach protested at the mention of an all-you-can-eat smorgasbord. Never a first choice, but she could probably make do. "Buffet's fine if that's the only option, but I'd prefer something else."

"I know. I don't like it either." He rubbed his hands down his pant legs and watched the bartender stack clean glasses. He was still studying the glassware when he spoke again. "The only other thing I know of is room service."

Like a neglected appliance, her body sputtered to life. Her skin tingled, her heart sparked, and a pleasant buzz settled over her.

Did she really want to do this? Go back to a complete stranger's hotel room?

She took a deep breath. Her creep radar hadn't gone off once, and men this companionable were a rare find.

She bit her lip. If things went sideways, she knew how to handle herself.

He cleared his throat. "I'm sorry. That was—"

"Room service sounds great." She hopped up.

He stared for a moment, but then stood and threw two twenties on the bar. "After you."

Known for being somewhat reckless and impulsive professionally, she'd never been accused of such things in her personal life. If anything, she'd kept herself overly buttoned up, letting no one get too close.

Would she regret spending the night with a perfect stranger? Maybe. Was she going to change her mind? Not a chance.

CHAPTER 4

Nate glanced at Angie, then away. He couldn't seem to keep his eyes off her as they rode the elevator to the ninth floor. She'd been running her hands through her hair. The long, silky mane had taken on a messy, tousled look that set off her dark, smoky eyes.

She studied him through lowered lids, irises shining. At first glance, her posture appeared reserved, but he felt the singe of her gaze.

He'd been silent for too long. He cleared his throat. "How long are you in town?"

"Not sure." She leaned her shoulder against the wall. "I've got some business to look into. It'll depend on how that goes."

He stared at her lips, a beat too long. Her eyes sparked, holding an alluring glint of lust, and he imagined catching her plump bottom lip between his teeth. A moan inched up his throat, but he shoved it back down. He needed something to take his mind off the images swirling around his brain. "Where are you from?"

"California originally, but I live in D.C. now."

"What do you do for a living?"

She waved her hand and blew out a dismissive puff. "Boring government job. You?"

"Family business. Me and my siblings."

"Siblings…" Her voice trailed off. "I'm an only child."

The transformation in her voice from upbeat to monotone happened so quickly it was jarring.

"Take it from me, siblings aren't all they're cracked up to be."

She blinked, then averted her gaze. "I'm an only child. By default."

Nate swallowed. He almost didn't want to ask. "By default?"

A shadow passed into Angie's eyes. "My sister died when I was fourteen."

Shit. He couldn't imagine if something happened to one of his siblings. Well, actually he could. He'd spent most of his life imagining exactly that.

"That must have been hard." Pain and loss had been his constant companion for as long as he could remember. He didn't seek comfort and rarely provided it, but God help him, he wanted to enfold her in his arms. "Were you the oldest?"

She nodded. "She was eight. I'm not sure I ever really processed her death. My parents never talked about it, never showed their grief. At least not to me."

What could he say? That he understood? That his parents had also fallen short in the nurturing department? No, she didn't need to hear any of that. "I'm sorry."

"Thanks. I've had a long time to get used to it, but it never really goes away. You know?"

Did he ever. The past and people he'd never see again occupied his thoughts more than he cared to admit.

The door dinged. They stepped off the elevator. He motioned her to the right. "I've got the last room at the end of the hall."

He waved the plastic keycard in front of the electronic pad, turned the handle, and held the door so she could enter. A whiff of her earthy fragrance mesmerized him as she brushed past.

Instinct prodded him to pin her against the wall and tear off her clothes.

He flicked on the light.

"Hey, this room is a lot bigger than mine." She circled the small sitting room and peeked into the bedroom. "Mine's just a regular hotel room."

Her enthusiasm was adorable.

"Free upgrade. I haven't been coming as often. They're trying to lure me back."

She sank into the couch. "I guess it worked."

He picked up the room service binder and settled next to her. "As good an excuse as any to get away."

Opening the menu, he handed it to Angie. She flipped to the page and assessed the options.

A lock of her dark hair fell forward. She tucked it behind her ear, and the motion gave him an opportunity to study her profile. Thin brows curved around the outside corner of her eyes. She had a small, round nose, and his fingers ached to touch her flawless, golden-brown skin.

He'd not been with a woman since before his dad died, and that was over a year ago. Before that, he'd had several short-term girlfriends but had never been good at one-night stands. For some reason, he couldn't be intimate with a woman and then walk away. Maybe that's why he'd resigned himself to being alone. Because real connections always felt out of reach.

The faint, familiar burn of the scotch he'd nursed earlier lingered on his tongue, a reminder of his usual comforts. Those rituals that offered predictability when everything else in his life was uncertain.

"Would you like a drink?" He stood to retrieve a bottle of wine in a bucket behind the sofa, a congratulation perk from the hotel manager for advancing to day two of the tournament.

"Sounds great."

The ice in the bucket had melted, leaving the label a soggy mess. He stepped into the bathroom to grab a hand towel, then handed her a glass and removed the cork. "Say when."

He filled the glass to the halfway mark and stopped. She raised a brow and tilted her glass back toward the bottle. "When."

He didn't care for wine but wasn't about to let her drink alone. Another generous pour went into his glass. He set the bottle down and took a sip. A taste of bitter wood hit the center of his tongue. He shook his head and smacked his lips.

"Not a fan?"

"I guess my palate isn't that refined."

She spun the bottle to see the label. "There's nothing wrong with your palate. This isn't exactly high end. Besides, you seem to have a taste for expensive whiskey."

"I know what I like." He stared for a moment, unable to form a coherent thought, then shook it off. "What do you want to eat?"

She tilted her chin and studied the menu again. "California club with fries."

Nate dialed room service and placed Angie's order, plus a burger for himself and two bottles of water. He set the receiver down and returned to the couch.

A moment of silence followed. He opened a streaming music app on his cell. "What do you like to listen to?"

"Eighties music is always good."

The small Bluetooth speaker he'd set up on the coffee table played The Smiths. Not the most romantic option, but she'd not given him much to work with. At least the background noise helped eliminate some of the awkwardness. Although to be fair, she was amazingly easy to talk to. He relaxed into the sofa, recalling their easy banter in the bar.

She took another sip of wine. "You said you work with your siblings. How many of you are there?"

"Three. My sister, brother, and me. We used to work with our dad. He died last year."

Her gaze went distant for a moment. He caught a flicker of recognition in her eyes. "Something wrong?"

Shaking her head, she gave a light laugh. "What you said reminded me of something, but I'm not sure what exactly." She set a warm hand on his forearm. Her voice was soft. "I'm sorry about your dad. That's tough."

Tingles crawled up his arm and spread across every inch of skin. *Jesus*. If this was any indication of how his body reacted to her touch, he was in for quite a night.

Another song came on. She swayed and mouthed the words. He sucked in a breath, his gaze returning to her lips.

The goblet squeaked as she ran her finger around the rim.

"Refill?" He leaned over to pour and froze. That scent. He closed his eyes and inhaled. "What is that perfume? You smell like a summer night." The words surprised him even as they were leaving his mouth.

"Vetiver."

He'd never heard of it, but whatever it was, it drove him crazy.

Their faces almost touched. Their breaths mingled. Without thinking, he bent his head closer and traced the shell of her ear with his finger. "Can I kiss you?"

She wet her lips. "Please."

He wove his hand into her hair, unable to remember the last time he'd wanted anyone quite this much. If they only had tonight, he wanted to savor every minute. His fingertips grazed the skin behind her ear, and he felt a tremor ripple through her. He leaned closer, pressing tender kisses against her neck. Her husky sighs made his body ache. He sat back and brushed his thumb over her satiny lips. The warmth coiling through him went straight to his cock.

Her hand against his chest was like a foot on the gas. His turbo engaged and his heart zoomed from zero to sixty in nothing flat. God, this woman. Something about her made him feel things he hadn't let himself feel in a long time. Like maybe this could be more than a one-night stand. *No.* He couldn't think about that. Not when he might never see her again. Especially not when she lived hundreds of miles away.

He grazed his lips against hers and knew immediately that one taste wasn't enough. A low, guttural rumble rose into his throat as he teased her lips open. Her warm mouth, laced with the rich, smoky flavor of wine, ignited his need.

Fingertips dug into his shoulders. Their light, exploratory kisses turned into a frenzy of teeth, lips, and tongue.

Tap. Tap. He pulled away, dazed and panting. A cute pink flush crept into her cheeks.

The knock came again. "Room service."

Damn. Angie hadn't been kissed like that since...well, ever. For a moment after Nate pulled away, she kept her eyes closed, yearning for the return of his lips. Instead, he muttered a barely audible curse and stood, leaving her body and mouth abandoned and aching for more.

What were the chances? She'd chosen the casino to give herself some balance between work and her need for a vacation. A one-night stand had never factored into her plans. But she wanted this, and if his kisses could turn her to jelly, she couldn't wait to find out what he did to her between the sheets. She'd be nothing but a sated puddle of goo by the time he finished.

Nate jerked open the door, took the tray, and shoved a tip at the startled-looking young man. He kicked the door closed with his foot and returned to the couch, setting the food on the coffee table. The smell of hot fries filled the room.

"I'm sorry about that." His hungry gaze lingered on her face, then raked her body.

"Me too."

Ignoring the food, he pressed her against the arm of the sofa, his tongue teasing and prodding. "We should eat before it gets cold." His voice rumbled against her lips.

"I'm starved," she murmured, still claiming him with greedy kisses.

He returned her kiss. Ravenously. Clutching her breast, he ground against her, his hot breath warming her neck, his erection pressing into her leg.

Then he stopped and pushed his forehead to hers. "God. I want you," he panted. "But you need to eat. An empty stomach and alcohol don't make the best combination for decision making. If we're going to do this, I don't want either of us to have any regrets."

He smiled down at her, his eyes warm and admiring.

There it was again. That feeling. The pleasant tingle spread through her chest like wildfire. Nate was more than a handsome face. He was kind and thoughtful and protective. The kind of man she could fall for—if she did that sort of thing. "I appreciate that."

He lifted himself and sat back. She smothered her desire while he inspected their dinners.

The plastic lids covering the plates had steamed up, making it impossible to see inside. Nate lifted a plate off the tray, peeked under the lid, and set it on the table in front of Angie. She reached for a bottle of water.

Avocados and bacon squished out the back of her sandwich as she lifted it to her mouth. She set it back on the plate and rearranged the ingredients.

"So, what do you do besides enter poker tournaments?"

He gave a half-hearted shrug. "Not much, to be honest. The business takes up a lot of my time."

"I know the feeling. Work goes everywhere with me. I can't seem to help it." She bit into her sandwich while secretly studying her companion. The guy was ripped. The sleeves of his short-sleeved tee hugged strong, shapely biceps, and earlier, she'd noticed his chest flexing beneath his shirt. Either he did manual labor for a living or he worked out. "Are you into sports?"

"Soccer, but I haven't played since I was a kid. These days, it's just something to watch on TV. I try to get to the gym to lift in the mornings. They've got a boxing ring, and sometimes I spar with a friend. Occasionally, I'll get in an evening jog, depending on the heat."

Yep, that explained it.

"Why do you ask?" He gave her a sly smile.

Uh oh. Busted. Well, hopefully soon enough she'd get a better look at his body. His hard, naked body. She shoved a clump of fries into her mouth.

"What about you? You look like you stay in shape."

She swallowed her food. "I like to swim. Started when I was a teenager."

"Oh yeah? Long distance?" The look of admiration on his face made her stomach twist in the most delightful way.

"Sometimes. I've done a few triathlons."

"Training for an event like that must be time consuming."

"It can be." A strange sensation fluttered over her. She hadn't even considered doing a triathlon since she'd joined the

Caribbean task force, and that was almost three years ago. "It gets me out of my head. Swimming is good for zoning out."

"I'm not super competitive," he said, stacking their empty plates. "Did archery for a while, but that was more for my sister. She's fantastic with a bow and arrow."

"That was sweet of you." She unscrewed the cap of her water bottle and took a swig. "Doing an activity just to spend time with your sibling."

"I don't know if it was sweet as much as indulgent. After my mom left, I felt responsible for my brother and sister. Tried my best to give them a normal childhood."

There was a gentle, aching pull to his words that seemed to unravel something inside of her. These were not typical one-night-stand feelings. Giving in to the sudden, urgent need to be near him, she lifted herself up, climbed over and straddled his lap.

She settled her ass on his thighs and ran her fingers down the front of his shirt. "Do you bring every woman you rescue from drunk creeps to your hotel room?"

"Never." Dark, earnest, hungry eyes stared back at her. "I'm not usually this lucky."

She pressed a soft kiss to his lips. "That's okay. If my blackjack winnings are any indication, I've got luck for both of us."

His hands slipped under her T-shirt, skimming across her skin. He cupped her breasts and tweaked her nipples through her bra. "I can't wait to see these."

She took off her shirt and tossed it onto the floor. He stared at her chest, nostrils flaring. His thumbs stroked across her nipple, and he gathered her breasts in his hands. "What about the bra?"

"Why don't you lose your shirt first?"

"Gladly." He leaned forward, lifted his shirt over his head, and dropped it beside the couch. "Now?"

With a small nod, she reached her arms behind her back to unclasp the hook. The bra fell slack. She slid her arms out and sent the lacy undergarment on a similar trajectory as her shirt.

Her small breasts had never been a favorite feature, but the way Nate stared, his chest heaving, a barely restrained growl climbing up his throat, made her feel desired in a way she'd never felt before.

He brought his mouth to her nipple and sucked, groaning like a starved man with his first meal. Her breasts weren't terribly sensitive, but something about watching him lose his shit—over her—sent lust straight to her core. Her breaths turned to pants. Jesus. How could she be this turned on?

Leaning in for a kiss, she let her hand slide down to grip his erection through the stiff cotton of his pants. "I think we should do something about this, don't you?"

He dragged his teeth against her bottom lip and moaned.

"I'll take that as a yes." God, she loved feeling this way—assertive, sexy, in control. She tugged on his zipper and marveled at the way his bulge seemed to expand before her eyes. Her pulse fluttered in her ears as she stuck her hand into his boxer briefs and stroked.

"Oh fuck, Angie." His words were ragged, broken at the edges, and it imbued her with a new sense of power. Tightening her grip, she gave a series of long, slow pumps.

He kissed her again, but this time he wrapped his arms around her and eased her to the couch. "I want to touch you, taste you."

"By all means..." She heard the smile in her voice.

"Take off your pants," he ordered, his tone low and authoritative.

Her inner walls clenched. Another turn on. Who knew?

He lifted away from her, allowing her to kick off her boots and shimmy out of her jeans. Then he was hovering above her again, his hand sliding down her stomach and into her underwear. She tried to relax into the cushion, but the moment his hand found her slick entrance, she jolted.

Her arousal gathered and grew. Her breaths and moans turned desperate. Release pulsed through her. Blinding. Consuming. Electric.

Still panting, she drew his mouth to hers. His lips were fuller and softer than they looked. He kissed her back. Wet, hot, urgent.

She pulled away. "Please tell me you have a condom."

"My brother gave it to me before I left. Said I needed to get laid." His words vibrated against her lips. He gave her another long, slow kiss before standing. Taking her hand, he tugged her to her feet. "How 'bout we move this to the bedroom?"

"Feeling lucky, are we?" she teased.

"That jackpot is looking pretty damned good tonight."

CHAPTER 5

A ngie scooted onto the bed and let Nate wedge himself between her thighs. His mouth crashed into hers, his tongue searching. She moaned into him, and then his hand landed between her legs. Something about the friction of him rubbing her through her underwear had her writhing like a cat in heat. She was shameless and didn't care in the least.

"Fuck, you're wet." The curse came with a growl, rumbling against her ear and stealing her breath. He wasn't wrong. No way would she be wearing these panties again tonight.

"That's your fault," she said, her voice huskier than she'd ever heard it.

He trailed kisses down her neck to her collarbone, all the while dragging his thumb in lazy circles across her cotton-covered clit. A musky scent rose from their heated skin, and she couldn't resist skimming her hands over his hard, sculpted stomach. She went lower, dipping into his underwear to cup his erection and rubbing her thumb over the slick head.

"These panties need to disappear." He stopped stroking and slid the bikini briefs down her legs. Next, he stood and removed his own underwear.

She sat up and gawked openly at his broad shoulders. His strong, muscled body. His thick, heavy erection. He disappeared into the bathroom and when he returned was already rolling on the condom.

He climbed back onto the bed. "You sure about this?"

"Yep. You?" She tried to sound cocky, but any show of bravado was offset by her body shaking with anticipation.

In response, he threaded one hand into her hair, wrapped the other around her waist, and kissed her. No, not kissed. Claimed. In a way that was commanding, firm, possessive. His mouth pushed hers wider, his tongue conquering, plundering, owning. Surrender was her only option. She gave in, let go, and lost herself in the man she'd met only hours ago.

Nate maneuvered her back onto the bed, placed the head of his cock at her entrance and pushed inside. They groaned in unison.

She wound her hands around his neck and raked the short hairs at his nape with her fingernails. He thrust in and out slowly, as if they had all the time in the world. Oh, if only. Now that she was here, beneath Nate, she never wanted it to end. He lifted her leg over his arm and pushed in hard, deep. Her breath hitched, and her body clenched. He kept going, winding her tighter and tighter.

Then, almost as if he knew she was close, his hands found hers, their fingers lacing together. And it felt *right*. God, what was happening?

A dizzy, disorienting euphoria crashed over her as Nate's rhythm hastened. Her body clenched around him, and waves of pleasure coursed through her. His grip on her fingers tightened.

He buried his head in the crook of her neck and came with a groan.

Her body continued its pulsing as he collapsed against her, warm breath feathering her skin. "Fuck," he murmured into her hair.

She reveled in the weight of him, the heat of his sweat-slicked body. She didn't want to move. Not yet. Not with her brain still reeling. She'd had lovers—some of them pretty spectacular—but never had it felt like *that*.

Eventually, he lifted off of her, stripped the condom and tossed it in the garbage can. Then he settled back in bed, tugging the sheet to cover them both. They lay there, staring at one another, and Angie sensed she wasn't the only one who felt like she'd crash landed in unfamiliar territory, unsure whether to run or hang around and see what came next.

"That was..." Nate puffed out his cheeks then made an explosion gesture with his hand while blowing out his air. "Wow."

She tried to keep her face serious but couldn't hold in a laugh. "Definitely adequate."

"Adequate? I was fantastic." His happy, teasing tone stirred something dormant inside of her.

"Aren't you smug?" She poked him in the ribs.

"Rightfully so, I'd say." He pressed a soft, lingering kiss to her lips, then pulled her close, wrapping his arms around her tightly.

She nestled into him, her back against his chest. His fingers plucked absently at her nipple. The night had been perfect. Nate was perfect. She felt more like herself when she was with him than she'd felt in years.

Suddenly, she wanted to absorb everything she could about this man.

"How do you like working with your brother and sister?" Pillow talk? Her?

She felt him shrug against her. "We've always been together and always been around the business." His voice vibrated with tension. "Other than last year after our dad died and my sister ran off to live in another state."

He'd clearly taken his sister's leaving personally. Probably tied to his white-knight complex. *Shit*. She was doing it again.

"She's back now?"

"Yeah." He snorted. "Along with Mr. Wonderful."

Angie couldn't stop a laugh. "Should I assume he's not actually Mr. Wonderful?"

"Oh, he's okay. To be fair, he helped her out of some trouble—a lot of trouble—actually." His hard exhale rustled her hair. "Probably saved her life."

"Wow." She hooked her leg between his. "Sounds like it's a good thing she met him."

"He works for the FBI, even transferred to the Miami office to be with her."

A tiny alarm sounded in the back of her brain, a niggling awareness she couldn't quite identify. "Working in D.C., I've interacted with agents from different agencies. Most of them are good people."

His exasperated breath feathered her hair. "I should probably try to get to know him. He doesn't seem to be going anywhere."

She nodded, ignoring the dread pooling in her gut. "What sort of business do you have?"

"We own a small airline. Charters and flying lessons."

Angie stilled. That niggling feeling she'd ignored earlier returned but louder and sharper this time. Her heartbeat slowed to a leaden thud. "That's an interesting occupation." She spoke slowly, as if wading into icy water. "Where do you operate?"

"Key Largo. We've got six planes. Technically seven, but one's out of service for the foreseeable future." His voice changed. Low. Quiet. Bitter.

Her lungs seemed to collapse in on themselves. She closed her eyes and held her breath. *Fuck. Fuck. Fuck.* Everyone in the intelligence community knew the story of the undercover FBI agent who was captured by a crime lord and fell in love with the mobster's granddaughter. Angie hadn't been interested in the story itself so much as the person involved—her asset's daughter.

Her stomach clenched, her food threatening a rebellion. A metro area with millions of people and she ended up in the hotel room of the one guy who was completely off limits. The gorgeous man who'd fucked her into tomorrow was Nathan Hughes, son of Rick Hughes, the man whose suspicious death had brought her to Florida.

It also made him the grandson of Aleksander Koslov, a notorious gangster known as Papi. And Nate's mother hadn't just left her family. She'd gone into hiding when another crime family put a price on her head.

Dear God. What had she done?

Nate felt Angie stiffen against him. In an instant, she went from loose, relaxed, and happy to tense and drawn. She extracted her leg from its spot between his and sat on the side of the bed. Maybe he shouldn't have said the thing about the plane. She didn't need to know about his family drama. Hell, he'd barely come to grips with the truth about his dad the drug smuggler. He certainly shouldn't be saddling someone else with his problems.

He cleared his throat, hoping to steer the conversation back to lighter topics. "It's probably not too late to order dessert."

She popped off the bed. "Shoot. I just realized I was supposed to wait for a text from my boss. He had something he wanted me to look into." She darted about the room like a stark-naked bouncy ball.

Nate sat up. What was going on?

She ricocheted into the sitting room. "Pants, pants, pants," he heard her murmur, followed by, "Bra...shirt...boots."

When she reappeared, fully clothed, she held up her phone. "Yep. Boss texted. Work emergency. Wants me to give him a call." She bent over to retrieve her panties, which she crammed into her brown, slouchy purse. "There's no telling how long it'll take. I should go."

She's leaving? He lifted himself from the bed and pulled on his boxer briefs, an angry growl rising in his chest.

There'd been a connection. She'd felt it too. He was certain. Is that what this was about?

He couldn't let her leave, not without knowing what happened. "Did I offend you?"

"Of course not." She spoke quickly, as if she'd just discovered he was a serial killer and wanted to get away before he realized she was onto him. "Just one of those things."

For a moment, he thought he saw regret flash in her eyes. His pulse raced, and his chest tingled. His fingers itched to keep her from walking away. Why was she doing this? There was something between them, and it wasn't just physical. It was deeper than that.

She turned and left the bedroom. He followed, hoping she'd change her mind. An ache of disappointment knotted his stomach. *It's only a one-night stand. It doesn't mean anything.* Liar. "Can I get your number?"

She caught her bottom lip with her teeth, then moved her purse across her body. The tightness in his shoulders and behind his eyes eased. Maybe she really did have to do something for work. Maybe this wasn't the only night they'd ever have. He picked his phone up off the coffee table.

Instead of her cell, she extracted a wallet from her bag. "What do I owe you for dinner?"

He clenched his jaw. "My treat." A prickle crawled up his neck and onto his face. He braced his hands on his hips.

"Well, okay. It was nice to meet you."

Despite her words, passion smoldered beneath her lowered lids. Maybe there was still a chance. *Do it.* Kiss her. Remind her how good it was. He leaned forward. She tilted her head and licked her lips.

Then, with one deft maneuver, she ducked his mouth and stepped closer to the exit.

"It's been great..." She yanked open the door, and by the time it closed with a soft thud, she was gone.

CHAPTER 6

Nate's sister nodded at him as she put a box of files on their dad's desk. "Okay. Done with this one."

She set down another stack of folders, and though he'd never admit it, he enjoyed letting his youngest sibling boss him around. For most of their lives, he'd been the one keeping everyone in line, shouldering the burden of their safety, dictating who did what and when. Knowing those days were over brought a strange mix of regret and relief.

Elise rifled through the disorganized folders, rustling aged paper. Dad had owned the business for over twenty years and threw nothing away. Unfortunately, he also didn't have any discernible system for storing or organizing his paperwork.

With a groan, Nate picked up the box and moved it to the tower forming near the back door. How he got roped into the grunt work while their brother Jack manned the front desk was a mystery. He grumbled. Mostly for show.

They were getting rid of their dad's old documents. Elise had finally convinced him to go digital. He'd missed her when she ran away to Colorado, but hadn't been ready for the get-things-done office manager who returned.

In truth, Nate didn't mind the physical work. Other than Elise's nattering, it gave him time to think.

Stew would be more accurate.

That woman. *Angie.* Just her name made his jaw clench. He shook his head. Future Nate would be dealing with a cracked tooth and dental bills if he didn't cut it out. But dammit, he couldn't put her out of his mind. He'd tormented himself for three days straight.

His sister dropped a thick stack of papers on the desk. On its own, a piece of paper was nothing, but cram thousands of them into a box and suddenly the weight was almost too much to lift. That's how his night with Angie felt. One more slight, combined with a multitude of failures that buried him under their weight.

He let the numbness settle over him with a dull, distant thud.

The morning after she'd rushed from his room—her sprint of shame—he'd walked the entire casino hoping to see her. He loitered near the reception desk in case she checked out or came through the lobby. He even asked the front desk clerk if there was anyone named Angie staying at the hotel. The guy refused to look, but it didn't matter. She was gone. Nowhere to be seen.

"How about lunch?" His stomach rumbled.

Elise glanced at her watch. "Taco Tony should be in the parking lot."

With no food court or restaurant, the small airport relied on a regular rotation of food trucks. Elise sorted the chaos of files into two neat stacks before going out the front. "Do you want the regular?"

Nate nodded and watched her leave, stopping to get Jack's order. He sighed and took a seat at the desk. There'd been something about Angie. Something that made him believe he wasn't destined to be alone. But that was crazy, wasn't it? It was only one night.

So why was he still obsessing over her soft body and sweet kisses?

A too-tall tower of boxes caught his eye. Something to get his mind off that woman. He stood, walked to the stack, and lifted the top box.

And that body—a contradiction of soft, womanly curves and strong, hard muscle.

Stop it.

She didn't want him. She'd had him and decided he wasn't for her. He needed to accept that. The fact he couldn't bring himself to believe it? That was on him.

He dropped the box onto the floor, then reached for another.

Perhaps it wasn't her he was fixated on, but rather the idea he'd stumbled upon someone who might allow him to forget the burden of his daily life. A life he sometimes worried would swallow him whole.

This probably wasn't about a woman at all. It was about the abrupt shift in responsibility.

He'd hidden the truth about his family's identity for years, believing it his duty as the oldest son. But then, Dad died and Elise ran away, and the carefully constructed façade collapsed in a heap of lies. Their grandfather, the crime lord. Their mother's escape to South America. Stolen birth certificates. Made-up lives. And on top of all that, the plane crash that revealed Dad's drug smuggling.

It was too much.

His brother and sister were lucky. They didn't remember their old life. When a gangster—their grandfather's rival—kidnaped Elise a few months ago hoping to lure their mother out of hiding, Nate could no longer conceal what he knew about their criminal connections.

He'd expected waves of relief. Instead, feelings of failure dogged him. If he hadn't pushed his sister away, she might never have ended up in Vincenzo Alario's clutches. In the end, everything turned out all right, but Nate still struggled to let go of the need to protect both his siblings and the family secret.

"You okay?" She'd returned and now stood in front of the desk, holding out a red and white checkered tray with a burrito and tortilla chips.

He blinked away the memories. "Thanks."

She pulled a chair to the other side of the desk and devoured a taco in three bites. "Eric wants to smoke a brisket this weekend. We'd like to have you over for dinner."

Nate nodded and chewed. "Sure. What should I bring?"

"A twelve-pack ought to do it."

He pried the lid off the plastic dipping container. Tomatillo salsa. His favorite. He started to dip a chip.

"There's a woman Eric works with—"

"No," he blurted, his shoulders sagging. Not this again. Ever since Elise discovered true love, she'd been trying to shove women at him. She didn't understand. Not everyone was fated to find their soul mate.

She pulled her dark hair through an elastic and folded her arms into the quintessential little sister huff. "Well, we've already invited her. Her name is Susan, and she's wonderful. You two will get along great."

"Not interested."

"Nate, I'm worried. You've been grouchy for months. I thought the poker tournament might be a good diversion, but your mood is worse than ever."

He crammed the second half of his burrito into his mouth so he wouldn't have to talk.

Of course, that did nothing to stop Elise. "I don't want you to be alone. I want you to find someone. Like I did."

With his mouth full, all he could manage were exaggerated motions. He made a cut-it-out signal with his free hand.

"I've already told Susan about you, and she's looking forward to getting together."

He finished chewing and swallowed. His tone came out harsher than he'd intended. "Peanut, no."

She leaned back, her amber eyes round and earnest. "I'm only trying to help."

He spoke again. This time in a softer tone. "I know, and I'm sorry. But I'm not interested. Fix her up with Jack."

"She's not right for Jack. Besides, he's already seeing three women."

He couldn't hold back a bark of laughter. "No shit?" He didn't know how his little brother managed it.

"Can't you just meet her? If there's nothing there, I'll never bring it up again."

Nate blew out a lungful of air. Who was he kidding? He couldn't deny his baby sister anything. He opened his mouth to surrender—

"Nate?" Jack stepped into the office, pushed the door mostly shut and rubbed his brow. "There's someone here to see you."

He didn't have any appointments. "A customer?"

"Uh, no." Jack touched the back of his neck. "A woman."

A hush fell over the small office.

Nate frowned. "And?"

"And she's hot." His brother's mouth twitched, an obvious attempt to keep his face impassive.

Elise gasped and brought her hands to her mouth, her eyes lit with glee.

Jack peeked through the door crack. "She said you met last weekend at the casino."

An uncomfortable flush of heat crept up Nate's neck and settled on his cheeks. Had she found him? Surely not.

CHAPTER 7

A ngie stood at the flight school counter and waited for the man to return. He sure looked a lot like Nate. He had to be the younger brother, Jack.

She closed her eyes and took a deep breath. It had been three days since she'd figured out her would-be paramour's identity and fled his warm body and hungry kisses and still, the specter of his touch lingered on her skin. Since then, she'd packed her bag no fewer than ten times, her finger hovering over the purchase button on the airline website.

But then she'd think of Rick and the first time they'd met—a fact-finding mission in Jamaica. A veritable who's who of law enforcement and the intelligence community. Through it all, he'd remained calm and collected. Not the least bit intimidated.

Memories of Rick inevitably led to thoughts of his big, sexy son. The kind of man you knew could swallow you in his arms, tell you everything would be okay and make you believe it was true.

Her insides rolled themselves up and twisted into the world's worst pretzel. She'd fucked up. Big time.

How many times had she thought of Nate over the last seventy-two hours? Replaying his kisses. The heat of his mouth.

The way he moved against her and inside of her. Wondering if she should have stayed.

She drummed her fingers on the counter, then pressed the button to set a swimsuit-wearing Santa into motion. His hips rocked to a tinny version of the Beach Boys' *Little Saint Nick*, a reminder the holiday season was supposed to be about spending time with people you loved.

Which begged the question, what was she doing here?

Part of her desperately wanted to run out the front door, flag a taxi, and never think about this family again.

But Rick had been a good man. A man she and her department had manipulated, shamelessly using his family secret—a secret she knew he'd do anything to protect—to ensure his participation. Participation that got him killed.

She'd failed. Again. But maybe—just maybe—she could catch his killer and finally silence that restless voice in her head. The one that told her she was a liability. That she was the reason people died.

Rick's family deserved to know he wasn't a smuggler, and she owed it to them to figure out what happened. Asking for their help wasn't fair, but it was her best shot at getting out of the country unnoticed. That last conversation with Gary about the investigation into Rick's death looped through her memory.

She had to do something. Even if it meant career-ending consequences, possibly even serious legal trouble. She couldn't live with herself if she didn't find out what happened to Rick and why.

But how could she face Nate after their encounter in Miami? She could only pray his desire to find the truth about his father would be enough.

The door flung open. The man in question stalked into the small area behind the counter, his brows drawn. He wore a white tee beneath an unbuttoned short-sleeved shirt. His short dark hair formed a messy peak on top of his head. Her heart thudded out an anxious rhythm at the sight of him. He looked every bit as handsome as he had the other night.

The younger man and a woman peered through the open door. When she'd imagined how this would go, she'd focused on Nate. Given the situation and the closeness of the family, that wasn't realistic.

"How did you find me?"

She pushed back tense shoulders and forced herself to meet his glare. "You're the reason I'm here. In Florida."

His face registered confusion and surprise. Then his back stiffened and his features hardened. Distrust oozed from him like gas seeking a spark. "Explain."

She fought to keep her voice steady. "Your brother and sister should be here for this too."

Without taking his eyes from her, he backed up and pushed open the door. This was a man who didn't let his guard down for anyone. Especially the woman who ran out of his hotel room three nights ago.

"Can you two come out here?"

They had similar coloring to Nate's, but where his eyes were a rich, dark brown, theirs had a lighter, honeyed hue. They stared at her in silence.

She cleared her throat, pulled her badge from her pocket, and held it so everyone could see. "My name is Angela Liu. I work for the CIA." She forced herself to keep going. "I worked with your dad."

Nate's already cold gaze seemed to frost over before her eyes.

The woman—Elise, if she remembered correctly—gasped. Jack placed a hand on his sister's shoulder, the muscles in his forearm flexing as he massaged her back with his thumb.

Angie shifted awkwardly. "Is there somewhere we can talk?"

"No," Nate snapped.

Elise clenched her jaw and shook her head before shooting her oldest brother a what-the-fuck look. "Don't be an asshole. I want to hear what she has to say."

"It's okay." Angie took a deep breath. "I work for Transnational Organized Crime. Your father was helping us investigate a Jamaican drug lord."

Nate's posture stiffened again.

"What do you mean 'helping'?" Jack asked.

"He used connections in Jamaica to affiliate himself with the gang and had started transporting drugs."

"You mean he was undercover?" Elise's voice shook.

Angie offered a sad smile. "In a manner of speaking, yes."

"Is that why you're here? To tell us he worked for the CIA?" Nate's voice was sharp, gruff.

"Not exactly," she stammered. "Though technically, he also worked as an informant for the DEA. They recruited him and shared him with us and the FBI."

Huffing like a bull, Nate let out an exasperated puff of air. "Our dad worked for the DEA, the FBI, *and* the CIA? You must think we're idiots."

"I don't think that at all." She crossed her arms, fingers digging into her biceps, wanting to appear resolute. "The operation was terminated after your father's death. I was told to drop it."

"Let me guess, you're not." He mimicked her cross-armed pose. "And we're supposed to thank you?"

Her stomach fluttered, keeping rhythm with the percussion of her heart. This was the make-or-break moment. "Something your dad learned got him killed. I want to know what it was. Since the case is closed, I no longer have access to agency resources. My investigation will be completely freelance."

Nate's sister closed her eyes. "I need to call Eric." She moved around the counter.

Shit. Elise's boyfriend worked for the FBI. No doubt he'd start asking questions. She would have to reach out and make sure he didn't talk. No matter what she did, she couldn't help but shovel more dirt out of an already too-deep hole. She held up her hand. "I understand you need to process the news, but could you hold off on talking to him until you hear the rest of what I have to say?"

Elise nodded and returned to her position beside her brothers.

"How do we know you didn't have something to do with Dad's death?" Jack's voice was quiet, even. "Now you've got a guilty conscience and you want to involve *us* in something that could get us killed too."

A fair question. She bit her bottom lip. "The truth is, it's only a matter of time before someone else comes knocking, wanting to use one of you as bait. That's how this works. When an asset gets killed, everything stops. Eventually, they start looking for someone to take the asset's place. That often means going back to the original source."

"So, you want to involve us now to save our involvement later?" Jack smirked. "Lady, your logic doesn't make sense."

Angie shook her head. "This is going to be an old-school investigation. Asking questions on the ground. Up close and personal." Dangerous. "I don't want you anywhere near it."

"So why are you here?" Nate scowled.

"I need to get into Jamaica." She lifted her eyes to his. "I'm desperate."

"Commercial airlines fly into Kingston, Montego Bay and Ocho Rios." Jack took a stance very similar to his brother.

"I could be flagged leaving the country. Since I work for the CIA, I'm not supposed to leave without permission, and I can't risk alerting my department. Even if I said it was a vacation, the location would be suspicious." She paused. "I'm doing this on my own time and with my own money."

"So, you're hoping for a free trip to Jamaica?" Nate practically growled the words. He turned to his siblings. "Give me a minute. I want to have a conversation with the *agent*."

Elise didn't ask questions. She darted around the counter and headed for the stairs, probably to call her boyfriend. *Shit.*

Jack's response was different. His face tightened. "I don't know if that's a good idea."

"Go away." The words might have been directed at his sibling, but the tone was all for Angie.

Jack frowned, gave Angie a wary glance, and pushed through the door beside the counter.

Nate paced back and forth a few times, then turned a cold and intense look on Angie.

She gulped. "I'm sorry about the other night. Once I realized who you were, I freaked out. It was wrong of me to leave like that."

He swallowed and looked away.

She'd pissed off plenty of men in her life—co-workers, bosses, boyfriends, her father. Seeing the wounded expression on this hulk of a man was almost too much.

Thank God there was a counter between them. Otherwise, she didn't know what she might do.

She was sorry? If he was in his right mind, he'd tell her it was too late for that and throw her out on her ass. But he couldn't. Because despite everything, there was nothing he wanted to hear more than her confession of regret.

He'd thought of almost nothing else for days, allowing himself to picture her returning to his hotel room to grovel for forgiveness. In his fantasy, she'd promised to make it up to him while shedding her clothes one article at a time. He'd played the scene in his head so many times, he could almost hear the whisper of her clothing sliding to the floor and taste the pinot noir on her lips.

But that woman didn't exist. The flesh-and-blood female standing across from him was more complicated than anything his brain could conjure.

He gave a self-deprecating snort. Her being here was a coincidence. The rest of it? Delusion. Still, he wouldn't mind hearing her acknowledge the mind-blowing sex and the fact she'd never get it again. So, he did what any wounded idiot would do. He lied. "It was just a fuck."

Her shoulders fell. *Good*. Now she knew the sting of rejection.

She looked away, but not before he saw the faintest tremble on her lips. Her pained look slammed into him like a gale-force wind. Damn it.

If she were to be believed, she'd left not because she wanted to get away, but because of her connection to his father. The knowledge helped to repair some of his wounded ego. But what were the chances? Was this another example of the universe screwing him over? Or was it all a little too convenient? Maybe sleeping with him hadn't been about attraction, but access. Or leverage.

He scanned the airport lobby. No customers and nothing on the schedule.

"Let's go into the office." He held open the door. Her perfume wafted toward him as she stepped into the room.

She stopped short and scanned the chaos. "Whoa. Did a tornado touch down in here?"

Right. Elise's mess. "My sister decided to digitize our records. It's turned into quite the project."

"It's probably time. Looks like you've hung on to paper much longer than you needed." She ran her fingers along a dusty box top labeled 2005.

He watched, remembering the feel of those hands skimming his face, his chest, his torso.

"She has a system for what to keep and what to get rid of. I'm only here for menial labor."

Angie brushed her knuckles beneath the collar of her V-neck t-shirt. Her jeans hugged her body, and she wore little red flats, making her appear much smaller than the other night. She'd pulled her almost-black hair into a ponytail and applied smoky makeup that made her dark eyes pop.

He pushed down the stirrings that were prodding him to pull her in for a kiss. She wasn't here for him. He needed to remember that. "Were you close to my dad?"

"We only met a few times." She shook her head, then added, "But I liked him."

He rubbed the back of his neck and looked away. Avoiding emotions was easier than the alternative. His sister thought if he dealt with his shit, he'd feel a lot better. Unfortunately, he didn't know how to handle more than one feeling at a time, and all of this—Angie, his dad, the family secrets? It was too much.

She flicked her fingertips up the side of a stack of folders, fluttering papers and creating a soft whirr.

"Something I don't understand," he said, knowing he was skirting dangerously close to admitting that her exit the other night had nearly blown him in two. "If you still planned to come here after figuring out who I was, why did you leave? Why didn't you say something then?"

Thick lashes hooded her eyes. She shuffled her feet. "Because I didn't know if I'd have the nerve to go through with it." Her gaze shifted. Her eyes met his.

Silence pulsed between them. His anger ran out of him like water down a drain. He cleared his throat. "Tell me what you need to do in Jamaica."

Her demeanor turned serious. "Rick—I mean your dad—worked as a pilot for a crime lord named Bear Golding. The CIA was trying to help the DEA locate his American distributor."

"Did my dad know this Golding guy?"

"Golding runs a huge operation. I'm not sure they ever met or if Golding even knew of your dad's existence. Rick had started forging connections and learning the workings of the enterprise." She hesitated. "I don't believe his plane ran out of gas. I think someone sabotaged his fuel tank."

Nate's chest compressed his heart like a stress ball. An hour ago, he believed his dad was a drug smuggler, an irreconcilable revelation he'd somehow learned to live with. Now he knew differently, and all because of the perplexing woman standing before him. The same woman who'd taken him to bed, only to disappear, walking away like it meant nothing.

Regardless of his jumbled feelings toward Angie, he needed to know what happened to his dad. "I want answers. I'll do it."

"It doesn't have to be you. I understand if you don't want to see me again, much less fly me to a Caribbean island."

"I know the airstrip Dad used. We can skip customs and the landing permits." He leveled his gaze on her, needing to make his position clear—for both their sakes. "Once I get you there, you're on your own."

Her voice cracked. "Thank you."

Corralling his emotions, he sucked in a deep breath and cleared his throat. "We'll leave tomorrow."

She flashed him a smile that sent warm tingles through his chest. He ignored fingers itching to touch her.

He was doing this for Dad. Not for her.

Regardless of what it felt like.

CHAPTER 8

"So, what's your deal?" It took a moment for Nate's words to register through the muffled isolation of Angie's headset. She wrested her gaze from the endless ocean.

They both sported giant earphones with mics, which only enhanced Nate's appeal. His rugged good looks, those aviator glasses and the commercial earphones made him even sexier. Something she'd not thought possible.

She, on the other hand, couldn't ignore the weight or the feel of the headset and had accepted shortly after donning the headgear that she probably looked like a bobblehead.

"My deal?" Surely he didn't want to rehash the fiasco in his hotel room.

"What do you do? At the CIA?"

She relaxed. "I'm an analyst. Organized crime."

"You're not a spy?"

She shook her head. "Operations officers are in the field. I work in an office."

"You were my dad's handler?"

"No, I'm a deputy task force commander. Your dad was recruited by the DEA. Someone over there managed his case."

He nodded and looked out the side window. They'd flown north because of the weather and had just made the turn to the south. The deep, persistent thrum of the engine would make it easy to slip back into silence, but now that he'd started talking, she didn't want it to end. "Do you like being a pilot?"

He flashed her a dazzling smile she hadn't seen since before he discovered her real identity. "Flying is great. It's all I ever wanted to do."

His infectious energy made it impossible not to grin. It must be nice to have a passion, to have always known who you wanted to be. Sure, she was passionate about catching criminals, but that was more about atonement than natural inclination. Everyone in law enforcement had a "one who got away." Never mind that hers happened when she'd barely hit her teens.

She shook her head. No point dwelling on the past. "You're lucky. There aren't many people who actually get to do what they love."

His mouth twisted into a bittersweet smile. "My dad taught me to fly. Some of my best memories are me and him up in the air."

The sound of longing combined with loss that threaded his voice created an all-too familiar ache in her chest. She choked back the hard lump working its way up her throat.

"As a kid, I wanted to go into the military. Maybe fly fighters, but it wasn't meant to be."

"Why didn't you enlist?"

He exhaled. His tone took on the inflection of someone reciting an answer. "I had to watch out for my brother and sister. Make sure no one figured out who we really were."

Right. The big family secret. "It must've been hard always having to lie about your identity."

"After a while, it stopped feeling like a lie." He shrugged, and if it hadn't been for the slight wince that accompanied the gesture, she might have bought his nonchalance. "Dad told me to make sure Jack and Elise never revealed our identity. Guess I took it upon myself to make the lie seem real."

Wow. That would have been a big burden for a teenage kid. "Did they ever let anything slip?"

He shook his head. "Jack knew we were hiding, but he didn't understand why. My dad and I spent a lot of time drilling him and testing him on his identity."

"What about Elise?"

There was a resigned sigh. "She was so young. Didn't know anything other than Mom left. She grew up believing our mother didn't love her. Since I couldn't tell her the truth, I did my best to make it up to her."

"Like archery?"

"Yep. Taught her to ride a bike. Took her to the library every Saturday. Read her bedtime stories. The one thing I didn't do was tell her the truth." His voice faltered. "And then she was kidnapped."

Angie could see how Nate might blame himself for his sister's abduction. Because in his mind, if he'd done a better job protecting her, she never would have been taken. He'd created a fallacy of failure and tortured himself with it.

Guilt was a weight Angie knew all too well. One she recognized it in the slump of Nate's posture and the ache in his words.

Rick had seemed a good guy, but the burden he'd saddled his eldest son with wasn't fair.

It explained a lot though. The need to be in control. An inability to form deep attachments.

"What about you? Were you destined for law enforcement?"

Talk about a loaded question. "Maybe? It's never felt like a choice."

She could see him trying to find the right words. Might as well put it out there. "Things that happened when I was a kid had a big impact."

"Things?"

"My sister's death." Twenty years had passed and still, talking about Cindy was like taking a knife in the gut. "She was everything I wasn't. Agreeable while I was obnoxious. Well-behaved when I was in trouble. Her even-tempered disposition the exact opposite of my hot-headedness." She shook her head, remembering her precocious little sister.

"Trouble? You? *Noooo*," he teased.

She couldn't help but laugh. Something about Nate—maybe his own childhood trauma—made it easier to talk about Cindy. "She was sweet and kind and really, really smart. That kid lived for culture school."

"What's that?"

"Where parents send their kids to learn about Chinese culture. There were language classes, dance classes, things like that." She shook her head and smiled. "I never took to Mandarin, but Cindy was a natural."

"What was your favorite class?"

So many years and so much anguish had passed since then, it was hard to recall. "I liked to Dragon Dance. Boy, did my arms ache afterwards though. Those bamboo poles were heavy." Goodness. How had she forgotten that detail?

"Sounds like fun."

"It was." So why had she fought so hard not to go? "Cindy loved it." She stared out the window and imagined the memories drifting away on the clouds.

Nate cleared his throat. "So, tell me about this Bear Golding guy."

"He moves thousands of kilos of cocaine and marijuana through Jamaica and the U.S. every day. Sounds like a bad guy, right?"

His lips twitched. "Is that a trick question?"

"Nope. He also invests loads of time and money into his community. People love him."

"So, he has a hero complex?"

"Despite his wealth, he still lives in the neighborhood where he grew up. It's the poorest part of Kingston. He's built schools, housing, rec centers. In that regard, he's a man of the people. As a kingpin, it's a different story. He's ruthless. He doesn't hold grudges, he retaliates."

"Retaliates how?"

"Drive-by shootings, executions, disfigurement, mutilation. You know, normal gangster stuff." The moment the insensitive words left her mouth, she regretted them.

Nate didn't seem to notice. "Sounds vicious."

"He's extremely protective of what's his and wants to expand his organization and his power across the Caribbean."

"My dad worked for this guy?"

Angie pursed her lips, but knew she could avoid the conversation only so long. Maybe it was best to get it out of the way. "Your dad was involved in the organization, but nowhere near the boss. I doubt he was ever in the same room with Golding."

"Bear is an unusual name."

"His real name is Teddy."

Nate groaned. "Are you serious? That's a little on the nose, don't you think?"

She loved that he picked up on the irony. "I think that's the point."

His Adam's apple bobbed. She braced herself for the one question she didn't want to answer.

"How'd Dad get involved?"

Her turn to swallow. Hard. The truth was, she'd manipulated the man, knowing he wanted to quit. The DEA had already pressured him for intel. He'd thought he was almost done, but they were close to figuring out Golding's operation, and she pressed him to keep going.

"I don't know how it started. Someone in the DEA recruited him."

Nate rubbed his hand against his chin. "What I don't get is why he agreed to it. He severed ties with my mother's family and relocated to Florida. After that, protecting us was his only goal."

What was she going to say? That his father's DEA handler told her the easiest way to get Rick's cooperation was to threaten to expose his children's identities?

He caught her gaze. After a long silence, his words reverberated in her headpiece. "Unless they had something on him."

She forced herself to look him in the eye. She owed him that. "They—" She cleared her throat. *Tell him.* "We knew who he was. Used it as leverage."

His nostrils flared. "How? It's been so long. Who figured it out?"

"I don't know." At least, that was the truth. But how could he ever forgive her after she'd just admitted using his father so shamelessly?

The cockpit seemed to shrink around them, the silence heavy and constricting. "I thought the feds were supposed to be the good guys."

"Compared to the alternative—" *Shit.* What was she thinking? She had zero right to tell this man how to feel. When would she learn to think before she spoke? She started again. "We are the good guys, but it's complicated. Sometimes you have to weigh the risk against the common good."

He stared at her, and she sensed the question he wanted to ask. *What was your involvement?* His lips parted, then closed.

Not knowing what else to do, she lay her hand on his forearm, noting the soft hair and warm skin. "I'm deeply sorry about what happened to your dad."

If ever there was a woman he should avoid, it was this one. And still he shuddered at her touch. Sitting next to her in the cramped cockpit of his Piper Cheyenne was pure torture.

He needed to divert blood flow back to his brain. He cleared his throat and steered the conversation to neutral territory. "Did you know we flew through the Bermuda Triangle?"

"We did?" Her eyes lit with amusement.

Maybe he wasn't the only one eager to change the subject.

"Go back. I want to see a UFO."

Her smile warmed him like sunlight on a chilly day.

"Sorry. We've got a schedule to keep. Maybe next time."

Her lips parted into a sensual little pout. "Next time?"

He clenched his jaw. What was wrong with him? There wouldn't be a next time. He knew that. He opened his mouth to clarify, but she interrupted and saved him the effort.

"Seriously, I didn't think the Bermuda Triangle was a real thing."

His muscles relaxed. "It's really just a heavily trafficked shipping lane. More boats and planes mean more wrecks."

"Ah well, it's fun to pretend there are forces at work we don't understand."

An incomprehensible energy hovered between them, heavy and intrusive, and he'd been an idiot to think he'd be impervious after nearly three hours in the tiny compartment.

He glanced at the navigation display, hoping a change of subject would be enough distraction to get them on the ground. "We'll start our descent in about twenty minutes. What's your plan for the airport?"

"Plan? What do you mean?"

Nate faltered. Surely, she didn't expect to wander into Kingston and start asking questions about a drug lord.

"God, you're easy." She snickered and gave a dismissive wave. "I'm going to ask around to see if anyone remembers the day your dad took off. After that, I'll get a taxi to the resort."

"Don't you think a random American asking questions might attract unwanted attention?"

She hesitated. "Since you mentioned it, have you been to Jamaica since your dad died?"

Clearly, there was more to this trip than a simple drop off. He should've known she'd try to pull something like this. A growl rumbled in his throat.

"I'll take that as a no." She wiped invisible dust off the copilot control wheel and gave him a sideways glance. "Since this is your first time back, it's only natural you'd want to ask around, talk to people who knew your dad."

A sharp pain hit him just above his right eyebrow. Jack had warned him she couldn't be trusted. "What didn't you understand when I said I would take you to Jamaica and that was it?"

She shrugged like this was an every-day request. "You were perfectly clear, but I also know you aren't going to head back to Florida immediately. You'll get out, stretch your legs. It only makes sense you'd chat up a few of the locals." She gave him a goading smile. "This is the only thing I'll ask of you. I promise."

Dammit.

Her eyebrows drew together. "But keep in mind that any of these people could have sabotaged your dad's plane."

Reality seeped into him. This wasn't some half-cocked adventure, and while Angie gave off an I've-got-it-covered vibe, what she planned to do was dangerous. She could get hurt. Or killed.

Like his dad.

He felt a slight pressure change in his ears. They were getting close to their destination. He checked the artificial horizon and leveled off before pulling back on the throttle and lowering the nose.

"Thank you, by the way." She gave a crisp nod. "For everything."

Good God. He felt like a tetherball the way she wound him up and banged him around.

Her bolting from his hotel room finally made sense. This wasn't the kind of thing she could screw up or approach haphazardly. It could be life and death. Literally.

She stared out the window for a long moment. "There's a foreign agent at the airport. I don't want him to see me."

He frowned. "Really?"

"Yeah. He was a contact for your dad. Bald guy, goes by the name Doc—"

"Doc works for the CIA? You're fucking with me." The man was a fixture at the airport.

"I'm not, I swear. He's already been debriefed on the day your dad crashed, but I wonder if he'll tell you any more than he told the task force."

This was starting to feel less and less like a quick favor. But he saw no point in arguing. He'd do it. How else was he going to find out what happened to his dad?

"So, you want me to talk to Doc." It wasn't a question.

"It would be a big help. If he sees me and reports back to the agency, I'm screwed. Not to mention, I'll never get to investigate your dad's death."

Might as well stop acting like it was up for discussion. "We'll be on the ground in a few minutes. Get the cash and your passport ready."

"Cash?"

"We talked about this. A thousand dollars in cash. Fold it up and put it in the passport."

"All of it?"

"You wanted to get into Jamaica unnoticed, didn't you?"

"Yes."

"This is how we do it."

She hoisted her bag onto her lap. "How do you know this?"

"You think you're my first client who wants to enter another country illegally?"

"Guess I hadn't thought about it." She pulled a stack of bills from her wallet. "I don't think it's going to fit."

"It's fine. Fold it in half and stick it in the middle. No one will care how it looks."

She muttered a curse, dug through her bag, and crammed a wad of bills into the little blue book. "I hope you know what you're talking about."

CHAPTER 9

Nate's heart clenched the moment the airstrip came into view—a swatch of concrete nestled among green hills and blue water. Memories smacked into him like an unexpected headwind. The buildings, the runway, all of it so familiar. And so colored by regret.

The last time they'd been here, Dad was making a cargo run for a client, an islander who owned a South Florida liquor store. They'd flown in to pick up a shipment of rum. Or so he'd been told. If only Nate could go back and ask the right questions. Maybe he could have talked his dad out of working for the feds. Maybe they could have avoided all that came after.

Now he was flying into the same airport and making another mistake. No. He couldn't think that way. This was the right thing to do—the only thing.

Nate set the approach flaps and lowered the wheels and landing gear. A few moments later, the plane touched the ground with a gentle bounce.

He glanced at his passenger, and his stomach soured. He'd fulfilled his part of the deal and delivered her to Jamaica. Now all he needed was to complete one last task. Then she'd go on her way and he'd be headed back to his regular life.

"Earth to Nate."

A hand waved at him from the passenger seat. So caught up in his memories, for a moment he'd almost forgotten she was there. Another lie. His body had been attuned to her since they climbed into the plane, the scent of her lemon-grass perfume wafting toward him every time she moved. Each and every fidget and wiggle in the co-pilot seat had been catalogued by his body.

Even worse, this wasn't a new phenomenon. She'd been a constant fixture in his mind from the moment he saw her standing at the counter in the lobby yesterday afternoon.

He'd told himself to move on but couldn't shake the sizzle of attraction between him and the beautiful woman at the casino who'd not needed rescuing, but who'd accepted it, nonetheless.

He shook his head. Remembering their encounter in Miami didn't help. In fact, it probably made things worse. He said he'd talk to Doc, and he would. But after that, he was leaving. The sooner he could get back in the air and put her out of his mind, the better.

"Can you hear me? Is this working?" She pointed to the giant headset.

The microphone blocked his view of her mouth, but her dark eyes pulled at him, just as they had when he kissed her in his hotel room. *Shit*. Was he on this again? This whole endeavor was about Dad and finding out what happened to him. It had nothing to do with getting closer to the vexing woman sitting next to him. "Sorry. Concentrating on landing."

She nodded, but he didn't think she bought the lie. Might as well come clean. At least about Dad.

"Thinking about the last time I was here." He steered the plane onto the tarmac and parked on the airport apron.

She removed the headset and leaned toward him, brows knitted together. "I know returning is hard, and I appreciate your bringing me. I hope to pay you back one day."

"Figure out who killed my dad, and you won't owe me anything."

Her face softened. She laid a hand on his wrist, and a pleasant tingle zinged up his arm and into his chest.

She broke eye contact and removed her hand. "I'd like to get an idea of what to expect now that we're here. What can you tell me?"

"Haven't you been here before? After my dad's death?" And if not, how had she known this was where they would be going?

"The airport? No, Doc's debriefing was at the U.S. Embassy."

Nate studied her, trying to determine whether she was being truthful.

"We're at a private airfield about fifty kilometers from Kingston. They've got a few personal hangars, a maintenance hangar, and a small terminal building. On the other side of the terminal, you'll find a tall iron fence with armed guards. Normally, that's where you'd go through Customs, but we're going to take care of that now." He glanced out the window. A man in a tan uniform approached.

She nodded and held up her passport. "I guess Doc will be in the maintenance hangar?"

"Most likely. When the officer gets here, we'll show him our documents and should be good to go. Then I'll find Doc."

She smiled, and his fingers itched to trace the outline of her lips, to remove the tie holding her hair in that ponytail, and to run his hands through the silken strands.

Nope. Not going there. Once he was back in the air, this inability to keep his body from reacting to the most mundane gestures would be a thing of the past.

An uncomfortable realization squeezed his chest. Once he left, Angie would be on her own, trying to get information from dangerous criminals. Sure, she worked for the CIA—in an office. She'd not mentioned anything about field work. Protecting her wasn't his job. She probably wouldn't want him inserting himself into her investigation anyway. Putting distance between them was the smartest thing he could do.

So why did he hope she'd ask him to stay?

—ееⅇ—

Angie handed over a poorly concealed wad of cash in an over-stuffed passport, and Nate provided his own non-lumpy identification. The official pocketed the cash, then opened each of the little books, holding it up as though verifying the biographical data matched the flesh-and-blood humans standing before him. He scanned Nate's passport with a device that looked like a phone but ignored Angie's.

"Enjoy your stay in Jamaica." The officer handed back the travel documents and gave them each a bright orange exit ticket. He turned to amble back toward the terminal.

Without a word, Nate shoved his hands in his pockets and took off for the maintenance hangar, his posture slumped, his gait halting.

Angie's heart constricted. Since their first meeting, all she'd done was make him miserable. She was part of the reason he and his siblings had a hole that could never be filled, a pain that would never go away.

She'd never expected to see the consequences of her actions. The truth of it was, she hadn't regarded Rick as anything more than a means to an end. Sure, she'd liked the guy, but she'd not thought about him beyond what he could do to help the mission. And while she'd not initiated the relationship, she'd leveraged his family's safety to get what she needed.

Just like everyone else he'd dealt with in the intelligence community.

Prickles of shame spread across her skin, skittering and multiplying like a swarm of ants. She'd never forgive herself for putting him in danger. And while she couldn't bring him back, maybe she could catch his killer.

Nate disappeared into the maintenance hangar. She had no business getting close to him or wreaking any more havoc in his life. Hell, she'd had plenty of that in her own life and had done a damned good job of ignoring it for twenty years. Last thing she needed was to get involved in someone else's mess.

This attraction to Nate had slammed into her like a punch in the face. The way he'd claimed her in front of Nemo, draping his arm over her shoulders and pulling her against him. A simple gesture with a lasting impression that had yet to fade. Even in his hotel room, there'd been a sense of rightness, a feeling that it was only the beginning.

No point thinking about it now.

A deep, hollow ache for the relationships she'd never have spread through her. Better to focus on finding out what happened to Rick and bringing closure to his family. That way, when she left, she'd know she'd done at least one thing right.

The faint aroma of exhaust fumes and sea salt hung heavy in the air. She wandered toward the terminal, noting its mold-covered façade and cracked stucco exterior. Upkeep of the pastel-blue monstrosity may have been neglected, but its fortifications had not. Just past the open-air building, two guards paced in front of a tall iron gate, M-16s angled toward the ground.

Hopefully, getting through security wouldn't be a problem.

Multi-colored huts crowded a tract of flattened grass and foot-worn paths on the other side of the bars and made for a jarring juxtaposition. A nonstop murmur of patois came from the market as vendors tried to lure sunburned clientele their way. Reggae music spilled from a speaker as tourists haggled over woven baskets and hats.

Maybe if her life had taken a different turn—maybe if her sister hadn't died—she'd be one of those normal people enjoying a normal vacation. How foolish of her to imagine something so ridiculous. She'd learned long ago not to bother dreaming about things that would never be. Tightness pulled at her eyes. She blinked the past away. The present was too important to get distracted, and first things first, she needed transportation to the resort. And maybe to do some furtive digging regarding the day Rick died.

In an alcove near the women's bathroom, Angie noticed a collection of vendor booths. Scuba diving, snorkeling, scooter rentals. She approached a young woman in a blue polo shirt manning a stall advertising jet ski tours.

"Wa gwaan." The woman's dark curls were streaked with gold and bounced when she spoke. Her words were smooth and lyrical. "Tell me what you need."

"I'm looking for car service to Kingston."

"Hold on. Let me get the driver for you. Nina!" The woman stretched her neck, and her hoop earrings jiggled as she waved at another employee on the far side of the loggia. She pointed at Angie. "This lady needs a taxi."

A small, middle-aged woman walked their way. She wore the same blue polo and had a soft bronze coloring. "Where you wanna go?"

"Casa Tortuga." Just saying the name of Golding's resort made her ill. Staying at a property owned by the man she'd be investigating had seemed like a good idea when she'd been a thousand miles away. Now? Not so much. "Can you take me?"

"Cash only."

Her chest loosened. Thank God she'd only given the customs agent a fraction of what she'd brought. "Not a problem."

"You ready now?" Nina asked.

Angie gazed at the planes lined up outside the terminal. No sign of Nate. "I need to say goodbye to a friend."

Nina shrugged and pointed to a shaded niche. "I'll wait over there."

Angie thanked her and turned back to the rental attendant, whose nametag said Jada. "Do you get a lot of business here at the airport?"

The woman bobbed her head casually. "Sometimes, y'know. People get so excited when they reach Jamaica, they want to plan the trip right away. If you're ready, I can sort it out for you."

"I'll probably wait until we get to the resort." Angie pretended to peruse the prices on the laminated service menu.

"You staying at Casa Tortuga?"

Angie nodded.

"We don't work out of that resort."

Angie bobbed her head like she was considering the information. "A friend told me about a crash that happened out of a small airport about a year ago. Was that someone who flew out of here?"

Jada's eyes flickered, and her smile faltered. "That was Mr. Rick."

Excitement at finding someone who knew Rick bubbled up. Angie fought to keep her tone casual. "Did you know him?"

"He would drop in and chat sometimes. Nice man."

"Were you here on the day of the crash?"

"Yeah."

"Anything stand out? Anything unusual?"

"Yuh full of questions, eh?"

"My friend knew him. Said he was a good pilot. Couldn't believe something like this would happen. I guess I'm just trying to make sense of it."

Jada's earrings wobbled when she shook her head, her reply slipping into Jamaican Patois. "Mi not notice nuttin strange."

"Did you see him before he left? Did he stop to talk?"

"Not that time."

Any hope she'd found a lead fizzled. "Well, thanks for talking to me about it, and thanks for the help with the car."

"No worry. Have a good day."

Angie walked to the tarmac and took a seat on a concrete bench. She twisted her hands together. Soon, Nate would return, tell her what he learned from Doc, and then go back to South Florida. Once that happened, they'd both be better off.

And yet, she couldn't ignore the truth. She wanted him to stay.

CHAPTER 10

Doc was in the office at the back of the hangar reading a magazine, feet propped on the desk. Nate stared for a moment. Even now, he had a hard time imagining that this man with his shiny bald head and affable demeanor was an informant. Or that he'd be involved in the activities that got his dad killed. Nate rapped his knuckles against the doorjamb. The sharp crack made Doc startle.

"Nate!" A huge smile spread across the other man's face. He popped to his feet, shoved the magazine under his arm, and came forward to clap Nate on the shoulder. "Wah yuh doin' here?"

The words rolled together in that easy Jamaican rhythm Nate remembered from childhood.

Doc and Nate's dad had been friends for more than two decades. Nate met the man when he was fifteen years old, and Doc had been a fixture at the airport ever since. Was Doc the reason Dad got involved with the Feds? Or had it been the other way around?

Nate cleared his throat. A mix of guilt for knowing he planned to pump this man for information and regret for the way things had turned out rendered him speechless. He gave himself an inward shake. Get the information and get the hell off this island.

"Brought a client over. Thought I'd drop in to say hi."

"I'm glad you came. Jack comes 'round now and then, but I wasn't sure I'd ever see you again."

Though Doc's smile appeared genuine, Nate realized he was one more person whose motives would forever be suspect. As if he hadn't had enough disillusionment for one lifetime.

"Coming back..." Nate shook his head as though willing the words to come to him. "It was time."

"About your father..." The paper crinkled as Doc rolled his magazine into a tube. "He was a good man. That accident never shoulda happened."

"That's kind of why I stopped in." Nate rubbed a hand against the back of his neck. "I've been thinking about Dad a lot lately."

A wary expression flittered across Doc's face. "Yeah?"

"Did you see him that day? The day of his crash?"

"I did, but only for a few minutes."

"Anything you remember would be appreciated. I'm just trying to get a picture of what happened."

Doc tilted his head and considered Nate for a long moment. "You thinking it was something other than an accident?"

"How can I not? There's no way Dad would have taken off without making sure he had enough fuel."

"All I know is, he called ahead and asked me to fuel the plane. Wasn't like him. Then he got here and was in a big, big hurry. Said he didn't have time to see the 1940s biplane I been fixin' up. Promised to stop by the next time he was on the island."

"Did you? Fill him up?"

Doc's lips pressed into a tight line. "Yuh serious askin' me that? Of course, I filled the tank—put in about two hundred gallons. Your dad told me to put it on his credit card."

Nate hadn't looked at his dad's credit card statement after he died, but Elise had gone through and settled all the accounts within a few weeks of learning about the accident. Would she remember a fuel charge?

"I meant no offense. Just trying to figure out how this could have happened." Nate put his hands on his hips and looked around the hangar. "Any chance the tank was sabotaged?"

Doc shrugged. "Don't think so. The plane went from here to the runway. Didn't see even a drop of oil."

The clank of tools sounded from another part of the hangar, followed by gruff, hurried shouts.

Nate watched the other man. He should have asked Angie for tips on how to tell when someone was lying. But Nate's gut was telling him that everything Doc said was the truth. "Did you notice anyone suspicious?"

"Not that I remember. I was called to tow a plane with a flat tire. Was gone maybe thirty minutes."

Was that enough time for someone to compromise Dad's plane? What would they need to pull this off? A hose and some sort of container to siphon the gas, as well as something to transport the fuel once the tank was drained. Dad's fuel gauge used a float sensor. Anyone with a bit of mechanical knowledge could jam the float into the up position, making the gauge read as full.

"Was this after you filled up the plane?"

Doc rubbed his chin. "Think so. I did only just get back in the hangar when your dad showed up."

"Anything else stand out?"

"Right before he climbed into the plane, he said, 'Trust is a currency, but you have to spend it wisely.' Wasn't sure whether he was talking to me or himself." Doc shook his head. "Thought 'bout that the whole time I watched him taxi and take off."

The comment didn't sound like anything Nate had ever heard Dad say, but it made him think someone Dad considered a friend may have betrayed him.

"Sorry, I don't have anything else to tell you," Doc said.

"It's more than I knew before."

Nate stuck out his hand. Doc gripped his fingers in a firm handshake as though trying to communicate something important.

"You take care of yourself." Doc's gaze was intense and unwavering. "Poking the beehive is not always the answer. Especially if someone hurt your dad on purpose."

"Appreciate your concern." He held Doc's stare. "I'll be careful."

Nate stepped out of the hangar and into the warm sun. He slipped on his sunglasses and gazed across the tarmac. From somewhere nearby, a prop engine buzzed to life. Angie sat alone on a bench near the terminal building. All he needed to do now was fill her in. Then he could leave.

He walked toward her, keeping his pace slow, then stopped altogether. Why was he hesitating? He should be climbing into his plane, not staring at a woman who rejected him—a woman who'd hijacked his brain and refused to leave.

The closer he got, the more she consumed him, filling him up with a need to be near her. Whatever was happening to him, he didn't like it.

Forcing his feet to move, he trudged forward. Angie pulled the tie out of her hair and shook out a long mane of dark, silky locks. Saliva flooded his parched mouth. He was not going to drool, dammit.

Every glance in her direction brought back the sting of abandonment, the memory of the hotel door shutting, not knowing what he'd done wrong. And then the kicker. Her appearance at the airport counter and the admission she knew all about him.

Now he knew who she was and why she'd fled his hotel room.

And despite it all, he still wanted her. His cheeks scalded with shame. So much for the family-first mantra that had been drilled into him—initially by his grandfather and then his dad.

"How'd it go?" She shielded her eyes from the sun and looked up.

Tell her about the conversation with Doc. Fly home. Forget they ever met. "I think he only talked to me so I'd leave."

Angie leaned forward, bottom lip caught beneath her teeth, questions in her eyes.

He inhaled, letting the hot, humid air fill his lungs. *Get it over with*. "Dad called ahead the day of the crash and asked him to fuel the plane. It was his habit to hang around and shoot the shit before taking off, so the phone call stuck out. Doc said the tank was low, so he added fuel."

The cock and bull story about his dad running out of gas never sat right with Nate or his siblings. Doc claimed to have topped off the tank, but could he trust anything the man said? Until today, he'd had no idea Doc worked for the CIA.

"That tracks with what he said in the debriefing."

"He also said Dad was in a big hurry when he got here. He wanted to show Dad his restoration, but Dad said he couldn't stay. Promised to see it next time." Nate swallowed back the lump rising in his throat. "According to Doc, just before takeoff, he mumbled something about trust being like currency and that once it's spent, you're left with nothing."

Angie's eyebrows drew together. "That's new. I wonder why he didn't share that with the team."

Nate shrugged. How could he possibly know what went through Doc's mind? "Maybe he forgot about it."

Angie's pupils tracked up as if she could pull the answer from the sky. "It's possible. Or maybe he didn't realize the significance. Doc was pretty stressed out about being summoned to the embassy."

"Any idea what Dad might have been talking about?" Nate gazed down at her, noting the way her thick, dark hair shone in the sun. He could almost imagine how it would feel cascading through his fingers.

"I doubt it had anything to do with Golding. Like I said, your dad wasn't high enough in the organization to have contact with him." She twisted a lock of that wonderful hair around her finger. "It sounds like someone he worked with directly, someone he thought he could trust might have betrayed him."

"It took a lot to rattle Dad." Nate pursed his lips, trying to remember if he'd ever seen his unshakeable father back down from anything. "Whoever it was, it must've really scared him."

Angie stood and paced the length of the bench. "He obviously thought he was in danger. Otherwise, why would he have been in such a hurry to leave?" She stared at Nate as if expecting an answer. "What about Vincenzo Alario? He went after your sister not long after your dad's death."

Nate shifted. Not enough penance in the world could make up for Elise's kidnapping or the fact it happened after she left home to get away from him. "Who was at the debriefing?"

"Some DEA guys, the task force commander, the department chief, a few of the other agency officers." She paused. "Me."

He took a reflexive step back, as if distance would give him clarity. She'd told him she was at the meeting at the embassy, but talking to Doc put things into perspective. What did he actually know about Angie Liu? Only what she'd told him. The whole thing might be a setup. The casino, the hotel room, showing up at the airport saying she needed his help. She already knew about their connection to the Koslov crime family. His eye began to twitch. What if she betrayed his family to the Alarios? What if she was responsible for what happened to Elise?

He took a shallow breath and forced himself to give some semblance of a smile.

Angie lifted her bag to her shoulder and grabbed the handle of her suitcase. "Thanks again for your help. I appreciate your talking to Doc. I know it wasn't easy." She jerked her thumb over her shoulder. "I've got a ride lined up. I should get going, and I'm sure you want to start for home."

She extended her hand.

This was it. Time to say goodbye and get on with his life. He stretched out his palm, then stopped. "How will you get home once the investigation is done?"

She gave a hadn't-thought-about-it shrug that tugged at his conscience. He knew she could take care of herself but didn't feel right about leaving her stranded. Not to mention how he would feel if he left her here and she got hurt.

"Don't worry about me. I'll be fine."

"What if I stayed for a few days? I'm here. I want answers." He'd been looking over his shoulder his entire life. Enough was enough.

Her gaze locked with his. "Let's see if we can find you a room."

CHAPTER 11

A luggage cart rumbled past, its wheels rattling against the uneven concrete as Angie and Nate leaned against a wall, waiting for their driver. Angie barely even registered the sound over the clatter inside her own head.

Something was going to have to be done about the out-of-control hankering she'd developed for this man. Especially considering he wanted nothing to do with her.

Nate's eyes met hers, his gaze so intense it felt like he was inside her head. She gave her imagination free rein— his mouth tracing the line of her neck, her fingers gliding down his bare abs.

His eyes darkened. Was he remembering their hungry kisses in his hotel room? The way their bodies fit together?

Time for a diversion. "You're going to need a change of clothes." He'd dressed for the flight in cargo shorts, a T-shirt, and sneakers.

He shrugged and pointed at a black leather duffel at his feet. "I have my overnight bag. After that, I'll pick something up at the resort. If I even need it. I'm only staying for a day or two."

"The guy I spoke to at the hotel said there was one room left. I told him to add it to my reservation."

"Let me know what I owe, and I'll pay you back."

Was he serious? They weren't even close to square. "Not necessary. You got me here. A hotel room is only a drop in the bucket." She didn't know how much the flight over would have cost him, but it certainly wasn't free.

Nate opened his mouth, presumably to protest, but didn't get a chance.

"Yow!" Nina's waving arm drew their attention.

"Guess she's ready for us." Nate pushed off the wall and put his hand on Angie's shoulder, guiding her toward their driver. His palm lingered for less than a second, but her skin tingled, even after he pulled it away.

It was going to be a rough few days.

They stopped at a gate. A uniformed officer waved a metal detector over a passenger's body. Two other officers crowded the man and asked what he planned to do in Jamaica. The man fidgeted and blinked.

Angie resisted the urge to clutch her purse to her side and prayed the guards wouldn't find the Sig Sauer she wore in the concealed carry holster at her waist. The bribe to the customs official was supposed to take care of this, but she'd not told Nate she had a weapon. Maybe he didn't think to mention security because he didn't know she'd be armed.

Nina took their customs tickets, handed them to a guard, and motioned them through the gate, bypassing the search. Relieved to have passed another hurdle, Angie let her attention wander to the pop-up market with its colorful tents and stalls. With all the noise and activity, the little bazaar seemed to exhale energy.

"My car's over 'ere." Nina led them to the sidewalk and down the block. They followed her into a narrow mud alley between two dwellings that ended in a gravel parking lot.

"Wait 'ere." Nina ran around the corner of the building.

Angie watched for a moment, wondering if the car service was on the up-and-up, then turned to Nate. "I'm glad you decided to stay, but I need you to understand I can't involve you in anything that might put you in danger."

An angry scowl settled onto his face. "Yet you had no hesitation when it came to my dad."

Crap. "The DEA trained your dad. He learned about surveillance, countersurveillance, handling risky situations, avoiding detection—"

"How'd that work out for him?" His voice was flat, but she couldn't miss the current of anger threading his tone.

Having a civilian tagging along wasn't ideal, but a partner could be useful. Besides, this wasn't a typical mission. Nothing she would be doing here was sanctioned by the CIA. An unconventional investigation with an unconventional partner. It just might work.

"When we get settled in our rooms, let's meet and go over the game plan. I'll fill you in on what I know."

His shoulders relaxed.

Tires crunched over dirt and gravel. Nina rounded the corner in an old Toyota. Nate climbed into the front passenger seat, while Angie took the seat behind the driver.

The drive took them along the Jamaican coast, weaving through small towns and offering spectacular views of the Caribbean. Thick, lush forests stretched between the highway and the sea, and rocky hills grew from the land on the other side of the road. Angie watched for a time, but the beautiful scenery was no match for the man in the front seat. She studied him. The way his eyes crinkled when he smiled, how he made easy conversation with the driver, the pulsing of his jaw when he was deep in thought. Every gesture provided insight into the man she wanted to know better but had no business even thinking about.

Now, all she had to do was figure out how to keep her libido in check and keep him safe. Because she'd never forgive herself if anything happened to him.

Eventually, she dragged her gaze away and watched the coastline for the rest of the ride. Forty-five minutes later, they were at a guardhouse waiting to be admitted to Casa Tortuga.

———ℓℓℓ———

The driver dropped them at the first door she saw. Nate waited for Angie to hand the woman a couple of bills before exiting the car.

The automatic doors swooshed open, and they entered the resort's casino. Lights flashed, bells clanged. Customers sat on stools, sipping drinks and mindlessly pressing buttons on screens. A film of smoke hung in the air.

The casino was small and only featured slots and pokies, but that was to be expected. As Nate knew from the few nights he'd spent in Jamaica, all other types of gambling were illegal. That didn't mean you couldn't find a card game. You just needed to know where to look.

They entered a long hallway and finally emerged into the lobby of the hotel. The turquoise ocean stretched for miles beyond the open glass doors at the far side of the large room.

He scanned the space, but then his gaze snagged on the sway of Angie's hips. *Shit.* Not here. He closed his eyes, but all he saw was her beneath him on the sofa in his room in Miami.

Just knowing she was in the same hotel would be hard enough. Because as much as he wanted to dislike her for her role in his dad's death, he couldn't find it in him. There was something that drew him to her, like a magnetic needle finding true north.

He glanced around the atrium. Thankfully, the resort looked to be quite large. He needed to be close enough to know what was going on with her investigation, but otherwise, he'd keep his distance.

"Welcome, Mr. and Mrs. Connor!" A voice boomed from the check-in desk.

Nate looked behind him. They were the only ones there. *Connor?*

"Oh no. We're not a couple. Just travel companions." Angie smoothed her shirt and gave a self-deprecating laugh.

"Are you Sarah Connor?" The desk clerk's braids shook when he tilted his head, the beads on the ends knocking together.

Angie shifted her weight uncomfortably while Nate stifled a laugh. Of course, she'd used a fake name—and of course, it was *that* one.

She turned and glared.

It fit, somehow. Not just the alias, but the whole vibe. Like she was one step away from pulling out a sawed-off shotgun and declaring today judgment day.

"Shut up." She said to him before turning back to the desk.

"Honeymoon suite, no?" The clerk leaned forward. His gaze flicked to Nate, then back to Angie. He bit his bottom lip and waggled his eyebrows.

"No, we have two rooms." She fidgeted with the pen on the counter and spoke in a low voice. "We *need* two rooms."

"No mistake, miss. You were given a complimentary upgrade." The man sported a wide, bright smile.

"While I appreciate that, I reserved two rooms." The pitch of her voice increased. "I had one, and I called to request another."

Nate's cock, clearly a fan of sharing a room—maybe even a bed—took notice. *Breathe.* He squeezed his eyes shut, exhaling slowly and imagining himself beneath a stream of cold water.

"Let me check the reservation for you." The man, whose name tag said Isaac, tapped away on his keyboard. "I see in the notes you called to add a companion to your booking. You accepted the offered room."

The hair on the back of Nate's neck rose and sent a shiver to his shoulders. He needed his own room with his own bed. Preferably as far from Angie as possible.

She must have had the same thought. Her voice took on a panicked edge. "I need two rooms. I had a room for me, and I added one for him." She held up two fingers. "Two. Rooms."

The man's braids clacked again. "Sorry. The suite is the only one left."

"That can't be right."

Nate's entire body pulsed with the beating of his heart, though the pounding grew more pronounced in his groin. He couldn't do this. He couldn't share a room with this woman.

"The Caribbean Economic Partnership Summit is this week, so all the rooms in the city have been booked."

"But you had a suite available?" She shook her head in disbelief.

"Cancellation." He shrugged. "Sometimes things just work out."

"This isn't working out. This is wrong." Both the volume and pitch of her voice rose in frustration. "There must be something you can do."

Her eyes met Nate's. She wet her lips and turned back to the clerk.

They were adults. Working together to find out who killed his father. He swallowed a hard, dry lump. No reason it had to get weird.

"Your original room has been reassigned and is occupied." Isaac gave a small smile. "In the living room, there's a couch. If it helps, I can send up extra bedding."

Angie gave a half-hearted shrug. "Fine." Her sharp tone conveyed the opposite.

Looked like Nate would be sharing a room. With Angie.

The desk clerk slid a piece of paper across the counter. Angie scrawled out a signature. He handed her two room keys and presented her with a map of the building.

Maybe it wouldn't be all bad. The close quarters would make it easier to keep himself in the loop and figure out whether she could be trusted.

She turned to Nate and took a deep breath. "Honeymoon suite it is."

CHAPTER 12

They rode the elevator in silence. Angie leaned against the side wall and tried to avoid looking at the man she'd be sharing a room with. God, what a disaster. They might have made peace had they both had their own space, but this? Crossing the Atlantic in an inner tube seemed less daunting.

Nate cleared his throat but said nothing.

The door dinged open. Distant laughter and the thud of a door closing down the corridor made the anxiety between them that much more obvious. He motioned for her to go first, and she stepped into an impossibly long hallway. The placard on the wall pointed to the right.

She dragged her suitcase to a door near the end of the corridor, while Nate followed one step behind. Once again, they stood outside a hotel room. An awkward tension simmered. She pressed the keycard against the pad above the handle.

Nate held the door. The aroma of stagnant air and lemon Pledge greeted them. A quick survey of the main room revealed a small kitchen, a bathroom, a sitting area, and a balcony.

The door clicked shut behind Nate, the sound final and deep. He dropped the scuffed overnight bag onto the chair, and she stifled the urge to fill the space with words. Even though they'd been on a plane together and in their driver's tiny Toyota, the deep blues and yellows of the lushly appointed room seemed to close in around her. She couldn't have been more aware of Nate's presence if they'd been crammed in a closet.

"Maybe this is a good thing." Forced optimism pushed the pitch of her voice higher. "People thinking we're a couple. You know, as a cover."

His gaze strayed toward the bedroom. He didn't need to speak for her to know what he was thinking. Looking at him, with the day-old scruff on his jaw and his dark, intense eyes, a few forbidden ideas fluttered through her mind as well.

All foolishness she didn't have time for right now.

"You want to pretend to be married?" He shifted closer. "Newlyweds? Deep in love?"

"Sure." She tried to sound upbeat, cavalier. Hell, maybe this really would help them find out what happened to Rick. "Piece of cake, right?"

"I suppose." The words dragged over his lips.

"We did it once before. With Nemo."

"That was only for a couple of minutes."

She drew in a breath and held it. Could they really do this? Pretend to be a couple? Probably not. There was too much between them for it to work. Too much anger, too much regret, too much desire. "You know what, stupid idea. Don't worry about it. I was only thinking out loud—"

"I'll do it."

"Besides, who'd believe—" *Wait, what?* "You'll do it?"

"If you think this is the best way to find out what happened to Dad." He gave an unconvincing shrug, then grabbed her suitcase and wheeled it through the French doors and into the bedroom. A moment later, he returned, cupping the back of his neck with his hand.

"What's wrong?"

He glanced back at the bedroom, but didn't say anything, instead choosing to stand stiffly in the middle of the room.

"Regretting our pretend marriage already? Do we need to find a pretend divorce attorney?"

"It's fine, really."

A pang of hurt feelings squeezed at her heart. Was the thought of being married to her so unpleasant he couldn't stand to think about it for more than thirty seconds? Dammit, if he didn't want to do this, he should just say it. "You're a terrible liar."

Ignoring her, he moved to the couch and turned on the television, flipping through until he landed on a sports show. She shuffled her feet. Oh well. She didn't have the energy to get into it now anyway.

Diverting her attention from the annoying man on the couch, she took a closer look at their surroundings.

The suite must have come with some sort of romance package. In one corner, she spied a bouquet of white roses. In another, chocolate-covered strawberries and a bucket of champagne.

A warm flush edged up from the collar of her shirt. Just because there were tokens of romance scattered everywhere didn't mean it had to be uncomfortable. Besides, she'd never understood the allure of strawberries. What could be less sexy than watching someone eat?

She strode across the room and picked up a strawberry by its little green leaves. Nate had taken off his shoes and was leaned back against the sofa, clearly trying to avoid acknowledging the situation. Overcome by the strangest desire to provoke a reaction from him, she imagined dangling the fruit over his face, his chin tilting up to see what she was doing. The mental image alone nearly made her laugh.

Lifting the strawberry to her own mouth, she let the bitter scent of chocolate tickle her nose. She bit into the bottom half of the candied fruit. The chocolate coating cracked, and sweet juices oozed onto her tongue.

She wiped her mouth with the back of her hand, and her gaze landed on Nate, who was no longer staring at the television. Instead, he'd twisted his body toward where she stood by the sliding glass door. Wide-eyed and with one arm draped over the back of the sofa, his full attention was on her.

A tingle spread up her neck to her ears and across her face. She gave herself an inward shake and spun slowly, pretending to survey the room—anything to take her mind off the man watching her every move.

Pretty standard. A living area with a couch, a chair, and a television. A sliding door to the balcony overlooked the pool and ocean. And then there was the bedroom. Situated directly behind the couch, it had French doors that framed the room and revealed a king-sized bed with a plush, white comforter.

Covered in rose petals.

She remembered the funny look on Nate's face when he came out of the bedroom. Was this the reason? She squelched the hysterical laugh crawling up her throat.

Everything would be fine. She was a professional. This was no big deal.

She turned back to Nate, still on the couch. He ran a hand over his jaw. A slight but strangled sound passed his lips.

Her heart thundered like a thrash metal drum solo as tension rippled between them. Somehow, they were going to have to move past this. Her mouth went dry and her voice cracked. "I'm hungry. How about you?"

Something flared in his eyes. He startled, then gave his head a small shake and blew out his breath. "Food sounds great."

"Excellent. Give me a couple of minutes to shower and change."

Nate sat on the couch, flipping through the channels on the television without seeing anything, the drum of the shower boring into his brain. Angie. Naked. A couple of thin doors the only thing separating them.

His head throbbed. *Fuck*. The image of her eating that strawberry would not leave him alone. Her teeth scraping against the candy coating. The dribble of juice that leaked between her lips.

No. This was wrong. All of it. Staying had been a complete mistake.

He sniffed his shirt—the same one he'd put on before leaving Key Largo earlier in the day. The overnight bag he kept in the plane contained only a pair of boxer briefs and a clean T-shirt. At some point, he'd need to visit a store.

He leaned forward and covered his face with his hands. What was he doing? Waiting to go to dinner with his pretend wife? He'd clearly lost his mind.

Though the alternative wasn't any better. Staying in this room with her would drive him crazy. He slumped against the couch. Never did he imagine when he said he wanted to stay that they'd end up sharing a hotel room. As newlyweds.

He groaned. People would expect them to behave a certain way. Could he do it? Unfortunately, he thought he could.

And that scared him more than anything.

Continuing to deny the attraction wasn't rational at this point. Neither was the fact that despite all the uncertainty surrounding Angie's appearance and his father's death, he *wanted* to trust her. Honestly, what ulterior motive could she possibly have that involved tricking him into inviting her to his hotel room in Florida and then coercing him into flying her to Jamaica?

He'd created this situation when he insisted on staying. Now he had no choice but to deal with it.

There'd been a collection of storefronts in a corridor off the lobby. The front desk would know when the stores closed. If not tonight, he'd go down and buy a few items in the morning. He leaned over to pick up the handset of the phone.

He read the speed dial to the right of the keypad and had his finger poised to push the button when a movement in his peripheral caught his attention. He turned his head and sucked in a breath.

Angie stood just outside the door to the bedroom, looking amazing in a white summer dress with a vibrant red floral pattern that brought out the russet tones in her skin. He dropped the handset back into its cradle and stood as if seeing her for the first time. Thin straps accentuated lean arms and shoulders. A low-cut V-neckline plunged to her breastbone and emphasized the plump, round mounds of her breasts. The instrument of torture stopped just above her knees, revealing toned, bronze legs.

He clenched his fists at his sides and looked away. He had no right to want her. But God help him, he wanted nothing more than to pick her up and carry her to that bed. Maybe if he didn't already know how good she smelled, how her mouth on his made him hard. Maybe then, resisting her wouldn't feel like climbing Kilimanjaro in flip-flops.

He glanced at his cargo shorts and t-shirt. "People are going to wonder why you married such a slob. Will they even let me in dressed like this?"

"I called downstairs. They said it was fine."

Hard to believe, but he wasn't going to argue it. "Shall we?"

Without thinking, he held out his elbow, as though escorting her to dinner was a common occurrence, and to his surprise, she slipped her hand into the crook of his arm. His nerve endings took notice of her touch, sending urgent messages to his brain to catalog the feel of her hand on his skin.

They exited the room, and halfway to the elevator, she let go. "Thanks for going along with the married thing." She lowered her gaze and crossed her arms. "I know it wasn't what we planned, but it works. No one will give us a second thought."

He responded with a lame, "No problem."

After the longest elevator ride ever and a trek past the enormous pool, they arrived at a restaurant overlooking the ocean.

"Welcome." The hostess offered a broad smile. "Do you have a reservation?"

Angie nodded and held out her room card. The attendant swiped it and gazed at the computer for a moment, then offered a wide smile. "We just love newlyweds." She winked and grabbed menus.

Nate bowed to Angie and motioned with his hand. "After you."

The route to their table zig-zagged through candlelit scenes with couples sharing desserts, holding hands, and sipping drinks. Some sort of jazzy Caribbean music played softly in the background.

Nate had always considered such displays self-indulgent but couldn't ignore the tightness in his chest as he imagined a romantic dinner with Angie.

Clearly, this newlywed thing was really messing with his head. He'd spent his whole life pretending to be someone he wasn't. You'd think he could handle a few days in a make-believe marriage.

A soft, barely audible orchestral tune played in the background. Near the back wall, they took a sharp right and were seated in an alcove behind a water feature.

Dark. Private. Romantic. Nate concealed his groan and pulled out Angie's chair.

They were about to embark on a dangerous investigation to find his dad's killer, and he didn't know if he could make it through dinner.

A server arrived with a bottle of wine.

Booze was the last thing he needed. He held up his palm. "We didn't order that."

The man flipped over the stemware and began to pour. "On the house."

Angie leaned over. Her scent brushed his nose. "It's included with the meal."

Introducing alcohol to the situation was probably a bad idea. He rubbed his hand along his jaw and stared at the drink.

Angie lifted her glass, held it up and waited for him to do the same. "Here's to a successful investigation."

They clinked glasses. Nate lifted his to his mouth. One sip couldn't hurt.

"And to doing whatever it takes to make our marriage believable." She froze, seeming to catch the implications of her words.

He almost spit up his wine, but when he looked at her, the most delightful flush colored her cheeks.

"That's not what I meant."

"I know." He chuckled. "Maybe we should just acknowledge the elephant in the room."

"What sexual tension?"

Nate laughed. It sounded nervous and forced. *Fuck*. He wanted her.

But no, he couldn't have these thoughts. Not here. Not now. Not ever.

His body didn't agree.

They shared a mutual attraction. Now that it was out in the open, maybe they could put it behind them.

The server returned to take their orders. He grinned and motioned his finger back and forth between them. "You two are going to make it."

"What makes you say that?" Nate asked.

"I can see it in the way you look at each other. The body language says it all."

Man, this guy was full of it. Nate opened his mouth to set the record straight, but once again, Angie commandeered the moment. "You're too kind." She reached across the table and grasped Nate's hand, just like the couples they'd passed on their way to the table. Her fingers were soft, and when she rubbed her thumb across his knuckles, his skin heated. But it was her eyes that pulled him in. Warm. Kind. Sincere.

"I can see you want to keep things private. No problem." The server winked again.

The moment the guy rounded the corner, she let go. "I think we need to maintain the cover as much as possible."

The way she'd gazed at him. For a moment, Nate had wanted it to be real.

"Sure." He forced his face into a neutral expression. "You're the boss."

"We should strategize, determine our first steps." Angie leaned her elbows on the table and clasped her hands together, the motion accentuating her cleavage in the most alluring way.

He swallowed hard and poured himself another glass of wine.

"What do I need to know?" He refilled her glass and shook the empty wine bottle. "We're going to need another one of these."

Her eyes sparkled in the candlelight. What would she do if he leaned over and kissed her? Would she pull away? He didn't think so.

But now wasn't the time and it never would be.

CHAPTER 13

Angie kicked off her sandals, picked them up by the heel straps, and let the cool sand squish between her toes. They'd finished a bottle of wine at dinner and had a glass of sambuca with dessert. That buzzy warmth she associated with just the right amount of alcohol spread through her chest. Her limbs were loose, her smile easy.

She leaned into Nate and wrapped her hand through his arm. "I think I'm a little tipsy."

"Really? I couldn't tell." He smiled and led her toward the water, where the wet sand made walking easier.

Frothy waves lapped at her feet. She rested her head on his shoulder and inhaled the salty ocean air. If only they were here for a different reason. She could almost forget it wasn't real.

Why did being close to him feel so good?

Whether it was the wine or something else, Nate seemed to have relaxed during dinner, and now things felt more like they had the night they met—easy and comfortable. The smart, sweet, funny guy she'd met at the casino had finally returned.

The bright moon cast a silvery shimmer across the water. It left one side of Nate's face in shadow but accentuated his handsome profile—the sharp line of his jaw, the gleam in his eyes.

God, how she wanted to kiss him.

What if that night in Miami she hadn't freaked out and taken off? What if she'd told him the truth? She let out a sigh. Foolish to even speculate. They were doomed from the start.

Knowing that should have been enough. But still, her desire for this man kept finding a way to seep through the cracks in her previously impenetrable armor.

Was it the alcohol? Drinking certainly made her more inclined to give in to her impulses. Always a bad idea. Touching him was another bad idea. She extracted her hand from the crook of his elbow.

They passed a couple in a passionate embrace.

Nate cleared his throat. "The resort is nice."

She let out a shaky laugh. "It is. Especially considering it's owned by a drug lord."

He stopped. "Drug lord?"

"Bear Golding."

He wheeled to face her. "We're staying at a resort owned by the man who may have killed my father?" His voice was a growl.

Angie winced at her thoughtlessness. "Your father heard rumors of a trafficking enterprise at the resort. A waypoint for the cartel. He mentioned someone named Wayne. It made sense to stay close to the action."

Nate was quiet. The darkness obscured his expression. What must he be thinking?

"I know you don't trust me. I should have told—"

Cupping her face in his hands, he cut her apology short. "Took me by surprise, is all." His voice was soft, his breath warm on her lips. "But if you think being here, close to the source, is the quickest way to get answers, then I believe you know what you're doing."

Her pulse quickened, and a rush of heat spread across her skin. His touch, tender but firm, sent a shiver down her spine, and the air between them seemed to thicken, pulsing with energy, drawing them together and igniting the tension until it was almost impossible to ignore.

Maybe they should just get it on and get it out of their systems. Though truly, she didn't think that was going to do it. She already knew the feel of his hands on her body, the way he moved insider her. Once hadn't been enough. She didn't know if it ever would be. He held her gaze. The warmth of his palms traveled from her cheeks to her core. Neither spoke, and she twisted her skirt in her fists to keep from touching him.

He let go and took a step back. The cool air nipped at her skin where his hands had been. Her stupid heart thrummed against her chest.

Without missing a beat, he resumed walking, apparently unaffected by the intimacy of the moment. "Is it normal for a crime lord to own a hotel?"

"Yes, actually. The hospitality industry has a complicated relationship with dirty money."

"Why's that?"

"Hotels and restaurants tend to do a lot of cash business. It's the perfect cover for moving money into banks and making it look legit—Ouch!" She sucked in a breath as pain flared across her foot. "I stepped on something." Bracing a hand on Nate's shoulder, she inspected the damage. "Just a shell. A sharp one."

He leaned closer. "Are you bleeding?"

She shook her head and straightened. "I don't think so. I'll be fine."

His hand lingered on her forearm, then slid to her hand. Their fingers intertwined.

Grinning, she concentrated on the swinging of their joined hands and the rightness of the connection.

She moved her thumb along his calloused palm, liking the texture, the imperfections. Hands that knew hard work. She longed for that rough skin to skim across her body. Her stomach. Her chest.

He couldn't know what she was thinking, but her face warmed nonetheless.

"Do you know what Golding is up to?" he asked.

"I have some ideas. I'll start investigating in the morning. After that, I want to visit a connection on the Kingston police force."

"You trust this person?"

She nodded. "Fitzroy is a good man. If he can't help us, he'll have an idea where to look."

They walked in silence for a few moments, alone on the beach, the rhythm of the waves whispering that she needed to savor the moment. She inhaled, letting the briny air fill her lungs.

"I hope my being here isn't a problem." There was an unspoken question in his words.

Her stomach fluttered again, a reminder that lying to herself wasn't going to work. "Why would you think that?"

He shrugged.

She tugged him to a stop and faced him, her heart softening. "I'm glad you stayed." She touched his cheek. The coarse stubble of his jaw made her palm tingle. "It's nice to have company and certainly better than being alone."

He held her gaze and nodded. "Much better." His voice was a low rumble.

He leaned forward at the same time she stretched onto her toes. Her shoes dropped onto the sand with a soft *thunk*. She wrapped her arms around his neck and he drew her in.

Their lips touched.

Soft and tentative but filled with an electricity that sent shivers coursing through her.

When she closed her eyes, their tongues collided. This was different from the night at the hotel. That had been about two strangers enjoying each other for an evening. But they weren't strangers now, and this kiss communicated a need that went beyond a onetime passion.

Everything melted away with her moan. *Yes.* It seemed neither of them could get enough. Nate pulled her tight against him. His arousal pressed into her stomach. Her womb throbbed in response, and she ground against him, wanton and out of control.

He cupped a breast through her dress with one hand while the other lifted her leg to hook it around his hip. With only her thin panties between them, her clit rubbed against the coarse material of his shorts.

She grunted her desire.

He withdrew his hand from her breast and found his way to her thigh. Bunching up her skirt, he inched his fingers into her panties. Fire erupted the moment his fingers slid over her slick sex. She pushed into him, wanting more. He teased and stroked, finally dipping inside. Her breaths quickened.

He pressed his thumb against her most sensitive spot, and she cried out. Her back arched. Her hamstrings quivered. Her body tensed and trembled.

A tsunami of pleasure, warm and fast, cascaded through her. Only his firm grip kept her from crumpling to the ground. She squeezed her eyes shut and struggled to catch her breath.

Had she really just done that? Made those sounds? Let him touch her like that? Her stomach hardened. Her face grew hot.

Once her breathing returned to normal, she opened her eyes and met Nate's stunned stare. A quick glimpse of his expression—overwhelmed, bewildered, confused—made her heart twist. His shoulders and chest rose and fell on a deep inhale as he averted his gaze, and then his eyes locked on hers and his features turned to stone. "That was a mistake."

Had he been toying with her? Trying to get her to drop her guard so he could manipulate her and make her feel like a fool? Well, mission accomplished.

God, she was dumb.

She couldn't change what they'd done, but she could make sure it didn't happen again. "You're right about that."

She picked up her shoes, then turned to walk back to the resort.

CHAPTER 14

A door clicked. Ten seconds later, a steady pattering of water hissed against the tiles. Nate pulled the pillow over his face. He should suffocate himself for being such an asshole.

He'd barely slept, tossing and turning on the too-narrow, too-short couch all night. But that was only part of the problem. The real issue was knowing Angie lay in the next room.

With his face covered, he couldn't see the closed door to her bedroom, but he could picture it. He'd certainly spent enough time staring at it, wondering what she wore to bed. Tiny shorts and a tank top was his bet, but he'd gladly fork over the entire pot if it turned out she slept in the nude. When he wasn't imagining what she had on beneath the covers, he'd debated whether he should go to her. Apologize. Pick up where they ended things on the beach.

Instead, he'd glared at the door, irrationally blaming her for the way the evening ended, all the while knowing it was his fault. A knot formed in his belly. She'd come apart in his arms and he'd ruined it.

She'd been his. To touch. To tease. To arouse. He'd tossed her aside like she meant nothing. Why?

Because he was a fucking dumbass.

And because he'd felt himself being drawn to her, the impulse to steer into what she offered nearly irresistible. She was magnetic interference. She disrupted his internal compass and distorted his ability to interpret signals from his own brain.

He didn't trust himself to make sound decisions where she was concerned, and rather than admit his discomfort and confusion, he'd made her think he didn't want her.

When there was nothing further from the truth.

He rubbed his hands against the rough stubble of his face hard enough to make his palms sting.

After the fiasco at the beach, they'd returned to the room in silence. He'd not known how to explain his actions—or if there was even any point. Her silence was angry, an inferno seething just beneath the surface. He'd been afraid that anything he said would set her off, so he said nothing.

He'd been a coward.

When he hadn't been torturing himself, he searched for something to justify his behavior. Being a dipshit was certainly part of it, but there were other, more complicated layers. He just couldn't find a way to reconcile his desire to be with her when his dad was dead and his siblings' lives had been blown to bits.

The physical attraction and the raw, hungry desire to touch and hold her didn't change the fact it would have been a mistake. They weren't on vacation. This trip was about his dad. He shouldn't be wasting energy trying to get laid.

But that was just an excuse. Angie took the entire endeavor seriously. She knew the dangers. She hadn't asked him to stay. He'd invited himself.

Last night had been incredible. He'd never behaved in such a way in public. Even better, no woman had ever reacted as she had. They were in sync. He couldn't put a name on it, but there was something there. And he blew it. Just like everything else.

What could he do to make it up to her? To feel her hard, tight body writhe against him again? A tight throb pulsed, low and deep. His cock stiffened. The thought she might come out and see what he was doing—and know that it was because of her—made him ache.

He wet his fingers, then stuck his hand down his underwear and pumped toward the mushroom-like tip of his dick. He closed his eyes and opened his mouth but kept the moan inside his throat.

The patter of the shower mesmerized him and lulled him into a lustful, dream-like state. Angie nude under the water, her long dark hair slicked back from her face. Soapy bubbles clinging to her curves. Probing and cleaning her most intimate places.

This time, his moan was audible. She'd almost been his.

A door latch clicked. He opened his eyes. The spray of the showerhead no longer beat against the tile.

Fuck. Maybe he didn't want to get caught after all.

He threw off the blanket and stood. Cool air blew from the vent, chilling his torso. He glanced at his shorts and t-shirt, but movement in Angie's room set him into motion. He hurried to the spare bathroom in only his boxer briefs to finish in private.

A few minutes later, he emerged and headed for the coffee pot. Once he'd had his morning caffeine, he'd get dressed and be ready to talk. An apology would be first. An explanation second.

The whoosh of the waves hitting the shore caught his attention. He turned. The sliding glass door stood open. Angie leaned on the balcony. She wore a straw hat and a two-piece swimsuit with a sarong. A simple bow between her shoulder blades and another at her neck was the only thing standing between him and her smooth, bare skin.

She turned and regarded him coolly.

The black bikini top consisted of two fabric triangles and not much else. The wind caught and tugged at the wrap tied around her waist, giving him a glimpse of equally skimpy swimsuit bottoms. His fingers twitched—it would be so easy to unfasten those little bows.

She stood unnaturally still, and if not for the flaring nostrils, he might have confused her for the world's most perfect department store mannequin.

He should say something. Tell her he was sorry.

His gaze raked her body from the wide-brimmed hat to her tiny top and the gauzy wrap skirt. Finally, down her smooth, shapely legs to sandals and red-painted toenails.

Wait. Wasn't she supposed to be starting her investigation today?

Some self-destructive impulse compelled him to say the first stupid thing that came to mind. "Looks like you have a busy day planned."

She shook her head ever so slightly, then lifted a large pair of sunglasses and slipped them on her face. "I was going to suggest you go get yourself some clothes—maybe a pair of swimming trunks—but you can take care of yourself. I've got things to do."

With her nose high, she strode past him—her footsteps hard and angry—and out the door.

That now-familiar pain stabbed Nate just above his right eyebrow. Getting through the next few days with his heart and his ego intact would not be easy.

Angie stomped past the pool and its two-person canopy chairs already filled with reclining couples.

Who did he think he was? Standing there in his boxer briefs looking good enough to eat? This wasn't a vacation. They weren't in a relationship. And yet, last night, she let herself pretend.

He'd been sweet and funny at dinner. Then serious when they spoke of the resort and his father. Then passionate when he pulled her into his arms and introduced her to a new brand of ecstasy.

His deft fingers had played her, and she'd lost control.

She'd compiled dossiers on some of the world's worst criminals, yet she'd let this man get into her head. Pathetic.

Her face warmed. Despite the utter shame of falling into his trap, the memory of their tryst on the beach—the fact they could have easily been seen—made her body tighten with need. She slowed her pace and took a few calming breaths, pretending to dig through her bag in search of a missing item. Her fingers brushed over a tube of sunblock, a tank top and her worn paperback copy of RBG's autobiography. Beneath the soft cotton towel, she felt her real cargo—her gun.

The perfect reminder. She wasn't here to play house. They weren't lovers. They were working together, and that was it. Whatever happened last night was a one off. It wouldn't happen again. Couldn't.

Nate was right. It was a mistake. Finding out what happened to Rick was more important than her attraction to his son. Today, her mission was to start piecing together the events of Rick's last day.

She resumed her trudge to the beach.

Her feet pressed into the warm sand, such a contrast to last night when it had been cool and damp. She walked along the water, pretending to be on the lookout for the perfect spot. In truth, she wanted to get a look at the resort and the tourist traffic. There was a lot going on. A snorkeling tour, water ski-ing, a sand castle-building contest, and a reggae band. A lot of distractions for the average tourist. And the perfect place for blending in and conducting criminal activities.

She turned to study the cove and shielded her eyes. Her wan-dering gaze caught sight of a small thatch-roofed hut. Rentals. Retracing her steps along the water's edge, she made her way back to the grassy bank surrounding the beach.

According to Nate's dad, the go-between worked with boats and wave runners and was named Wayne. Normally, she'd try to go unnoticed, to walk that fine line of getting close but not standing out. Today, she needed to identify her target quickly. With only three weeks left of her leave, she wouldn't have time to conduct a typical investigation.

She approached the shed and peeked inside. It was larger than she'd expected and filled with gear. "Hello?"

A man in board shorts and a rash guard stepped out from behind a row of kayaks.

Angie blinked. The guy was attractive, and not at all what she'd expected. This man was movie star handsome with dark, wavy hair that accentuated prominent cheekbones and a square jaw. Quite the contrast from Nate's rugged good looks. When the man grinned, she almost expected his teeth to sparkle. His eyes flickered with interest, mesmerizing her until she remembered to speak.

"Hi." She stepped inside the hut. Had she been on her own, she might have flirted, but that wouldn't work given her pretend marriage. "I got in last night and wanted to plan my activities for the week."

"You're in Jamaica. No plans. Go where the day takes you." His speech rose and fell with the lilting rhythm of the islands. He flashed that dazzling smile again, and she noticed the way his shirt clung to broad shoulders and well-defined pecs. His skin had a lovely bronze glow.

She cast her eyes down, pretending to be a closeted list-maker. "That's not the way I do things. I need an agenda."

"Maybe you just need someone to show you the Jamaican way." He stepped closer, and though he gave the appearance of a flirt, she'd wager it was an act. This guy was what the intelligence world would call a gray man—a criminal hiding in plain sight.

This was her opportunity to establish her cover. She cocked an eyebrow. "Do you show husbands the Jamaican way too?"

He laughed, spread his arms wide and put a foot of distance between them. "Everyone who visits gets a taste of that irie spirit."

"Good to know." Angie tried to look nonchalant as she surveyed the space. Life preservers, paddles, inflatable inner tubes. It all appeared to be on the up and up. "What sort of activity would you recommend for a newly married couple on their first trip to Jamaica?"

"We have several options, but if it were me, I'd rent a boat. You can float around, explore the shoreline—enjoy each other's company." He waggled his eyebrows.

"Sounds nice." And it did. Angie would love to spend time lounging around with Nate, but as he'd proved last night, he wasn't interested in any sort of romantic entanglement. Which was just as well.

"We have one catamaran, a couple of small sailboats, and a few motorboats."

She put her finger to her lips, pretending to consider the suggestion. "A catamaran seems too big for two people, and we don't know how to sail. Are the motorboats easy to operate?"

"We give you a short lesson, and then you're good to go." He motioned for her to follow to a dock where several boats were tied up and ready to launch. "You can rent a boat for yourself and float around the shoreline or—if you don't mind a tagalong—you can go on a private tour with me or Matthew." He gestured toward a tall, thin man with dreadlocks, who was busy collecting paddleboards from a group of twenty-somethings.

"Let's say we decide to do a private tour, and we don't want to go with Matthew, who should we ask for?"

"Wayne." He bowed slightly. "At your service."

The steady hum of a motor carried over the water. In the distance, Angie saw a medium-sized boat heading toward the resort, its bow parting the water and radiating waves. She watched for a moment, mesmerized. Was it coming here?

The approaching boat made her think about the rental shack from an operational standpoint. The perfect blend of invisibility and access. Here, Wayne could monitor comings and goings, meet contacts, unload cargo.

"What brings you to Casa Tortuga for your honeymoon?"

"My friend's dad visited here and recommended it. He died last year—" She shrugged. "I guess I wanted to see what he loved about it."

"Sorry for your loss."

"He was a pilot. Died when his plane crashed into the ocean." The boat continued its trajectory toward the dock. "He'd actually just flown out of an airport near here."

Wayne stilled. "You don't say."

"Happened about a year ago." She shifted her bag to the opposite shoulder. "Did you know him?"

"There was a pilot. I met him a few times. Didn't know he died though."

Wayne was lying. Angie saw it in the way his pupils dilated.

"Is that one of yours?" She tilted her chin at the boat, now churning up bubbles and idling their way.

"Uh...no. They look like locals." The boat settled against the dock. A man hopped off and tied it to a cleat. "Come back inside, and I'll get you a price sheet." Wayne was clearly eager to move her away from those men and that boat.

She followed him to the rental shack, but glanced back just in time to see two men follow a trail into the trees.

Nate had overreacted in the hotel room. Once again, he'd opened his mouth and stuck his size twelve foot in it. In the lobby, he found a men's clothing store and purchased several items. He returned to the room and showered, then changed into his new swimsuit and flip-flops.

When he didn't find Angie lounging by the pool, he headed to the beach, passing the spot from the night before. The spot where he'd wrecked everything. Now he wanted to talk, to get it out in the open. See if they could salvage any part of their relationship, or whatever this was.

She was nowhere to be seen, but the recollection of her in his arms—the way her body quaked against him—was seared into his memory for all time. His skin grew warm, and suddenly nothing mattered more than finding her and pulling her close.

Then he saw her. On the pier. Talking to some other guy. Jealousy rippled through him like a shockwave. Sure, he'd been a first-class jerk last night—he could admit that. But to move on so quickly?

He stepped off the path and watched from beneath a shady palm. Angie and the guy moved toward the little hut and disappeared inside.

Nate ran a shaky hand through his hair. He should turn around now, go back to the room, pretend he hadn't seen her. But then what? Go back to acting like he didn't care?

There was virtually zero chance that would work. She had him tied in so many knots he could double as a string of Christmas lights. He took a deep breath and squared his shoulders.

Better to confront the inevitable. They needed to talk about what happened, and he wasn't leaving until they did.

He stepped onto the path at the same moment Angie came barreling around the corner. On instinct, he stuck his hands out to stop her.

"Nate." Her voice was breathless, and if he wasn't mistaken, contained a measure of relief.

He breathed a sigh. Maybe this wouldn't be as difficult as he'd thought. "I was coming to find you. We need to talk—"

She held up her hand. "Not now."

If not now, then when? "I came out here to explain what I said last night."

"I'm glad to hear it, and I want to talk about it, but not right this minute."

Nate clenched his teeth. Why wasn't she letting him apologize? She'd not struck him as someone to hold a grudge. "Does this have anything to do with the guy I just saw you with?"

"Yes...no...maybe." She took his hand and dragged him behind a small storage shed off the path. When she spoke again, her voice was low. "That was Wayne."

Wayne? Nate racked his brain. Was he supposed to know who Wayne was? Then it hit him. "The guy who knew my dad?"

She nodded. "Yes, and I'll tell you all about the conversation, but later. Right now, I need you to distract him for me."

"How?" And why?

"I told him I was here on my honeymoon with my husband and that we're looking for romantic activities. Pretend you're doing the same thing. Make him tell you about all the different options and the pros and cons of each."

"What will you be doing?"

"I'm going to sneak onto the boat that just pulled up and have a look around."

CHAPTER 15

N ate stared at Angie. Then at the forty-foot vessel tied to the dock. From what he could see, it looked like a standard fishing boat, including a row of fishing rods propped up in holders lining the back of the boat. The paint on the hull was faded and chipped, and the boat creaked against the pilings as it bobbed in the water.

What could she possibly expect to find on there? "You want to sneak on board? Why?"

"I was talking to Wayne when the men arrived, and it was obvious he didn't want me asking questions." She glanced over her shoulder. "But I saw the men who got off. They weren't tourists. Or your regular locals."

Nate scrubbed a hand down his jaw. He'd spent his entire life trying to avoid danger and wasn't sure he was wired to rush headfirst into it. "What does the boat have to do with my dad?"

"Maybe nothing, but I won't know anything until I get on board and have a look around."

He hesitated. The smart move was to walk away, to tell Angie it was too dangerous. But then he remembered his dad. The man had loved to fly, and he didn't deserve to go out with his plane at the bottom of the ocean. "What do I need to do?"

"Distract Wayne, but keep an eye out in case the men come back." She held up her phone, then pointed toward a trail that followed a small rise leading into the trees. "The men went that way, so watch, and if you see them on the path, text me."

Nate took a deep breath. He could handle this, just needed a little time to prepare. "Okay, when do you want to do this?"

"Now." Her voice was so matter-of-fact, he almost laughed.

She seemed to sense his hesitation. "We don't know how long they will be here or when they'll come back. It's now or never."

Of course it was. Nate swallowed his objections, along with a list of worst-case scenarios, and nodded.

Pulling off her floppy hat and stuffing it into her tote, Angie steered Nate toward the path leading to the rental shack. "Keep Wayne busy with questions about rentals. Once you've gone inside the rental office, I'll sneak onto the boat." She shoved her bag at him. "Hold on to my stuff and don't forget to keep me posted if anything goes down."

Right. As if he needed a reminder that there might be trouble. In one hand, he gripped the handles of Angie's bag. With the other, he cupped the phone in the front pocket of his swim trunks. "Sure. No problem. What could possibly go wrong?"

Angie ignored his sarcasm, either not noticing or not caring. Her eyes glowed with excitement as she gestured for him to get a move on.

He moved slowly along the path toward the rental shack, the rubber soles of his shoes crunching against the gravel. Wayne was nowhere to be seen. Nate approached the little open-air building and found the man at a counter inside. He looked up when Nate entered.

"Hello!" Wayne's tone was friendly. "How can I help you?"

"My wife sent me in here to choose an activity. Preferably something both fun and romantic." Nate wrapped the handle of Angie's canvas bag around his hand and forced a smile. "Newlyweds."

Wayne grinned knowingly and moved around the counter. "Have to keep the little lady happy. Come, step outside. I'll show you what we have."

Stalling, Nate moved to stand in front of a large, wall-mounted fan. "Maybe give me a moment to cool off." He waved his hand in front of his face. "This humidity is something else."

"Sure thing." Wayne grabbed a brochure out of a plexiglass holder and held it out for Nate. "Here's a list of your options, and what each one costs."

Nate opened the glossy leaflet and pretended to study the information but lifted his gaze to look outside where Angie had maneuvered a small ramp to extend from the dock to the aft deck. She stepped onto the boat and disappeared into the steering cockpit.

"My coworker's still on break." Wayne glanced at his watch. "I should have a jet ski rental due back any minute now. You mind if we step outside?"

Before he could respond, Wayne had moved through the door and into the sunshine.

———ell———

Angie stepped quickly and lightly onto the boat, keeping her feet wide for balance. She found nothing suspicious at the steer-

ing station, which was more or less as she expected. But there
were other places to search.

Though small, the vessel contained a below-deck cabin. With
soft footsteps, she descended the stairs, ducked her head, and
stepped into the stale, stuffy room. It had the usual fittings,
a kitchen and a small table that turned into a bed. She lifted
the bench cushion and peered inside. Blankets and pillows. She
poked around. Nothing.

She spied a utility knife lying on a pile of papers on the table
and grabbed it. Wouldn't hurt to have a weapon. Especially
considering her gun was in the bag she'd given to Nate. Prowling
the small room, she opened every door and drawer but found
nothing suspicious.

Maybe she'd been wrong. Maybe this really was a rental business that let the locals tie up. But where had those men gone?
Not toward the resort. They'd headed into the trees. To somewhere hidden.

There was one last place to look. Angie pushed open the
narrow door to the head, stepped inside and flipped the light.
A panel in the wall caught her attention. She pulled on the
top corners with her fingers, but the board didn't budge. She
opened the small knife and wedged it beneath the rectangular
plank.

The panel moved with a scrape, just enough she could hook
her fingers under the outer lip and pop it free. She leaned it
against the wall, catching a whiff of steel and gun oil. Her breath
caught in her throat when she saw the cargo. Man, oh man.
Guns. Dozens of them. Crammed into the hidden compartment. ARs, AKs, semi-automatic shotguns.

She lifted her phone to snap a picture of the contraband. And another. She ran her finger along the smooth barrel of a carbine rifle, feeling for the serial number, but found only a shallow gouge. Rotating the firearm, she snapped a picture of the scratched-out identifier.

Was Golding in the gun game now too?

She opened her messaging app, attached the photos, and sent a quick text to Nate.

Almost done. But look what I found. :-)

She tucked her phone into her waistband and pushed the panel back into the wall. Then, remembering the knife in her hand, she placed it back on the papers where she'd found it and started toward the stairs.

On second thought, maybe she should give the place another look now that weapons were in the mix.

Nate's mobile buzzed. He pulled his phone out of his pocket and thumb-swiped the screen to access the text from Angie. The moment he saw the images, his grip on the phone tightened. She'd found a cache of weapons. Lots of them. And she'd accompanied the images with a smiley face emoji. His breath stuck in his throat. He couldn't tear his gaze from the message.

"Everything good?" Wayne stepped through the door of the shed.

Nate hit the power button to turn off the screen, not wanting the other man to see what he was looking at. "Uh...yeah. Work stuff. I'm on my honeymoon. You'd think they could give it a rest, am I right?" He didn't wait for Wayne to respond and shoved the phone back in his pocket. "I don't need to deal with it right this minute."

Though a practiced liar, Nate had never been good on the fly. Still, judging by Wayne's bored expression, the man saw him as nothing more than another pesky tourist.

Wayne glanced through the open door of the hut, his brow furrowed. Had he noticed the ramp Angie propped between the boat and the dock? He picked up the brochure again.

"So, these boat rentals..."

Wayne turned away from the doorway and looked at Nate. "Yeah?"

"Well, I was wondering about taking a picnic lunch. Is that something we could do? Are there spots where we could tie up and have a meal?"

"There are some nice scenic spots with small docks, but no picnic tables, and you can't bring alcohol."

Nate bobbed his head as though considering. "What about in the evening? Could we take a rental and watch the sunset from the water?"

"Not really, no. The shack closes when dusk comes. If you wanted to do that—"

"What about the kayaks? Are those popular?"

"Yes, but they only fit one person, so not very romantic."

"No, no. I can see that." Nate tapped his finger against his lips. "What else have you got?"

"The paddleboats are popular with couples."

"That could be fun." Nate recalled taking his sister to a park about an hour north of their home in Key Largo to rent a paddleboat. She was only about ten years old, but she was barely pedaling. Then she spotted a gator and put in an Olympic effort to get back to shore.

"My wife would love that. We took a paddleboat out on our first date. Saw an alligator."

Wayne offered the placating smile of someone used to feigning interest in his clients and their stories.

"The paddle boats are down on the beach. You want to see them?"

Nate didn't answer, instead returning to the brochure in his hand. Wayne sighed and perched on his stool behind the counter. Nate glanced at him, then out the open door.

Two men. Coming down the trail. Heading toward the boat. *Shit.* Angie.

He fumbled to pull his phone from his pocket and moved toward the door, where he had a clear view of the dock. "I just remembered something. I need to send a message to work after all."

⁓

Angie felt her phone vibrate against her bare skin. She pulled it from her waistband. A message from Nate.

Get out now. Men coming back.

She grabbed the handrail and stilled. Voices.

"Mi tink mi tell yuh to pick up deh ramp."

"I swear mi did, y'know."

Footsteps, followed by the scraping of metal as the ramp was pulled inside the boat. Angie darted about the room like a squirrel in the middle of the road. She was trapped. Getting caught was not an option. She needed to hide.

Her gaze fell on the cabinet next to the sink. She'd searched it earlier and knew it was mostly empty. It would be a tight squeeze, but rather than a door, it had a cloth curtain which might give her a better chance of fitting inside.

Cramming herself inside the cabinet, she braced her feet against the interior wall, a motion that pushed her knees into her face. She pulled the curtain closed.

Please don't find me. Please don't find me.

Maybe if she repeated the mantra enough times, she'd get out of this alive.

The wood pressed painfully into her shoulders, and a bead of sweat trickled down her back. She rested her head against her knees and tried to slow her erratic breathing. Dear God, she'd really stepped in it this time. She could only hope Nate didn't panic and give her away.

There was a scrape, followed by a bump. The boat lurched to the side as though someone had given it a strong push. The cabin rocked just enough to indicate they'd moved away from the dock. Thick, pungent diesel fumes accompanied the deep hum of the motor.

CHAPTER 16

Nate's breath caught in his throat. His mouth opened in silent protest. The boat lurched away from the dock—with Angie still on board.

He needed to do something—anything—to help her. *Move!* His brain screamed, but his body locked like a zipper snagged on fabric.

His heart pounded into his ears, each beat a reminder of his utter and complete uselessness. *This.* This feeling—ineffective and powerless—was exactly what he'd spent his life avoiding.

It was why he'd tried to control everyone and everything. Because if things never got out of hand, he'd never have to confront his inadequacy and the inability to protect those he cared about.

This was Elise's kidnapping all over again.

Only this time, it was Angie putting her life on the line to find out what happened to his dad.

Fuck!

He turned to find Wayne watching, a curious look on his face. "You okay, man?"

"Oh...uh, yeah. Just got lost in my thoughts for a minute. Work stuff."

"You look like you've seen a ghost."

Nate forced a smile, the muscles in his face tight. "You have no idea."

Shielding his eyes, he watched the boat get further and further away. He could see both men still on the deck. Hopefully, they'd not discovered Angie yet. Surely, she was hiding, waiting for a chance to get away.

His gaze snagged on a couple of paddleboats pushed onto the sand. The chances of making it to the fishing boat were slim. But he had to try. "Can I take one of the paddleboats for a spin? Test the nostalgia factor before I get my wife out here?"

"Sure, but it doesn't respond as well with only one person."

"That's okay."

"Let me grab a life jacket and rental agreement."

The moment Wayne stepped into the little hut, Nate sprinted toward the closest paddleboat. He wrestled the boat off the sand, his feet slipping as the hull scraped the shallows. He nearly tripped, hoisting one leg over the side, then the other. But then he was pedaling. As hard and as fast as he could, steering toward the retreating boat.

Angie rested her chin on her knee. Though she heard the motor, they didn't seem to be moving very quickly. Could they still be in a no-wake zone? Close enough to shore that she could swim? One thing was clear. There was an expiration on how long she could remain crammed into this cabinet like a doll in a shoebox.

She wriggled her arm free from where it was folded against her torso and hooked one finger around the edge of the curtain and pulled. With her body contorted—shoulders hunched, knees drawn up and nearly touching her chin, movement wasn't easy. Still, she managed to twist her neck and get a look at the cabin.

A shadow fell across the stairs. Heavy footsteps echoed into the room. She dropped the curtain and held her breath.

The footsteps stopped. A cabinet above her hiding spot opened. Then the clink of something dropped onto the counter. The pop of the fridge, followed by the gurgle of liquid pouring out of a container.

Through the gap between the edge of the curtain and the side of the cabinet, Angie saw a hairy, bare leg.

Something slammed against the counter at the same moment she heard the *ahhhh* of thirst being quenched. The feet shuffled toward the head. The door slammed.

One man in the bathroom. One steering the boat.

This was it. Her chance to get away. Maybe her only chance.

She pushed the curtain aside, pressed her palm into the floor, and stopped to listen.

A guttural groan, low and breathy, rumbled from the toilet.

Hopefully, the guy would be in there for a while. Still, no reason to dilly-dally.

She leaned, forearm to the floor, and pivoted.

Softly, slowly, she swiveled one knee down, then the other. A sharp pain shot down her leg as her hip bone ground over the hard wooden shelf in the bottom of the cabinet.

Another grunt. Followed by the rattle of the toilet paper spindle.

Angie pushed herself onto her knees, then scrambled to her feet.

The mechanical slurping whoosh of the toilet pierced the silence.

Go, go, go!

She darted for the stairs and took them two at a time. Emerging onto the deck. She looked around to get her bearings. Off the back, she spied the rental shack in the distance. How far away was it? A mile? More?

And was that...a paddleboat?

Paddleboat or battleship, it didn't matter. She had to go.

The motor made jumping off the back impossible. Instead, she climbed up on the side.

"Hey!" the guy at the helm shouted. He let go of the wheel. Lunged.

Nate's heart pounded into his throat as he saw the man on the boat lurch toward Angie. A cry stuck in his chest. But then, she dived off the side like a starlet in a black-and-white film.

He jolted into motion, slamming the rudder lever as far to the side as it would go. The boat groaned in protest, resisting the turn and veering wide. Of course, Wayne had warned him. These things were built for two.

He pedaled harder, his legs burning.

Angie's head surfaced, and her arms sliced through the water with a practiced rhythm. She was a strong swimmer. Thank God—

A glint of metal. His heart slammed against his rib cage. A gun. Aimed at Angie.

He was too far away. He'd never get there in time.

Still pedaling, Nate lurched forward, waving his arms like a madman. "Gun! He's got a gun!" His voice cracked. His throat burned. Between the wind and the distance, could she even hear him?

But the man with the gun heard. He hesitated while the other man yelled something.

A beat later, the motor turned over with a screech. The boat's back end pitched down, churned up a foamy white wake, and sped away.

The men were gone, but Nate didn't stop. He couldn't. Not until Angie was safe. Back in his arms.

His legs screamed. Each rotation of the pedals seemed slower than the one before. Sweat dripped into his eyes.

"Come on! Go!" He yelled at himself.

He pedaled harder. Thighs cramping, lungs burning, a roar building in his throat.

Angie continued her progress in his direction.

He leaned, he pedaled, he pushed himself to his limit.

Dammit. Was he even moving?

Finally, the little boat angled into the turn, helped by the sudden push of the current. His quads ached. But he was closing the distance.

And then, like a miracle, her hand appeared, gripping the side of the boat.

He leaned over and hauled her inside, pulling her against him and burying his face in her hair. She gripped him back, and they rocked. Back and forth like a tree trembling in the wind.

Emotions clogged his throat. He'd almost lost her. Gripping her face, he stroked her cheeks with his thumb, studying her and assessing whether she'd been hurt.

"Are you okay?" He pushed the hair away from her face.

"Just wet." She felt the waistband of the dripping sarong. "And I lost my phone."

"I think that's the least of our worries."

"You got the pictures I texted?"

Good lord. After all of that, she was still thinking about the investigation? "Yeah, I got them."

"Thank God." She sagged into the seat and started pedaling.

He released a ragged breath, half laugh, half sob. "Jesus, Angie. When I saw the gun—"

"There was a gun?" She gave a grateful chuckle. "Glad I didn't know that."

The tension in his chest finally eased. Angie was okay. "You're impossible, do you know that?"

She met his eyes. Her mouth quirked up at the corner. "You're not the first man to tell me that."

He didn't want to think about other men. "Let's paddle this thing back to shore and hope Wayne doesn't see us."

CHAPTER 17

Angie swept from the bedroom in tiny blue shorts and a clingy white tank. Her face, bare of makeup, was flushed and damp from the shower, her hair bundled in a towel like she was waiting for a treatment at the spa. Nate stared. She looked soft, vulnerable. The intimacy of seeing her like this hit at something deep and unguarded inside of him.

"So..." She sank onto the couch beside him. "I think our next move should be following the trail I saw the men use when they got off the boat."

She wanted to keep going? After nearly getting caught? The contrast between her unruffled demeanor and his churning stomach made him feel like a total amateur. Did he want to know what happened to his dad? Yes, but not if it meant getting hurt. Or worse. "You don't think maybe we should cool it for a bit? Make sure no one got a good look at you?"

"I doubt the guy could describe me. He saw me for what, three seconds? His brain was in survival mode. It wasn't cataloging details. I'll be nothing but a blur."

Hard to argue with someone trained in behavioral psychology. Still, he wasn't ready to rush back out there, not after Angie almost got caught.

"What about Bear Golding? Do we really want to put him onto us?"

"There is almost zero chance those guys are going to confess that they let someone sneak onto their boat."

"And Wayne?" They'd ditched the paddleboat on the beach shielded from the view of the rental shack, but Wayne knew who took it. Not to mention Nate had done enough stalling that it seemed unlikely Wayne would forget him.

Angie appeared to consider this. She bobbed her head from side to side. "All you ever said was *wife*, right? You never described what I look like?"

"No." A cold dart of dread slithered through him. They'd just had a close call—a really close call. Was she really this unfazed?

"Good. He probably won't put two and two together. But just to be safe, we should steer clear of him for a while."

Nate felt his shoulders relax.

"Why don't we find a store where I can get a new phone? After that, we'll have an early dinner and talk about what we know. Later, after the rental shack closes, we can scope out the trail." She unwound the towel from her head and raked her fingers through the wet locks.

He watched her fluff her hair, remembering how it had looked spread across the pillow in his hotel room. *Get a grip, man.*

Adrenaline. That was his problem. Stress had always been an emotional trigger. How many times had fear made him overreact? The only difference here was that the response was desire. It wasn't her. It was chemistry—the aftermath of danger. His body didn't know the difference between relief and want.

She lifted herself from the couch with a smile and a wink. "You go shower. I'll find a phone store."

A couple of hours later, with Angie holding a shiny new phone, they approached the candlelit restaurant from the night before. The hostess looked up and smiled like she knew a secret they didn't. "Welcome back!"

Nate glanced inside. Dinner service had just started, and they were among the first to arrive, but the place was still decked out for romance. The lights had been dimmed, there were candles on every table, and a soft, orchestral tune played from speakers in the ceiling.

The hostess motioned for them to follow. "We're so glad you decided to join us for Newlywed Night."

The knot that had lodged itself in Nate's stomach the moment Angie showed up at the airline counter tightened. "Newlywed Night?"

"It was on the calendar. The one delivered to your room?"

Nate glanced at Angie. She shrugged.

The corner of the woman's mouth ticked up into a smirk. "Don't worry, you're going to love it."

He wasn't so sure about that but followed the hostess without argument. Tonight, they were seated at a table against the wall with a C-shaped bench seat meant for two. Nate waited for Angie to sit, then with no other choice, took the seat beside her, his leg pressing against hers.

"Your server will be with you shortly." The hostess spun on her heels and headed back to the check-in stand.

"So..." Nate fiddled with the corner of his menu. "They're really leaning into the couple thing."

She gave a half-laugh. "Yeah, Newlywed Night. Totally our vibe."

He relaxed. Maybe this wasn't destined to get weird.

"I think we should talk about what happened," Angie said.

Thank God. After the events of today, last night felt like a year ago now, but still, he needed to apologize.

"I have some thoughts." She leaned closer, her crisp, clean scent a reminder of their tryst on the beach.

The recollection of her in his arms slammed into him like a brick through a window. His skin grew warm, and suddenly, nothing mattered more than making things right.

"If Golding is getting into the arms business, the question is why." Her voice was all business.

She wanted to talk about the case. Of course she did. Nate hid his disappointment behind a sip of water. "What are your theories?"

"Well, there's the obvious—profit. Depending on the market, weapons can be sold at a high markup. It could just be another revenue stream. Gang violence is an ongoing problem. Maybe he's capitalizing on demand."

Nate leaned back and let the implications sink in. "What about a turf war?"

"It's possible. If he's worried someone else is encroaching on his territory, he might be trying to give himself an advantage. Or maybe he's protecting his infrastructure."

"So, it's about power?"

"Worst-case scenario? He's working with some sort of terrorist group or rogue state?"

"Is terrorism even on his radar?"

"He's an opportunist. If he sees a way to make money and increase his power?" Angie shrugged. "Who knows?"

"Welcome back." The same server from the night before appeared at their table with a basket of rolls and a bottle of wine. He placed the bread on the table and flipped over the stemware.

"None tonight, thank you." Angie held up her hand.

Was she trying to avoid a repeat of last night? He could hardly blame her. He still hadn't apologized for acting like a jackass.

The server removed the glassware from their settings and placed them on the edge of the table. "Are you ready to order?"

Angie glanced at the menu. "I'll have the grilled sea bass with the seasonal vegetables."

"Very good." The waiter scribbled onto his pad.

Nate handed the man his menu. "Filet mignon. Medium rare. Mashed potatoes." He hesitated, then added, "And a whiskey, neat."

"I'll be right back with your drink." He gathered the menus, then vanished.

Angie shook out her napkin and placed it on her lap. "I'm going to save the wine for after we investigate the path."

Right. The investigation. She really was single-minded. Might as well indulge her, especially if this was going to lead to information about his dad. "Where do you think Golding is getting the guns? And why were they on that boat?"

"My guess is he's swapping narcotics for the weapons. It's a known practice in the Caribbean."

"Speaking of known practices...shouldn't the CIA already know all of this?"

"Maybe. Maybe not. Sometimes we unconsciously suppress information. We might have all the pieces of the puzzle, but they could be scattered across departments." She tore a roll in half and smeared butter on the inside. "Human intelligence could also be lacking. Assets fall out of favor, become compromised, get themselves in trouble."

Like Dad.

She stopped chewing and her eyes went wide. "I'm sorry...I don't mean to be cavalier..."

"You think following the trail might really lead us to what happened to my dad?"

Her eyes locked on his, earnest and unblinking. "I don't know, maybe. Did your dad discover the guns? Did he threaten to go to the authorities? Or tell someone he trusted who betrayed him?"

Dad's words to Doc echoed in his brain. *Trust is a currency, but you have to spend it wisely.*

"It might be nothing, but I think it's still worth looking into."

Why argue? She was going to do what she wanted regardless of what he thought. And at least if he went with her, he'd know she was safe. He crammed an entire dinner roll into his mouth.

She took another bite of her bread. If he was going to say something about what happened on the beach, it needed to be now. He chewed and swallowed. "I'm sorry about last night."

Angie's eyes shimmered, and a pained expression crossed her face. She set down her knife and placed her hands in her lap. "What happened?"

Nate swallowed hard. "Guilt, I think. I realized I'd put myself first and had forgotten why we were here."

"I can understand that." She lifted her gaze to meet his eyes. "But that doesn't excuse what you said to me. The way you made me feel."

"I know. I panicked. Because I realized I'd let you in." Without realizing it, he reached for her hand. "Kind of like when someone ran out after the most incredible sex of my life."

"It was pretty great. And last night was fun—" She squeezed his hand, then pulled hers free. "Until you turned it into a whole thing."

He gave an eager nod. "Totally."

"Still, it's probably best if it doesn't happen again. Don't you think?"

His stomach clenched. Well, that was it. She was right, of course. Maintaining a professional distance was the only logical option.

"Glad we got that out of the way." Angie nodded at the almost-empty basket of bread. "Do you want the last one?"

"No, I'm good." Hard to have an appetite when his heart felt like it was splitting in half.

Without warning, the lights faded, and the room grew shadowy. A light popped through the darkness. An emcee made his way to the center of the dancefloor.

"Ladies and gentlemen, welcome to Newlywed Night."

Oh God, what now?

"Tonight, we celebrate love, and as it so happens," He waggled his eyebrows lasciviously. "We have some newlyweds in the house."

A sudden beam of light locked onto Nate and Angie's table, exposing them as the center of attention.

"Please welcome Mr. and Mrs. Connor to the dance floor!"

Nate shook his head and held up his hand in a clear no-thank-you gesture.

"It looks like our couple is shy. Help me get them out here!" The man moved around the room, encouraging the other diners to get involved.

There was a round of applause. Angie's brows knit together in a helpless plea. Nate forced a smile and tried again. "We're good. Thanks."

The asshole with the microphone wouldn't give up. He waved his hands in a get-'em-up motion. "It's just one dance."

Next thing he knew, the crowd was chanting. "Dance. Dance. Dance."

Fuck. He didn't want to dance with her. Not now. Not after she'd just told him she wanted to keep things professional. But aside from grabbing her and darting for the door, it didn't seem they had much choice.

Angie must've come to the same conclusion. "Might as well," she murmured, pushing herself to her feet. "Part of our cover, right?"

He nodded, taking her hand and leading her to the center of the room. The music started the moment they stepped onto the parquet floor. The slow, gentle twang of a guitar. Nate held in a groan. An old country song he recognized from hanging out with his cousin Sergei. The singer crooned about being shameless in love.

Angie wrapped her hands around his neck, and he pulled her against him. They swayed, awkward and formal, like two kids at their first dance. Her fingers toyed with the collar of his T-shirt. His palm pressed into the small of her back.

That scent—light and fresh and so totally her—drifted around him like a drug. He leaned closer just to breathe her in.

"Is this everything you thought our fake marriage would be?" he asked.

She lifted her gaze, her lips curling into a smile. "I'm not complaining."

That wasn't what he'd expected, especially not after the whole keep-it-professional conversation. He pressed his hand a little firmer into her back. "Me either."

"Sometimes I forget we're pretending." She feathered the hair at the back of his head with one hand and gripped his shoulder with the other.

He pulled her closer and let his thumb brush her waist. He was dangerously close to admitting how badly he wanted her. "You're not the only one."

The music played on around them. The distance between them melted. They settled into a slow rhythm, heat and admiration pulsing between them.

When he looked down, her eyes were on him. Her mouth was open in a slight pout, her lips full and soft and smooth. Good lord. Was he out of his mind? He lifted her chin and dipped his head. Their mouths so close he could feel her breath on his lips.

The music stopped. Angie blinked and stepped back—eyes glazed, expression confused. Nate clenched his jaw and dropped his hand.

"Is that love or what?" The emcee gushed while the crowd applauded.

Nate couldn't meet Angie's eyes. He took her hand and led her back to their table, the woulda, coulda, shoulda sparking like static between them.

CHAPTER 18

The sun cast a golden glow across the sky and reflected off the surface of the water. The rental shack would be closing soon, just as they'd planned. Angie walked beside Nate, pretending the almost-kiss hadn't happened, even as her mind played it on an endless loop. The path meandered between the bungalows and the pool deck. Lush tropical plants brushed the edges of the concrete trail.

They stopped at the infinity pool overlooking the beach. Couples leaned into each other and against the waterfall ledge, sipping cocktails and gazing at the cove. Angie barely resisted the urge to steal a glance at Nate. What she wouldn't give to be a normal person on a normal vacation in a normal relationship. She released a weary sigh. Why bother pretending it was even an option?

A woman raised her drink toward them with a grin, as if toasting an inside joke. How odd. Not knowing how else to respond, Angie gave a polite wave.

They headed toward the beach. In her bag, she carried two towels, a necessity for their cover, but also to conceal her firearm. She stopped and threw her flip-flops into the bag, then stepped onto the sand. The coarse grains rubbed against her toes.

"Congratulations!" a woman in one of the chairs yelled.

Angie paused to look around. There was a faint echo of laughter and the distant thrum of reggae music. Otherwise, she and Nate were the only ones there. "Thank you?"

"That dance was hot," said the woman's companion. "Oh, to be newlyweds again."

Great. Nothing screamed romance like almost kissing your fake husband and then pretending it didn't happen.

Nate stared at her for a beat, almost as though he had something to say. But then he turned away—jaw pulsing—to stare at the shoreline.

Awesome. As if they hadn't just endured the most awkward dinner in the history of humankind, now she had to deal with random strangers shipping her and Nate. On the bright side, at least she knew their cover was working.

"Hey, lovebirds!"

Her stomach knotted. She didn't know how much of this she could handle. "Come on. Let's find somewhere to sit."

Despite it being dinner time, more than half of the beach chairs were occupied, either by bodies or towels and clothes. Angie spied a pair pulled off to the side, but within sight of the dock. She trudged toward them and set her bag between two chaise lounges.

Situated on a small harbor, the resort angled to the west. The sun was just starting its descent, and judging by the red and orange streaks already shooting across the sky, the sunset would be magnificent.

They expected Wayne to close up shop sometime around dusk. And once he'd left for the day, they'd sneak up the dirt trail. In the meantime, they'd sit and wait.

Nate gripped the arms of his chair and leaned back with a sigh. "How warm do you think the water is?"

"You want to go swimming?" They'd gone back to their room after dinner to change into their swimsuits. All part of the disguise.

"Why not? You said it yourself. We want our cover to be convincing."

As if that were going to be a problem.

Right on cue, the water shimmered. "You go. I'll stay here."

He raised an eyebrow. "You sure? It's going to be dark before long. Then you'll have missed your chance."

The water looked amazing. So did Nate. She peered over at him, her admiration settling on the dark line of hair disappearing beneath his swim trunks.

Dammit. She couldn't resist this man. "Fine."

He rose and extended his hand, a wide grin illuminating his tanned face. She gripped his palm, and he pulled her to her feet with such force she tumbled into him.

"Whoops." His naked chest was warm, and she covered her awareness of him with a nervous laugh. "Sorry about that."

His hands lingered on her elbows where he'd steadied her. His dark eyes softened. "Let's go."

He turned and tugged her toward the water. She threw one last look at her bag, then followed the incredible man down the beach.

Nate walked straight into the sea, dunked his head, and came up with his hands already pushing his short hair off his face.

Angie was more deliberate. The chilly water hit her ankles. She stopped, stretched up on her toes and hugged her arms to her chest.

"Come on. It's fine," he coaxed.

She waved him off and took another step, wetting the tops of her shins. Knees were next, but this time her foot landed in a divot. The water rose to her hips. She squeaked.

"It's not that cold." He chuckled. "Weren't you already in the water once today?"

"That was different." Fleeing for her life, she'd not even registered the temperature.

"Just get it over with."

She shot him a dirty look. "I'll do it my way, thank you very much." In truth, she liked the feel of his eyes glued to her.

Another tentative step. Hip deep. She jumped up and down to prep her other half. Once the water reached her belly button, it would be time to submerge. Ready to go under, she closed her eyes and took a deep breath.

A quiet splash. Water lapped against her torso.

She opened one lid. Nate was gone.

A strong arm grabbed her from behind, lifted her in the air and threw her forward.

Cold water enveloped her, leaving the briny taste of the sea on her lips. She emerged, hair plastered against her face. She pushed it out of her eyes and glared. "What a jerk."

Nate's eyes sparked. He laughed and backed away from her. "I was only trying to help."

"You're going to regret that."

"I doubt it."

She launched at him, pushing on his shoulders with all her might. She practically scaled the man, but he didn't budge.

His arms coiled around her, anchoring her to him.

She should extract herself, but good God, that was the last thing she wanted to do.

Time slowed, his mouth once again hovering only inches from hers and carrying the faint scent of whisky. The gentle ocean waves rippled against their bodies.

Droplets of water ran down her cheeks, while those on her shoulders and arms beaded up and slowly disappeared. The humid air stuck to her sea-soaked skin, and the smell of salt lingered. Eyes the color of Brazilian cherry stared at her mouth.

Had something changed during that dance? They'd admitted the attraction was mutual. But he wanted to compartmentalize. To keep his personal life separate from his dad and the investigation. It was why she'd told him it was best if they didn't repeat the mistake of last night. Because it was what he'd wanted to hear.

Or was it?

He adjusted his grip, pulling her more securely against his torso and resting his chin on her shoulder. Soft breaths feathered the hair on her neck, calling tiny goosebumps to attention.

She closed her eyes and waited to feel his lips trailing up her neck. The moments ticked by.

Why wasn't he kissing her yet?

She opened her eyes and put her hands on his chest to push herself away to see what had caught his attention. He swiveled her around, her back pressing into his chest while her ass made tempting contact with his cock.

His deep voice vibrated in her ear as his hand snaked up and across her body, coming to rest on her chest. "Look who's leaving."

Wayne. He pulled the doors to the little shed closed and headed up the beach toward the resort.

Her chest tightened. This was good. It was why they were here.

And yet, she wished it weren't. *Story of my life.* If she ever wrote a memoir, she'd call it *Never Enough.* The title encapsulated so much. Her parents' indifference toward her after her sister's death, her never-sated quest for validation through work. And now Nate—a man she wanted but would never have—and to whom she was nothing more than a means to an end.

Her chest heaved with an unreleased snort. More important than the hand on her breast—or the way her nipples hardened in response—was the path through the trees the men had taken after leaving the boat.

The trail rose gently, winding through brush and low-hanging branches. Angie took the lead, squeezing the grip of her gun through the canvas of her bag. With no lights on the path and thick greenery blocking the moon, Nate used the flashlight app on his phone to light the trail from over her shoulder.

They hiked in silence, finally emerging into a clearing that contained a single picnic table. Huh. Angie hadn't known what to expect, but it wasn't this. She walked around the table, surveying the space but saw nothing special.

"Think this is where they eat lunch?" Nate's voice, warm and familiar, came from just over her shoulder.

She shook her head. "I don't remember that they were carrying anything when I saw them get off the boat. Certainly nothing that looked like food."

"So, what do you think is going on?"

"I don't know." She froze and pointed at the ground. "Hey, can you shine a light over here?"

Nate joined her at the end of the picnic table, flashlight aimed at the dusty earth. A line of boot prints angled toward the trees and trailing into the foliage. She didn't see a path, but that didn't mean there wasn't one there. She stepped forward and pushed aside a cluster of branches. Twigs snapped. Leaves scattered. She winced, standing motionless and listening, her sympathetic nervous system on high alert.

Reaching over her head, Nate held the branches aloft, and she stepped onto the overgrown path. She waited for him to follow and angle his light at the ground.

The path cut through thick tropical plants, winding back and forth, until finally, she spied a break in the trees.

Leaves rustled somewhere up ahead. She held up her hand, signaling to Nate to stop and wait. He clicked off the flashlight, and she inched forward, peering past the edge of the trail.

A man. Bald. Wearing a pair of coveralls. Stuffing a package into the hollowed-out trunk of a dead tree.

Nate pressed against her, watching from over her shoulder. He shifted his weight ever so slightly. The sharp crack of a twig reverberated through the night like a gunshot.

The bald guy's head snapped up. He turned, searching for the source of the sound.

Doc.

CHAPTER 19

Nate gasped, but didn't have time to process what he'd seen. Angie was shoving against him, urging him to turn around.

"Go!" she hissed.

They scurried along the trail, past the picnic table, and down the rise toward the rental shack. She clutched his hand and tugged him toward the beach, not slowing until they were nearly at the pool.

She squeezed his hand. "Act normal."

Was she kidding? Doc had been Dad's friend. A man Nate had known since he was a teen. "Do you think he saw us?"

"I don't know. Let's just get to our room."

She marched forward, still holding his hand. Had Doc killed his dad? The thought alone made his body seize. And yet, all the pieces were there.

Nate's foot snagged on the heel of his other foot, making him stumble. He staggered to a stop. "Did Doc—"

Angie whirled, gripping his face in her hands and forcing him to meet her eyes. There was fire in her gaze. "Don't do this to yourself, do you hear me?"

He nodded, dazed.

"We'll talk about possibilities later, but right now, the worst thing you can do is jump to conclusions." She searched his face, but he couldn't know if she found what she was looking for. "Let's go."

They trudged past the pool with Angie leading the way, her grip on his hand strong and firm. In the hotel lobby, he barely registered a pat on the back, followed by congratulations. Someone else yelled, "Don't do anything I wouldn't do!"

Even in the elevator, Angie didn't let go. Nate's hand clasped hers. Tight. Desperate. He hoped he didn't hurt her, but he couldn't loosen his grip.

When they got to the room, she pushed him onto the couch and, once again, clutched his face in her hands. Her fingers were warm, but her grip was firm. "Say whatever you need to say."

She let her hands drop to her lap, but her gaze never strayed from his face.

"It all makes sense." He shook his head slowly. "Doc has the know-how to tamper with the gas tank—to make it look full when it wasn't. He had opportunity. Dad's plane was parked just outside Doc's hangar, for Christ's sake!"

"Okay…" The word was long and drawn out. "If that's true, what's his motive?"

Nate didn't answer the question. "Dad trusted him." Still shaking his head, Nate let his hands fall limp and useless at his sides. "*I* trusted him."

"Why don't we talk about what we know? The men who got off the boat followed that trail up the hill, and we know that Doc left something in a tree." She shifted on the couch, leaning closer and somehow easing the tension clawing at his chest. "So, it's a meeting spot, a place to exchange information."

"Seems a bit old-school, doesn't it? Stuffing messages into a tree stump?"

"Old-school? Maybe. But also smart. No electronics, no signals to intercept." She shrugged. "And as far as hiding spots go, it's a pretty good one. Concealed but accessible."

"Does this mean Doc is feeding the CIA incorrect information?" He grasped her fingers and started tracing a slow, mindless path across the back of her hand.

"Maybe? It might explain why so many of these things—the summit, the guns—have fallen off our radar."

"What do we do now?"

"When we see my police contact tomorrow, we can ask if he has any information on Doc."

Nate nodded and stared, barely comprehending what she said. His mind whirred like a funnel cloud, flinging ideas and memories this way and that. But Angie was solid. And calm. And unshakeable.

He didn't think, just moved, leaning in and wrapping his arms around her, pulling her close. He needed to hold her more than he'd realized. She wound her arms around his back and held on tight.

With his forehead pressed to hers, he inhaled her familiar scent. And for the first time since he'd seen Doc, he felt like he could breathe.

CHAPTER 20

Angie stared at Nate's fingers splayed on the seat between them, only a few inches from her own. God, how she wanted to take his hand, to feel the warmth of his skin against hers. To reassure him and let him know she wasn't going anywhere. Instead, she watched him staring out the taxi window, the streets of Kingston sliding by.

Last night, when he reached for her, she'd wrapped her arms around him and savored the soft fabric of his shirt against her cheek and the weight of his head on her shoulder. She'd only wanted to offer comfort. But as he settled against her, something shifted, and she'd longed to kiss him and touch him and take him to bed. Rather than give in to the impulse, she'd held him for a long time—too long, if she was being honest—before finally pulling away, telling him to get some rest, and shutting the door to her bedroom.

Hours had passed before she fell asleep. She'd lain awake, wishing he was with her and wondering what she'd gotten him into. Learning Doc might be working for the other side was a huge shock—even for her. She couldn't imagine what Nate must've felt.

Worse than that? The danger and heartbreak she'd introduced to his life. And while she didn't regret the decision to investigate Rick's death, she had no business involving Nate.

She glanced at her companion. Strong, capable, handsome. Inexperienced. Sure, his grandfather ran a crime syndicate, but Nate didn't know that life.

Agreeing to let him stay was stupid. And selfish. She'd wanted him here, wanted his companionship. More than that, she wanted to know if whatever was simmering between them would eventually boil.

The taxi stopped across from the small police station. Angie turned to Nate. "Things aren't the same here as in the States. Stay close."

They crossed the street to a tan stucco building on the corner. Mold and peeling paint decorated the exterior walls, but it was the bars on the windows that stuck out. If the police needed protection, what chance did anyone else have?

At the entrance, a scissor gate was pushed to the side with one of the front doors propped open, a reminder that life outside the resort could be dangerous.

Angie glanced at her companion. It was hard not to picture him with those swim trunks slung low on his hips, his six-pack abs, and the contour of muscle forming a V across his lower abdomen.

A small spiderweb of cracks on the glass door snagged her attention. In the center, a smooth, round hole. Apparently, the additional fortification was warranted. At the very least, it was a good reminder that the rules were different here. Staying alert and not taking anything for granted. Those needed to be her priorities for the duration of her time on the island.

A row of orange plastic chairs and scuffed green and white linoleum tile formed the reception area. She was inside before she realized Nate was still at the door, staring at the bullet hole. What were the chances he regretted the decision to tag along? Nothing was keeping him here. If he wanted to leave, he could be in the air by the end of the day.

She should let him go.

As long as he was near, her emotions would be difficult to control, not to mention her body's barely manageable reaction to him.

This was a mistake. The words spoken on the beach after the most spectacular orgasm of her life had cut straight to her core.

He was right, but it hurt.

She shook off the regret of what might have been. Falling in love wasn't in her future. That dream was meant for someone else. Someone who was nothing like her.

Nate stepped next to her, but didn't speak. They approached the desk.

"Is Officer Fitzroy Brady available?" Angie gave her name to the desk clerk and prayed Fitzroy would help. They'd worked together on a lottery scam—her first case as a member of the Caribbean task force. He was an honest and hardworking officer.

Nate had taken a seat on one of the hard chairs near a small fan humming and pushing hot air into the room. She settled next to him. After a few minutes, a dark-skinned man in his late fifties rounded the corner. He'd gained weight, but she'd know that face anywhere.

"Angie Liu?" Her name sounded like a melody when said in his Jamaican accent. "That you? For real?"

She rose, a grin spreading across her face so wide it made her cheeks ache. He leaned in for a hug.

"My God. Lemme take a look at you." He clasped her hands and spread her arms wide. In addition to the extra pounds, he'd acquired more wrinkles and his hair now sported more gray than black. But when he smiled, the same creases appeared at the corners of his eyes.

He hugged her again, and she whispered in his ear. "I was hoping we could talk about Bear Golding."

He stiffened, then straightened, his gaze hard and worried. "Official business, yeah?"

She shook her head. "Not exactly."

Alarm flashed across his features. His gaze landed on Nate, who had appeared at her side.

"This is my colleague." She gestured toward Nate. "Can we speak in private?"

Fitzroy's gaze flicked about the room. "Not here. Meet me at the cafe down the street." He nodded to the desk clerk, who buzzed him into the back office. He turned back before the door closed. "Ten minutes."

Nate and Angie strode down the block and across the street until they found the place Fitzroy had mentioned. She led the way around the building to an old wooden picnic table.

Nate picked at the table's peeling paint. "You trust this guy?"

"One hundred percent." She kept her gaze on the corner of the building, watching for Fitzroy.

His belly appeared first, but then his face came into view. She couldn't miss the tension sketched across it. He maneuvered himself onto the bench on the other side of the table. "Tell me what's going on."

She motioned toward Nate. "His father was a pilot working for Golding, but he worked for us too. I believe he was murdered."

Fitzroy shook his head. "Golding is dangerous. More so now."

"Why now?" Nate leaned forward.

"He has a hand in just 'bout everything. Government, the courts, the banks." The man stared over Angie's shoulder, his gaze unfocused.

"The courts?" The island had a lot of problems, but she'd always thought the justices tried to do right.

"The cartel puts pressure on the judges. Prosecutors try to get convictions, but Golding scares off everybody and makes them obey."

"You talk like this is new." Nate crossed his arms over his chest. "From what Angie said, this guy's been in business for a while."

Fitzroy rubbed his brow. "Maybe, but his organization has almost doubled in the last couple of years. Things are heatin' up, and he seems to be behind most of it."

Angie forced herself to swallow through her tight throat. The possibility of continuing without alerting Gary seemed more remote with each revelation. "Are authorities working with the CIA?"

Fitzroy shrugged. "You tell me. The big thing happening right now is the economic summit."

The reason they ended up sharing a room. Nate shot her a look. He turned back to Fitzroy. "Are you saying Golding is involved with the summit? Isn't it a bunch of politicians?"

"In theory." The older man wiped away a bead of sweat that had formed on his forehead. Angie's own muscles tightened at his tense posture. "A couple of member nations suggest a coalition to deal with terrorism and money laundering. Several bills are up for a vote. Many could affect the drug trade. Golding's been buying up lawmakers to block the new measures, y'know."

Angie bit her lip. *Not good*. There was more going on here than whatever happened to Nate's dad. "What about the other nations? Do they have their own Bear Goldings?"

"Some do, I tell you. Players from all over the Caribbean are on the island. Everyone's jumpy." Fitzroy's eyes darted from Angie to the street. "I should get back."

Shoot, Angie had more questions. She reached for his hand. "Has Golding gotten into the gun game?"

"Not that I know of. Drugs keep the cash flowing. Gun buyers aren't usually repeat customers. Onetime deal, most times." Fitzroy's eyes narrowed. "Why you ask?"

Angie considered the wisdom of telling Fitzroy about the guns on the boat and how she discovered them. Admitting to an illegal search could ruin any chance of prosecuting Golding—if it ever came to that. She shrugged. "No reason. Just a feeling."

Fitzroy raised his brows. Doubt flickered in his eyes. "Be careful. Feelings can be dangerous, and Golding's got eyes everywhere."

"Including the police." It wasn't a question. She knew how these things worked.

The officer was clearly anxious to leave. Angie shot a quick glance at Nate. Even though they'd not spoken about Doc since last night, she owed it to him to ask. "There's a mechanic at the airport on the west side of town named John Henry Clarke—goes by Doc. You wouldn't happen to know whether he's an associate of Golding?"

"Don't sound familiar. I'll keep an eye out, but you gotta be careful who you ask."

Fitzroy pressed his hands against the table and stood. Angie rose, rounded the end of the table, and gave her old friend a kiss on the cheek. The two men shook hands and Fitzroy turned to leave, but then stopped and looked back at them. "Golding isn't the only big fish, y'know. Plenty of people think there's someone else running things. And the word is, the relationship not so friendly neither."

Angie's shoulder muscles tightened. Why would Golding go into business with anyone, let alone someone he didn't like? "Do you think it's true?"

"Not sure, but if it is, things could get messy." Fitzroy's eyebrows drew together. "At least Golding's a devil we know. Imagine the guy he's working for."

—ℓℓ—

Angie sagged into the taxi's vinyl seat, the conversation with Fitzroy settling in her stomach like a wreck on the ocean floor.

There was a common thread to everything they'd learned—the guns, Doc, the terrorism vote, Golding's new partner—and that was danger. And still, a tingle of excitement prickled along her skin. They were making progress.

"So," Nate said from beside her. "What are you thinking?"

"Not sure yet." Just that there was more going on than she'd guessed, that she didn't know what any of it had to do with Rick's death, and that she worried they were in over their heads. "At least we know more than we did when we started."

Nate blew out a breath, his lips vibrating. "Can't argue with you there."

"I wish I knew how all of it fits together—*if* it fits together."

"What's our next move?"

"I think we need to watch and wait—figure out if that boat ties up at the resort every day." She glanced at her smartwatch. "If it keeps the same schedule, we have about an hour."

The driver glanced at her in the rearview mirror.

"You know what? Let's talk about it when we're back in the room."

Nate nodded and turned away, but not before she saw the tension in his jaw and the look of defeat in his eyes.

He shook his head but kept his focus on the world outside. "I can't stop thinking about Doc. I can't believe he's involved in all this."

Her stomach clenched. Finding answers was great, but there was a clear emotional toll.

"We don't know anything for certain yet." Though it certainly looked like Doc might have been playing both sides. "Let's try not to jump to conclusions."

Without thinking, she reached over and gripped his hand. Why was her instinct always to touch him? She started to pull away, but his fingers closed around hers and squeezed. Not hard, but enough for her to take notice. That single point of contact—the heat of his skin, the pressure of his fingers—sucked the breath from her lungs.

Angie felt a ridiculous smile tugging at her lips. She tried to hold it back, and when the effort proved futile, she turned to stare out the window, still holding Nate's hand.

Colorful run-down buildings, shops, and office towers were a blur as the cab sped through the city streets. Angie and Nate stayed like that, fingers laced together, for the rest of the ride. She barely noticed when the taxi pulled into the circular drive of their resort.

Nate thrust a couple of bills between the front seats, and they climbed from the car.

Beyond the lobby, they stepped into the sunshine and walked across the pool deck and past a karaoke party in full swing. A pair of drunken vacationers were on the stage, swaying back and forth, belting out an Abba song.

The festivities had nothing to do with her—she knew that, but seeing the happy, carefree revelers felt like a slap in the face. A reminder that life should be filled with friends, family, and fun. All things that came easy to other people, but never for her.

Then Nate's hand brushed hers, and for a moment, hope wiggled its way in. Maybe it wasn't too late after all. Maybe it would be okay to dream. Maybe just a little?

They kept walking, but the singe of his touch lingered.

"We should get out of these clothes." Nate squinted at the pool for a beat, then slowed to a stop. "Swimsuits—I mean. We should put on our suits and come back out here."

Suddenly, it wasn't the sun making Angie hot. "I figured that was what you meant."

Neither of them spoke until they were inside the suite. Angie hooked her thumb over her shoulder. "I'll go get changed. We should look for a spot on the beach so we can see if the boat comes back."

She stalked into the bedroom, shut the door, and sank onto the bed. The line between professionalism and physical desire blurred more with each passing moment. It was only a matter of time before they crossed it.

And then, there'd be no going back.

CHAPTER 21

Nate sank into a beach chair beside Angie, stretching his legs out and digging his heels into the damp sand. On any other day, the steady rhythm of waves breaking against the shore combined with the distant cries of gulls would have lulled him into a quiet tranquility. But not today. Today, he had too much on his mind.

He looked at his watch. "Yesterday, the boat was already here by now."

"They may not keep a strict schedule." Angie shrugged. "We don't even know if they show up every day."

"Maybe they've come and gone."

"It's possible."

How did she manage to sound so nonchalant? Nate shook his head in frustration. He didn't even know if he wanted to see that boat again. Would it bring answers? More questions? Or worse? Danger.

Angie reached for his hand. The gentle pressure of her warm, soft skin did something to him—made him feel simultaneously weak and indestructible. He squeezed and didn't let go. Because right now, the last thing he wanted was to get lost in his head.

"Did you want to talk about last night? About Doc?" Her voice was tentative, concerned.

From the look in her eyes—a deep unspoken empathy—she thought he should talk about it. But he wasn't ready. The betrayal was too raw.

He did have safety concerns though. "Should I be worried about my plane? If Doc sabotaged Dad's plane, he could do the same to mine. It's sitting at the airport outside his hangar as we speak."

Her response was steady and certain. "You're not involved in the cartel. I can't imagine he'd have a reason to hurt you."

"What if he recognized us last night?"

"We don't know what he was doing or if he was even involved in what happened to your dad." Her fingers tightened around his. "But it's not a bad idea to take precautions."

"I guess I should have known this would be dangerous, but part of me feels like things are spinning out of control."

Angie paused, as though weighing her words carefully. "Things are more convoluted than I expected. And frankly, guns complicate matters. Weapons make everything less predictable, more dangerous." She chewed on her lip. "If you want to call it quits, I understand."

Was that what he wanted? To leave her here finishing the investigation without him?

Everything inside Nate felt like it was unraveling. But with Angie's hand still in his, her thumb casually brushing over his knuckles, she was an anchor. Holding him in place. Offering security and stability.

Maybe it was the adrenaline. Maybe it was needing to feel something other than dread. Whatever the reason, he couldn't stop looking at her. The way her arm rested on the curve of her torso. The lines of muscle that ran down her stomach.

Today she was wearing a red polka dot bikini with a little gold X in the center that caught the sun and drew his eyes to the gentle curve of her breasts. His gaze drifted up, following the delicate line of her neck. She rolled onto her side, facing him, a soft smile curling her lips.

He leaned in, just enough to catch the scent of her earthy fragrance. Her lips parted, willing and inviting.

Before he realized what he was doing, he was cupping her jaw. She didn't pull away but watched him with eyes that said she wanted it too. Their mouths were a breath apart.

"Hey, lovebirds! Pace yourself!" The voice was loud and loose, the speaker clearly inebriated.

Nate's head snapped up. A paunchy beachgoer with a sun-burned nose and a towel slung over his shoulder tipped a koozie-wrapped bottle of beer in his direction.

The guy kept walking, and Nate let out an annoyed sigh. He turned back to Angie, but instead of finding her still caught in the moment, her gaze was distant, her focus on the sea.

"They're here," she said.

He followed her line of sight. Sure enough, gliding through the water toward the dock was the boat.

Nate watched the boat's arrival from behind a yellow storage shed with red trim. He and Angie had vacated their spots on the beach to get a better look at the dock. Two shadowy figures exited and disappeared up the path into the trees.

He turned to Angie. "What do we do now? Follow them?"

"Yes, but not how you're thinking."

"You don't want to know what they do or who they meet when they get here every day?"

"I do, but I think we'll get more answers if we follow them on the water." She pointed to the rental shack. "We'll rent a boat and go around the bend out of sight. Then we wait. When we see the boat again, we'll follow."

Nate swallowed. It seemed simple enough. But potentially dangerous. Of course, so was following criminals into the woods. "At least Wayne doesn't seem to be around today." Nate had no desire to face the man after yesterday's stunt with the paddleboat. Best-case scenario, Wayne would think he was a weirdo. Worst-case, he'd suspect Nate was up to something.

And if Wayne had heard the boat left yesterday with a stowaway on board...Nate didn't even want to think about the implications of that.

"Come on." Angie grasped his hand and tugged him toward the boat rentals. "We don't know how much time we have."

Inside the hut, they found Matthew hanging up and organizing a pile of life vests.

"Wah gwaan. How can I help you?"

"We want to rent a boat." Angie pulled a wallet out of her bag.

Matthew sauntered toward the counter. "Gimme a sec. You need to fill out the rental agreement."

Angie bounced on her heels, restless and energized. If Nate didn't know better, he might buy the act. Impatient, but not so much that it felt overdone.

She took the pen and started filling out the form. "I hate to hurry you, but I saw a turtle offshore. We're getting the boat so we can get a better look."

Matthew shook his head slowly. "That turtle probably gone."

"I know, but what if it's not?" She checked the box to have the rental charged to the room, signed the form with her fake name, and pushed it across the counter. "Can we hurry this along?"

"What kinda boat you want?"

Having spent twenty-plus years living in the Florida Keys, Nate was as comfortable on the water as in the air. "Preferably something with a motor—in case we decide to do some exploring."

Matthew grabbed two life vests from the rack on the wall. "Come with me and put these on."

They followed him to the dock and a small skiff with faded paint. Matthew stepped into the boat, the hull rocking beneath him. He looked at Nate and Angie. "Either of you drive one of them before?"

"I have," Nate said, while Angie shook her head.

Matthew's hand touched various pieces of equipment as he spoke. He demonstrated each task, and the little boat sputtered to life. "Give the motor a couple minutes to warm up." He stepped out of the boat. "Life vests at all times, obey speed limits and no-wake zones. Don't disturb wildlife, and if the engine stalls or you run into any other sort of trouble, use the radio. Questions?"

"Don't think so." Nate looked at Angie. "You?"

"I'm good." She smiled but continued her excited fidgeting routine with some light foot tapping.

Matthew waited for them to step into the vessel, then cast the mooring line from the cleat. He tossed the rope into the boat. "Enjoy yourselves out there."

They pushed off and waved.

When they were clear of the dock, Angie pointed to the west. "Let's go over there and see if we can find somewhere to hide out."

A few minutes later, Angie spotted the perfect pocket tucked between two outcroppings of rock and half-hidden by over-hanging branches. Nate maneuvered the skiff into the narrow space and idled the engine.

They sat in silence for a long time, both staring into the distance, rather than each other. That didn't mean she didn't consume him. He couldn't help but replay that almost-kiss in his head. Over and over. The way she'd looked at him with fire in her eyes. Her soft lips almost touching his. So close. Again.

And again, it didn't happen. Was it for the best? A couple of days ago, he would have said yes. Now, he wasn't so sure.

She cleared her throat. "Have you spoken to your brother or sister since we've been here?"

Nate shook his head. "Not since we arrived when I called to say I was going to stay. Elise called this morning, but didn't leave a message."

"It sounds like you and Elise have a pretty close relationship."

There was something sad in Angie's tone, and Nate wondered if she was thinking of her own sister.

"You know most of the story," he said. "Dad drilled into me that it was my responsibility to protect our real identities at any cost. He said if anyone found out who we were, the consequences would be devastating."

Angie winced. "Why did it fall to you?"

"Probably because I was with them more. Dad had a business to run, but I had the ability to look after them at school." Nate shrugged, for some reason feeling the need to minimize the effect of his upbringing. "I was protective and overbearing, especially with Elise. I basically acted like a substitute parent."

"You said Jack remembered who your family was, but Elise never knew?" Her gaze scanned the horizon.

Nate closed his eyes and took a deep breath through his nose. In the end, keeping the truth from Elise hadn't protected her. It had endangered her. *He* had endangered her.

"Since she didn't remember, not telling her seemed the best way to keep her safe—and it probably was when she was a kid. But once she became an adult, I should have told her who we were. Not knowing made her vulnerable."

"You blame yourself for her abduction?" Angie certainly wasn't one to circle around the point.

"How could I not?"

She tilted her head, considering. "You did what you thought was best, right?"

Nate shrugged.

"There's no way you could have known what would happen."

He wasn't sure he agreed. He's spent a huge portion of his life thinking of possible catastrophes and how to prevent them.

"You know, I spoke with Eric the day we left. I wanted to make sure he understood what I was doing here and why."

"And?"

"He said he'd keep quiet."

"Why are you bringing this up now?"

"Because just from that short conversation, I could tell he loves your sister, and I can't imagine either of them blames you for what happened."

He didn't respond. What could he say? That she was right?

"At any rate," she continued. "You no longer have to protect the family secret. That should be a relief."

"Should be, but it's not."

A small crease appeared between Angie's brows as she studied him. He swallowed a sigh and continued. "I've not done a good job of letting go. People know who we are now. I know that. Logically. But emotionally, I still feel compelled to guard the truth and protect my brother and sister." He felt himself slowly deflate with the futility of it all. "Of course, Elise has Eric now, and Jack never really needed my protection."

Angie's mouth parted as though she were about to argue. But instead of speaking, her eyes snagged on something over his shoulder.

The cabin cruiser sped past, its hull bouncing and leaving a trail of foamy white wake.

Nate released the choke, then twisted the throttle.

"Don't get too close." The words were part observation, part command. Angie gripped the side of the boat. There was an edge of tension in her tight jaw and furrowed brow but also a wild gleam of excitement in her eyes.

"Hopefully, they aren't going too far. I don't know what sort of fuel range this thing has."

Angie stared, eyes wide and shouting over the drone of the engine, "Is the tank low already?"

"No, but we should keep an eye on it. If it gets to half, we'll need to turn around."

He pointed to the gauge. Angie nodded.

Twenty minutes later, the fishing boat turned at an inlet. When they reached the bend in the shoreline, Nate put the skiff in neutral, trying to balance the need to see with the need to remain hidden.

The area was remote, with overgrown vegetation and devoid of any signs of human habitation. The cabin cruiser continued for about a quarter of a mile, then docked against a piece of land with a concrete slab on top. One of the men got out and tied the boat to the dock. He went back inside.

A few minutes later, both men appeared, arms loaded with firearms. They disappeared into the trees.

"I want to get a closer look." Angie started to unhook her vest.

Alarm bells sounded in Nate's head. This felt like yesterday all over again. "What are you doing?"

"It's not far to shore. I can swim, then sneak over to see what they're up to." She pulled her gun from her bag. "Of course, if you get me close enough to wade, I can take this with me."

"Were you planning this all along?" He couldn't believe she'd do something so impulsive, especially after nearly getting caught yesterday.

"This specifically? No, because I didn't know what to expect. But getting close enough to observe what's going on? Yes, that was always part of my plan."

Nate let out a frustrated growl. They were separated yesterday and look how well that turned out. No way was he putting himself through that again. "I'm going with you."

CHAPTER 22

Angie hopped out of the boat and helped Nate drag the skiff onto the muddy bank. Her feet sank into the wet soil as they tugged the bow higher onto the beach.

A thick canopy separated them from the gunrunners—or whatever they were.

"Let's go." Angie stole a quick glance at Nate, glad to have him beside her. She didn't know what to expect, and if something happened, it was always better to have a second person.

They stepped over the knotty mangrove limbs tangling across the ground between the beach and the small rise to the woods. Nate didn't speak, but he stayed close as she picked her way slowly and deliberately between trees, turning sideways through the narrow spaces.

A soft breeze rustled the leaves on the trees and carried the sound of voices. Patois. Heavily accented. Angie couldn't make out what they were saying, but her instincts sharpened. They were close enough now that even the faintest sound from Angie or Nate—a gasp, a whisper, a snapped twig—could give them away.

She held up her hand, signaling for Nate to halt, and crouched behind a tree. Up ahead, she spotted the men carrying weapons across a ramp and into something built into the earth. She drew her gun and waited.

The unloading ceased. The men convened on the dock. Angie couldn't hear the conversation, but they appeared to be debating something. They disappeared back inside the boat. After a few minutes, the engine let out a sharp grind, then roared to life with a harsh growl.

They watched as the boat pushed away from the dock, swung into a wide arc, and reversed course. Angie released a breath as soon as she saw that the boat was back in the open water.

"Let's move," she said. "We don't know whether they'll come back."

Moving quickly, they made their way to the opening of what appeared to be a cave. Except, instead of a typical entrance, someone had built a set of stairs. Eight steps descended to a wooden walkway elevated above a shallow basin filled with a few inches of water.

With her gun still drawn, Angie ducked past a veil of hanging vines and stepped into the cavern. She inhaled damp air that smelled of earth and stone. The entrance was dark and narrow, but a few steps in, she spotted artificial light. Several feet later, the cave opened up to reveal an enormous chamber.

A wooden floor had been laid over the rock, and pilings reinforced the walls of the cave. Straight ahead, against the man-made back wall, were gun racks filled with every kind of semi-automatic weapon you could imagine.

"Jesus." Nate stepped beside her, ticking off groups of weapons with his fingers. His words echoed off the bare surfaces surrounding them. "There must be close to a thousand guns here."

Angie agreed. Not to mention dozens of wooden crates that might also be stuffed with firearms. She stowed her Sig in the holster clipped to her waistband.

"What the hell is this place?" She snapped pictures with her phone, taking one in panorama mode to capture the entire stockpile. "This seems more like someone building an army than a guy selling some guns on the street."

"No kidding. This is an armory." Nate walked around the room, a look of horrified awe fixed on his face. "I'd guess this has been going on for a while, don't you think? To have a setup like this?"

He was right. Someone went to a lot of trouble to create the infrastructure to store weapons here. Not to mention the daily deliveries. Had Rick found out? Is this what got him killed? It certainly seemed possible.

She lifted the lid off one of the crates. Yep, just as she'd thought. Filled with rifles packed between corrugated cardboard dividers. Another smaller crate contained boxes of ammo. Not good.

"Uh...Angie?" There was a heavy note of concern in Nate's voice.

Her gaze snapped to where he stood beside a workbench, and her breath caught at the object cradled in his hand.

A mobile phone.

"We need to get out of here." Nate returned the phone to the corner of the table. Whoever left it would probably be coming back to retrieve it. Should he grab a weapon? There were plenty around, but would any be loaded? And did he have time to find ammo?

"Cool yuhself. It nah tek long." The voice came from outside the cave. Boots scraped against the stairs.

Angie turned, eyes wide, and then motioned for Nate to take up a position against the wall on one side of the entrance. He did as she said, watching as she pressed her back against the rock on the other side.

A man in baggy shorts, a T-shirt and sneakers entered the cave. He went straight for the table, completely oblivious he had company. He may not have seen them yet, but he would as soon as he turned around.

Or maybe not. The guy tapped his phone a few times, then headed back toward the entrance, eyes glued to the screen.

Nate held his breath. They might actually get out of this without a confrontation.

And then, the man's gaze slid up to find Angie, his feet slowing to a stop and his thumb pausing mid-scroll. He knitted his brows together in a way that suggested his brain was still catching up with what his eyes were seeing.

"Eh! Wah yuh do in here?" A beat passed. Then he lunged at Angie.

Nate reacted without thinking, grabbing the guy and yanking him backwards. The man threw a punch—slow and wide and clumsy. Nate stepped to the side, letting the man's momentum carry him forward. Then Nate lifted his arm and drove his elbow into the creep's shoulder.

The guy fell forward with a grunt, but recovered quickly, gripping the edges of a crate and pulling himself to his feet. He charged at Angie. Her hand flew to the weapon at her hip. Before the guy reached her, Nate was on him, slamming him against the wall. He leaned into him, twisting the guy's hand behind his back and pressing his cheek against the rock face.

Adrenaline was still flowing through Nate's limbs. His breath was fast and heavy. He turned to Angie. "What do we do now?"

"Get answers." She moved close, a pissed-off look on her face. "Who do you work for?"

He didn't respond.

"What are you doing with the guns? What are they for?"

"Mi naw tell yuh nuttin."

She put her hand on the grip of her gun. "Is that so?"

"Mi know yuh. Yuh deh one from deh boat."

Another voice, sharp and impatient, came from outside. "Quick yuh ass up!"

Nate and Angie exchanged an anxious look. The situation was escalating quickly from bad to worse to how-the-fuck-are-we-getting-out-of-this.

The man with his face smooshed against the wall started to yell. "Help! Dwayne! Help!"

Fuck! These guys dealt in firearms. There was a good chance the guy outside had a weapon.

"We need to go. Now." Angie unholstered her gun.

Nate couldn't agree more. He considered the man pressed against the wall. He didn't know what to do with him and there wasn't time to talk about it. He yanked the guy backwards, spun him around, and pushed him backwards. Nate's heart banged against his ribcage, fast and loud. Then, in a single motion, he clenched his fist, shifted his weight, and let his punch slam into the guy's chin with a thwack.

The gunrunner's eyes rolled back, his mouth popped open, and he slumped to the ground like a bag of dirty laundry.

A look of delighted wonder lit up Angie's face, and for the briefest of moments, Nate wanted to thump his chest like Tarzan. In the next second, she was gripping his hand and dragging him out of the cave.

------ ❧ ------

Daylight smacked Angie the moment she exited the cave.

She blinked, but didn't give herself time to adjust. Cross-legged, she ascended the steps, gun pointed ahead, and Nate close behind. In the cave, one man lay unconscious. The other was out there—armed and on the lookout.

A few steps from the top, she stopped, scanning the dock and surrounding flora. Hard not to feel like a sitting duck. She didn't see him, but he was there. They had to move. "Go!"

They sprang into action, darting across the small clearing, but instead of running toward the forest, Nate headed for the narrow shoreline. "This way!"

A gunshot rang out. Angie ducked, but kept running, her footfalls fast and heavy. She and Nate tore across the narrow, wet embankment. Her legs burned. Her heart pounded. Her breath came in ragged gasps.

Another gunshot.

Fuck! She kept running, her feet digging into the soggy ground.

Nate was a few steps ahead of her now. *Keep going. Get to the boat.*

Footsteps. Behind her. Closing in.

Almost there!

Her foot slid. Her knee buckled. She fell.

Mud coated her hands. She still had the gun. But could she turn fast enough? The guy was close. Too close.

She scrambled to stand.

"Not so quick." The voice came from behind her.

Angie stood, then turned to face the man with the gun.

Was this it? Was this how it ended? She could only hope Nate would get away.

She lifted her gun, but his was already trained on her chest. If she was going to die, so was he. Her finger twitched on the trigger.

"Who yuh be?"

She released a breath. It seemed he wasn't going to kill her immediately. Not until he had answers. She mentally spun through her Rolodex of lies. "I'm a journalist. Heard a rumor that guns were moving through the area, and when I saw your boat yesterday, I got curious."

The guy stared, but he lowered his weapon just a fraction. Did he believe her? Would he let her go? "People know where I am. If I don't come back, they're going to ask why."

His jaw tightened. His eyes darted from side to side. Good. His indecision might give her the chance she needed.

A light rustling came from the forest.

Then, in a blur of motion, Nate exploded from the trees, tackling the man with the gun. They crashed into the shallow water, the firearm flying from the man's hand and hitting the water with a *plunk*.

Nate hauled the man to the shore and punched him in the stomach. The guy doubled over with a groan.

Angie moved to Nate's side. "Get his belt."

Nate undid the man's belt and pulled it through the loops. "What are you going to do with this?"

"Tie him up so we can get away." She held her gun on the guy and directed him toward a tree. "Sit."

Nate used the belt to secure the gunrunner's hands behind the narrow tree trunk. "Good?"

"Good enough." Angie nodded, high on the heady mix of triumph and reckless exhilaration. "Let's go."

They pushed the boat into the water. Nate started the motor, and they were on their way.

The skiff cut through the waves. Angie let out a shaky breath, the rush of escape draining into her chest.

They'd survived. This time.

But they'd set something in motion today. And this was likely only the beginning.

CHAPTER 23

The return trip was much quicker. Nate and Angie arrived at the resort less than fifteen minutes after fleeing the cave full of guns. Nate had the mooring line wrapped around the cleat before Matthew had a chance to assist.

"Did you find your turtle?" Matthew asked.

Angie hustled across the dock. "Nope. You were right. He was gone."

Nate took Angie's hand. They hurried along the winding path toward the pool.

"We can't stay here," she said. "We need to look for another hotel before those guys come looking for us."

The disturbing memory of what happened at the cave wouldn't leave Nate's mind—one man knocked out, the other tied to a tree. The thrill of adventure had soured into unease as they'd driven away.

Angie was right. They needed to get out of here. Those men recognized her. They knew she'd boarded their boat at this resort. Sooner or later—probably sooner—they'd come looking.

Nate squeezed her hand. "We'll do that as soon as we get back to the room."

They moved quickly across the pool deck.

"Try not to set off the smoke detector," someone yelled.

People cheered. Someone clinked a spoon against a glass. The words *afternoon delight* were uttered somewhere in the noise. Geez. One dance where you pretend to be newlyweds, and all of a sudden, the entire resort thinks it has a stake in your sex life.

The moment they entered the suite, Angie dashed to the bedroom, pulled her suitcase out from under the bed, and started throwing things into it.

Nate packed his few pieces of clothing into his duffel, then wandered to the bedroom to check on Angie. He leaned against the door frame.

She didn't look up from packing. "We need to call around, see if we can find somewhere else to stay."

He stepped forward and took hold of her hands. "Slow down."

"Slow down? I can't slow down. Those men—maybe others—are going to come looking for us. We need to get out of here."

"Shouldn't we know where we're going first?" He sat on the end of the bed and pulled her down beside him.

Her anxious eyes bounced across the room. "We don't have time for this."

"Take a breath and tell me what's really wrong."

"Besides the obvious?"

Not for one second did he believe Angie was this rattled by those men. Something else was upsetting her.

She blinked, then finally looked at him. "I dragged you into this. You're in danger. Because of me."

Nate let the silence between them draw out, figuring she had more to say.

"I can't let you get hurt." Her voice was steady, her jaw tight. "It was my idea to investigate your dad's death, and now you're wrapped up with a drug lord."

"You didn't drag me into anything. If you recall, I was the one who said I wanted to stay." He said the words because she needed to hear them, but he meant them. "You told me from the start it would be dangerous, and I wanted to be here anyway."

"Yes, but I bet you didn't think it would involve your dad's old friend or a cave full of guns."

He gave a half smile, trying to keep things light. "Cave, guns, drug lords—doesn't matter. I'm here because I want to be. And I'm not going anywhere."

"Good. Let's figure out where we're going. We have a target on our backs."

"I'm just following your lead."

She sat up and reached for her phone. "Let's find a room."

Thirty minutes later, they still hadn't found anywhere to stay. Holiday tourism combined with the economic summit made empty hotel rooms nonexistent. Nate even called a hostel. No luck.

"So," he said. "What's our next move?"

"I'll call Fitzroy." Angie let out a loud, beleaguered sigh. "I'll have to tell him everything we've gotten up to, but I'm not seeing any other choice."

CHAPTER 24

Angie put the key in the lock and pushed open the door. Since Fitzroy's sister was in the States for the holidays, he'd offered her third-floor apartment in Kingston's Southside neighborhood. She couldn't be more grateful.

"Home sweet home," she declared, dragging her suitcase through the entrance.

The apartment was neat and clean—and about the size of a standard hotel room. She suppressed a snort. And here she'd thought sharing the suite with Nate had been excruciating. These were significantly closer quarters.

The single-room apartment had a kitchenette, a table, a couch, and a bed. She stared at the mattress. It was small. Though technically, she supposed it was meant for two people, it had definite whoops-we're-spooning vibes. She took a sip of her water bottle.

Nate stood beside her, taking in the room. "Guess we better get used to being on top of each other."

She nearly choked. That wasn't what he meant. Clearly.

He cleared his throat. "Might as well make ourselves comfortable."

"Fitzroy said there were linens in the closet. We can make the bed later. First, I want to see the pictures I took yesterday and the ones from the cave today." She propped her bag on a chair at the table and pulled out her computer.

She opened her laptop, entered her PIN, and opened the cloud-storage folder with the photos she'd taken yesterday on the boat. Nate pulled up a chair and settled beside her. A smear of salt—probably from his tussle with the guy with the gun—stretched from his temple to his jaw, and she had the strangest urge to lick it off.

He must have felt her stare. "What?"

"Nothing." She redirected her attention to the first photo. Clicking on the little magnifying glass to get a better look at the weapons. A couple of ARs, some tactical shotguns, maybe an Uzi, and a bunch of other crap. A real mishmash.

A quick count showed thirty weapons, maybe more. Not a major acquisition, but if they did this every day, they were collecting a couple hundred firearms each week. And judging by what they saw in the cave, Golding had been at this for a while.

Next, she clicked the folder with the photos from today. She opened the panoramic first.

She blew out a breath. Man, that was a lot of guns. Her breath stuck somewhere between her chest and her throat. Only a few hours had passed since she'd physically been in the room with all these weapons, and still, the sheer volume astounded her.

And then it hit her. What was she thinking? Before this had been theoretical. Now it was real. And dangerous.

"I have to call Gary." She hadn't meant to say the words aloud.

"Who's Gary?"

"My supervisor."

Nate's gaze snapped to her.

"This is bigger than I imagined. Golding is planning something, and people are going to get hurt." She needed to tell Gary everything. The thought made her queasy.

Nate was quiet for an excruciatingly long moment. But then his fingers cupped her chin and forced her to look into his eyes. "Rather than rush into anything, let's take some time, figure out exactly what he needs to know."

She could read the questions in his eyes. Where did this leave them? Were they going to continue to look into his father's death? Or give up?

"I need to know what happened to my dad. And if Doc was involved."

The ache in her throat was sharp. Rick was a good man, and she'd failed him. "I want that too."

Silence pulsed around them.

"When I saw that asshole point a gun at you—" Nate's voice cracked. "I've never been so scared."

"You saved my life." Her voice was low and breathy.

"It was a team effort."

They'd agreed to keep this thing professional. Right now, she didn't care about that. She drifted closer. "Are we going to do this?"

His pulse fluttered in his neck. He nodded, his gaze never leaving hers. "I think so."

A wave of shivers rocketed up her spine and into her extremities. She'd not had many relationships. Sex? Sure. But a lasting, meaningful connection with another human being? Even her list of friends was pathetically short. After her sister's death, she'd fenced up her heart and not let anyone inside.

Nate took her hand and pulled her the short distance to the bed. He ran his hands up her arms, his thumbs rubbing soothing circles on the inside of her biceps. "Do you have any idea how much I want you?"

A warm current sparked through her veins.

"I think so." Because she wanted him too.

"Say it." His breathing grew raspy.

Her heart thudded. "I want you."

He pressed her flat on the bare mattress, grinding his pelvis into hers. Her muscles tensed in response, a deep thrum buzzing low in her belly.

She inhaled his sweet, earthy scent and savored the hard ridge cradled in her center. A wonderful pressure built, making her ache with anticipation.

Reaching under his shirt, she smoothed her hands over the hard ripples of his stomach, her fingers brushing the soft hair on his abdomen. A surge of power hit her nervous system.

Nate dropped onto his forearms, desire smoldering in his gaze. He nipped at her ear, and the erotic sting sent a shiver through her body.

"You do things to me I don't understand. It scares the hell out of me." The revelation escaped before she could pull it back. For so long, she'd protected herself, shielded every vulnerability. But with Nate, she laid herself bare. She wove her hands around his back, dug her fingertips into the spot between his spine and shoulder blade, and massaged the tense muscle.

He buried his face in the crook of her neck and dragged his teeth across her earlobe. A smile spread across his face when he lifted to look at her. "What are you thinking?"

"How right this feels."

A frisky glow bounced into his eyes. "We're just getting started."

Liquid heat rushed through her and flooded her most intimate parts, spilling into her panties. She shuddered and arched, grinding her sex against him. He kissed her forehead, then her cheek.

"I've never—" He searched her eyes. "I've never felt this way before."

She knew exactly what he meant.

His eyebrows drew together. "I feel whole when I'm with you. I don't know what to make of it."

God. This man. She couldn't take it a moment longer. Her fingers slid beneath the waistband of his swim trunks to wrap around him, his sharp inhalation inflaming her senses.

He moved away from her and tore off his shirt. She raised herself onto her elbows and gawked, unabashedly trailing her gaze from his broad shoulders to his torso and finally to the area still annoyingly concealed by his shorts.

Tugging her to a seated position, he lifted the tank top over her head, then yanked on the bow at her back and the one at her neck. The bikini top fell to her lap.

His appreciative growl said it all. With a gentle nudge, he pushed her further onto the bed. His fingers drew a lazy design on her stomach before cupping her breast. "God, you're perfect."

And then his mouth crashed into hers, the kiss deep and insistent. She moaned, clinging to him as he moved his focus from her ear down to her cheek to her neck and finally, her breast. Now that she knew his touch, Angie didn't know if she'd ever be complete without it. She ached to feel him inside her again.

He rocked against her, plucking her nipple before drawing it into his mouth. He sucked, then squeezed. "So beautiful."

She responded with quick pants. "More."

He kissed up her neck, slid along her jaw, finally arriving at her mouth.

In response, she squeezed his hair between her fingers and pulled. When he came up for air, she wrapped a leg around his and ran the side of her foot along his upper calf and knee. "Do you have a condom?"

A laugh rumbled against her ear. "I emptied the resort's gift shop."

His hands slid beneath her bikini bottom and rubbed along her slick entrance. A sharp electric current jolted through her as his fingers found her clit. "You're ready for me." His deep, husky voice rumbled against her ear.

He stroked and manipulated the little bundle of nerves. Her sex pulsed with an insistent demand, her body weakening as the ecstasy consumed her.

He slipped a finger inside. Then another, hitting her sweet spot and making her whimper. Curling forward off the bed, she clutched his shoulders and panted. "Nate."

"I love it when you say my name." He yanked down her shorts, then her bikini bottoms.

He wedged his thigh between her legs, still stroking, driving her near delirium. Pleasure coiled inside her. Then he slid down her body to place a gentle kiss on the sensitive skin just inside her leg. Before she knew it, his mouth was on her sex. One slow lick up her entrance, sweeping against her sensitive little bud. Then another. God, it felt good. She let her body relax into the rhythm and moaned with enjoyment.

He paused, pressing his tongue against her. Her body gave a soft shudder.

He resumed his rhythmic assault, making her entire body quiver, and when his tongue pressed against her one last time, her muscles clenched involuntarily.

She squeezed her eyes shut so hard she saw stars. She wanted to scream. "Please, inside me."

He held her in place as the climax tore through her, waves of sensation intoxicating her with pleasure. She collapsed into a sated heap, and he climbed the length of her body to press a kiss against her mouth.

"What do you want next?" He ground against her hard and rough.

"I want you to fuck me." Even as she said the words, she knew they weren't entirely accurate. She wanted more. Much more.

He took her mouth in a hard, urgent kiss. Desire flooded her. Those shorts of his needed to disappear. She tugged frantically at his waistband. "Off. Now."

He wriggled out of his swim trunks. She cupped his hardness, stroking up and down.

"Fuck." He breathed the word. His erection slid against her slick entrance.

She loved that he was as affected by her as she was by him. "Condom."

He scrambled to his bag. And then he was back, climbing onto the bed, pressing into her. She rolled her hips, her body stretching, yielding, accepting him. He pumped, slow and smooth. "Okay?"

She lifted into his thrusts. "Better than okay."

He increased his tempo, driving deep and hard. When he looked at her again, there was a wild gleam in his eyes. They were as close as two people could be, but she wanted more. Needed more. She tightened her arms around his back. He was hers—for as long as he'd let her have him.

His movements grew rougher, harder. The tension inside her grew with every twist, every thrust. Her core curled tightly, aching for release. He grasped the back of her knee and lifted her leg, opening her wider. Heat, bliss, euphoria multiplied, rumbling through her body like a shockwave. One more lunge and pleasure cascaded through her. She had to bite his shoulder to stifle her scream.

Her muscles tightened, her body trembled. She gave a soft sigh of pleasure.

Nate pumped one more time, buried his face in the bed and came with a loud groan.

*   *   *

Nate woke in a tangle of sheets and limbs. Angie nestled at his side, her head resting in the crook of his shoulder. He sniffed her hair. The sweet citrus scent of her shampoo loosened something in his chest. The fragrance felt comfortable, familiar.

After the most intense love-making he'd ever experienced, they'd put the sheets on the bed, then crowded into the too-small shower, exploring each other with warm soapy hands before tumbling back to bed and falling asleep in each other's arms.

He tipped his head onto the pillow and closed his eyes.

The dark-haired beauty beside him stirred. He wrapped an arm around her back and folded her into him. Zero chance he wasn't wearing a stupid grin. "Good morning."

He couldn't stop his hand from wandering. First to the small of her back, then her perfect buttocks. He squeezed. The things he still wanted to do to her.

Her hand glided across his stomach, edging dangerously close to his awakening dick. "You look like a morning person."

"Only when I have something to look forward to."

She wrapped delicate but strong fingers around his arousal and started pumping. Up. Down. Slow, then fast.

Her other hand slipped beneath the sheets and she moaned, writhing and panting against him. *Good lord. Could she be any sexier?* Just when he thought he couldn't get any harder, she grabbed a condom from the nightstand and ripped it open. Once he was sheathed, she climbed atop him and sank down.

Her body surrounded him, taking his entire length, her warm, velvety inside hugging his erection. And then she started to rock.

Warmth spread through his chest, but it wasn't just desire. It was bigger than that. Bigger than him. *Us*.

She lifted, then plunged him back into her depths.

Suddenly, they were one. Caught in a current, about to plummet over the edge.

"Fuck me," he moaned.

She leaned down and pressed her lips to his mouth, their slick skin gliding together.

Grasping her hips, he buried himself to his hilt, their bodies melding together. He held her there and rocked, fondling her swollen sex. His release was close, but he needed to see her, to feel her climax.

Her breath quickened, and her tight channel constricted and squeezed until he thought he'd go blind with pleasure. Before he knew it, they were careening toward the precipice. And he wasn't ever letting her go.

CHAPTER 25

A nutty aroma wafted into the room. Angie freed herself from Nate's grasp and raised up on her elbows. "Is that coffee?"

The half of his face that wasn't pressed into the pillow smiled. "Smells like it."

Sure enough. The coffeepot on the counter was burbling away.

"When did you do that?" Was there anything better than waking up to the smell of freshly brewed coffee? Obvious exceptions excluded. Her heart expanded at his thoughtfulness. If he kept this up, before long, she'd be able to park a pickup truck in there.

"Last night. Found the grounds and set the timer before bed." He gave her a peck on the nose.

She settled back onto her pillow. "I'm so glad you're here."

He rolled her onto her back and leaned over her. Dark stubble colored his chin and jaw. He looked like an outlaw. All he lacked was a lever-action rifle and a ten-gallon hat. For someone who worked in law enforcement, she sure did like the bad-boy look. Or maybe she just liked him.

He gave her an easy smirk. "Staying here sounds like the best thing in the world, but I'd wager you have plans for the day."

Dallying in bed was tempting. "I do. We should probably get moving."

Nate gave her a quick kiss and threw the sheet to her side of the bed. It wafted down on her like a parachute. Instead of kicking it off, she lay beneath the cream-colored sheet as if it were a shield, welcoming the solitude and using it as a much-needed moment of honesty.

Whatever this was with Nate, she didn't want it to end. It wasn't just that she wanted his hands all over her, but she wanted to make him laugh. She wanted a morning routine that included staying in bed to cuddle, cooking him breakfast and taking care of him when he was sick. Still shrouded, she lifted her hands to her face and groaned.

The clink of dishes being set on the counter and the thud of cabinet doors opening and closing reminded her she needed to get up. She flung Nate's half of the light blanket back onto his side of the bed and kicked off the sheets, then grabbed his T-shirt and pulled it over her head.

"Cream and sugar." He handed her a hot cup of coffee.

She took the mug with both hands and lifted it to her mouth. Her eyes shut when she took her first sip. "Thanks."

"So, what's first on the agenda?" He sat on the couch and looked at her expectantly.

"Before I fell asleep last night, I couldn't stop thinking about the cave. Initially, I didn't think the guns and the summit were connected, but now I'm not so sure."

"How so?" Nate's relaxed posture was replaced by something tense, alert.

"For one thing, why would Golding want to hold the summit so close to where he's stockpiling weapons? Is it possible that he has something planned for the event?"

"What are you thinking?"

She flung her hands out in frustration. "I don't know. An arms deal? A terrorist attack?"

His expression hardened. "What do you want to do about it?"

"I'd like to find some of the voting members who support the new banking regulations."

"How will that help?" He reached for her, tugging her down to sit beside him. She'd never been a hand holder before, but with him she wanted the connectedness. She laced her fingers through his, the now-familiar interlocking of their hands a comfort.

"At the very least, it might shed some light on Golding's scheme." She picked up her phone and scrolled through the contacts. "There's a member of parliament who lobbies for intelligence sharing and sometimes serves as a diplomatic back channel. I've worked with him before, so I'm hoping he'll see me. He represents a parish on the northeast side of the island."

"Is he in town?"

"My guess is yes, but I can call his office to make sure. Maybe they'll put me in touch with him."

Twenty minutes later, Angie disconnected a call. "My contact is staying at a resort about a mile down the beach from Casa Tortuga. He can meet us this morning."

Nate pushed himself off the couch and headed for his bag. "What are we waiting for?"

—— *ele* ——

Nate reached for Angie's hand as they climbed the steps to the lobby of the Grand Palace Jamaica, where her government contact was staying.

The outside of the resort looked dated and could use a pressure wash to remove mold, but Nate couldn't fault them for that. As a small business owner in South Florida, he knew all too well the headache caused by the unappealing black streaks featured on the sides of so many buildings.

Inside was another story. Clean and modern, the pool actually curled into the lobby. There were guests everywhere. He couldn't help but compare this resort to the one where he and Angie had stayed. The big difference? Kids. Adults lounged beside the pool, while children screamed and ran wild. Angie stopped to tell the concierge who they were looking for. He pointed to a tall, pale man with white hair.

"Mr. Morgan, it's such a pleasure to meet you." Angie extended her hand, and they shook.

"The pleasure is mine, Ms. Liu." He had a warm, friendly manner. "It's nice to put a face to a voice."

Angie turned to Nate. "This is my associate, Nathan Hughes."

Nate shook the man's hand, noting his firm grip and polished smile. "How do you do?"

"Have you eaten? I've arranged for a private dining room."

Angie's eyes lit up, and Nate suppressed a grin. She wasn't one to turn down breakfast.

"That sounds great," she said.

They followed the man to a secluded table. Mr. Morgan shook out his napkin and placed it on his lap. "Are you here investigating the banking regulation bill?"

"No, another matter, but it's come up in the course of our investigation." Angie selected a muffin from the basket and broke it in half. "As a member of parliament, can you tell me a little about the resolution and how it came to be?"

"If passed, the bill will require financial institutions to comply with anti-money laundering requirements. The main provision is the reporting of cash transactions over three thousand American dollars. The goal is to limit terrorists' abilities to use banks to support their enterprises."

Nate's mind raced. Three thousand dollars wasn't much. And banking regulations would be easy enough to sidestep. If Golding had an interest in the resolution, it had to be about more than a three-thousand-dollar threshold.

"How do you expect Jamaica to vote?" Angie's tone carried a subtle edge, as though she already knew the answer.

A stricken look crossed the other man's face. "Unfortunately, I believe enough of the voting members are compromised that passage is dead in the water."

Nate knew the basics of how legislation got passed, but that was in the States. This was the Caribbean. Still, he'd bet plenty of wheeling and dealing went on behind the scenes. "Is there a particular element or faction that wants to kill the bill?"

Despite being the only ones in a closed room, Morgan lowered his voice. "I'm almost certain Bear Golding is behind this. He's been working for months to secure the votes against the legislation."

"Is it possible Golding has aligned himself with extremists?" Angie pressed her lips together as though holding back information.

The MP shook his head. "No, I don't see it. He's never had strong ideology beyond protecting his people and making as much money as possible."

"If that's the case, what's his interest in the resolution?" Angie asked, buttering another muffin.

Nate couldn't help but feel a sense of pride as he watched her pull information from the man. She was smart, composed, relentless.

"He's already laundering money through his businesses. Would he really care that much about a three-thousand-dollar transaction limit?" she asked, echoing Nate's thoughts.

"There have been rumors that Golding has a partner. He's always been a force, but in the last year or so, he's gained considerable influence. One might think he has some sort of international backing."

The word *international* sent a chill down Nate's spine. Maybe a terrorism connection wasn't so far-fetched after all. "So maybe the mystery partner is pressuring him to vote a certain way. But why?"

"Can I ask—" Morgan's mouth set in a grim line. His gaze traveled from Angie to Nate, then back to Angie. "Why are you asking about terrorism?"

She took a deep breath. "We have information that Golding is hoarding weapons at a nearby location. Based on the extent of his supply, we think he must have something planned."

The MP inhaled sharply. "That's not good. How can I help?"

"Have you heard anything that might help us figure out who his partner is? Or do you know how we might find out?"

Morgan was quiet for a long moment. "Golding runs an import/export business. He uses shell companies to move money around. I could have a forensics investigator look into the accounts associated with the business and see if that leads us to his partner's identity."

Angie exchanged a glance with Nate, her eyes lit with hope. Something eased in his chest.

"Thank you," she said to Morgan. "This could be the break we've been waiting for."

As Angie and Nate crossed the lobby of the Grand Palace Jamaica, a man caught Angie's eye. Knee-length black denim shorts. A Miami Heat t-shirt. Short black hair and a beard. She'd spotted the same man across the street from the apartment this morning.

They were being followed.

Nate headed for the taxi parked at the curb. Angie grabbed his arm. "No, let's go for a walk along the beach."

He looked around, confused. "Really?"

"Yeah, just for a few minutes." She wrapped her hand around his biceps and leaned against him. "Don't look now, but I think we're being followed."

Nate twisted his head.

"I said, 'Don't look.'" She tugged on his arm, drawing his attention back to her.

"Followed by who?"

"Guy in jean shorts and a Miami Heat T-shirt."

Nate's mouth popped open. "I saw that guy in the lobby after we left breakfast."

"I didn't want to go straight back to the apartment because I wanted to see if he followed us."

"How will we know if we can't look?"

"See that bench?" She gestured with her chin. "When we get up there, I'll pretend I want to sit, and you can see if he's still there."

They approached the bench perched on the edge of the sand. Angie grabbed Nate's hand and pulled him toward it. When she tugged on his arm, he pivoted.

"Confirmation. Denim shorts is still there," he said, sitting beside her.

Sure enough, the guy was hovering, pretending to take a picture of the ocean.

Nate wrapped his arm around her shoulder, and she snuggled against him. It worked for their cover, but also, she enjoyed being close to him.

"I suspected as much." She kissed him on the cheek.

He pulled her closer. "Do you think he works for Golding?"

"That's my guess. I'd hoped the guys from the boat would've kept their mouths shut about us finding the cave." She'd counted on the men keeping quiet out of fear of Golding and what he might do if the gangster learned they'd been tailed.

"How long do you think he can mill around watching us before he decides it looks weird?"

"I don't know. Let's find out."

The guy wandered back and forth, taking pictures, pretending to look at shells, and staring at the ocean. All the while keeping them within his line of sight.

Finally, half an hour later, he ambled away.

Angie stood. "Should we head back to the apartment?"

They caught a taxi, then stopped at a corner market, where they picked up jerk chicken sandwiches and a couple of ginger beers.

"So," Angie said, unpacking the sandwiches at the little table in the apartment. "What do you make of our discussion with Morgan and what he said about the proposed policies?"

Nate took a bite and shrugged. "You said Golding does a lot of business in cash, and beyond that, he's laundering it through his businesses, right?"

Angie took a swig of soda and nodded.

"Well, if the reporting of cash transactions is the sticking point like Morgan said, why would Golding care?"

"It's not the cash limit that's the concern, it's the loss of anonymity. Any transactions over three thousand dollars will need to be reported, which creates a digital trail, and if you go outside of the regular banking system—to wire transfers or crypto—those are traceable too."

He shook his head. "I'm still not seeing it being a big enough deal for Golding to buy votes."

"I agree with you. Makes sense that some new person is pulling the strings."

"So, who would this be important to?"

A cold knot of dread formed in her gut. "I keep coming back to the guns. Everything points to extremists."

"Terrorism?" Nate blew out a heavy exhale. "Seems like this goes beyond anything with my dad."

"Maybe." She shrugged. "But maybe not. Maybe he found out what Golding was planning. What we've learned is definitely enough to get someone killed."

And that was the problem, wasn't it? Before this had been theoretical. Now it was real. And dangerous. Could she really go through with this? Put Nate at risk? The answer was no. Even if she didn't care for him—and God, how she did—she couldn't put him in harm's way, be responsible for him getting hurt. Or worse.

Before long, she'd need to tell Gary what she'd done. The guns were a game changer. Maybe he'd let her stay, continue to investigate. Seemed unlikely, but either way, she couldn't be responsible for Nate's safety. He needed to go home.

And yet, she couldn't bring herself to say the words. She cleared her throat. "What do you want to do with the rest of the day? We could wait for Doc to get off work, follow him, see what he does?"

"Would that be wise if we have a tail?"

He was right. "Maybe we can dig into Doc's financial accounts, look for unexplained income, new purchases, things like that." Without official resources at her disposal, her methods for doing that would be limited.

"Why don't we lie low for the rest of the day, figure out our next move?"

"Sounds like a plan." Staying in with Nate sounded a lot better than chasing bad guys.

And unfortunately, a lot more dangerous for her heart.

CHAPTER 26

Morning light streamed into the small room. Nate moaned, blinking himself awake. Angie was tucked against him, her back warm against his chest, her breaths slow and even. He tightened his arm around her and kissed the top of her head.

For the second morning in a row, he'd experienced the thrill of waking with her beside him. Also, for the second day in a row, he marveled at how right it felt. He'd stay here forever if he could.

But then reality clawed at him. Angie's plan. The one she devised last night. The one that could get her hurt. The one that was way too dangerous.

She stirred, mumbling something as she arched her back and stretched her arms above her head.

"Morning." His throat was dry. He wrapped his arms around her and squeezed.

"Sorry about the morning breath." She rolled over and kissed him. "But not really."

He'd take morning breath over breaking into a drug lord's hotel room any day. Maybe a full night's sleep had given her second thoughts.

"Macadamia nut pancakes," she trilled, casting off the sheet and stalking to the bathroom. "We better get moving. I don't want to miss breakfast."

The sight of her—bare, confident, fearless—left him speechless. The door shut. The water sputtered, then echoed off the plastic shower liner. He covered his face with his hands and groaned.

Last night, her idea had sounded so outlandish, he'd let her talk it out, thinking she'd realize it wasn't worth the risk. No such luck.

So now, after they were both showered and dressed, they were heading back to Casa Tortuga—where they remained registered guests—for the first day of the economic summit. Angie had reasoned that with the summit taking place at Golding's resort, he'd want to be there for opening remarks.

And she wanted to try the pancakes she'd read about in the hotel brochure.

Because of course she did.

She stepped from the bathroom with a towel wrapped around her hair and another covering her torso. "I was thinking I'd wear a swimsuit beneath my clothes, so it looks like we're spending another day at the beach."

"Okay." Nate pushed himself out of bed and into the shower.

Ninety minutes later, they were in the resort lobby on their way to breakfast with Angie leading the way. She looked around. "I haven't seen the guy in the denim shorts today, but that doesn't mean Golding doesn't have someone else following us."

Nate didn't respond. What was there to say? If knowing they were being followed wasn't enough to dissuade her, nothing he could say would change her mind.

They stopped at the hostess stand and waited for the maitre d'.

After a few minutes, a young, frazzled-looking woman appeared. Wisps of hair tumbled from what was meant to be a tight bun. She shoved a pen behind her ear. "Good morning, Mr. and Mrs. Connor. I apologize, but it may be a few minutes before we can seat you."

Nate peered into the restaurant. "Looks like a busy morning."

She blew a strand of hair out of her face. "It is. The symposium starts today."

A tall man with a silver-streaked beard and wearing a beige linen suit that contrasted his rich brown skin tone sauntered out of the restaurant. He patted a short, older man wearing a military uniform on the back. A group of young men in all-black tactical gear trailed behind.

The hostess fidgeted with a pile of menus as he approached. Beige suit handed her a folded bill and winked.

"Thank you, sir." She smiled and let out a huge breath.

Angie turned to Nate and mouthed a single word. "Golding."

Of course, he knew that. Angie had shown him pictures of the man last night. He turned to watch the retreating kingpin and his entourage.

Even though Golding lived in Kingston, Angie believed he'd stay at the resort during the summit or, at the very least, set up a home base in one of the rooms.

The hostess seated them near a large window with a view of the bay. The blue-green water rolled against the beach. He stared, thinking about Angie and unable to concentrate on her words.

Had it really only been a week since he'd met her? That couldn't be right. No way could he fall this fast.

But maybe he had.

He couldn't remember the last time he wasn't wrapped up in some family drama, worrying about the past beating down their door and wondering what new danger the future would bring. Now he had a whole new set of things to worry about.

"Nate?" The way Angie voiced his name suggested it wasn't the first time she'd said it.

He shook his head. "Sorry. I'm listening."

"Once we're done eating, you can go chat up the gal at the front desk, just like we talked about last night. Tell her we want to come back, but we're wondering if we could see their biggest suite before we decide. Since the hotel is booked full, she'll say the suite is occupied and not available for tours, but she might tell you where it's located."

He leaned into the chair back and clasped his hands. With that gleam in her eyes, there'd be no talking her out of this.

"Pester her for pictures or information about the suite if you have to—what floor is it on, what kind of view does it have, that sort of thing." Her voice was soft and conspiratorial.

Nate rubbed his face and groaned. His stomach roiled. And it had nothing to do with hunger. "You don't even know what you're looking for."

"If something's not right, I'll know."

He couldn't stop shaking his head. "What if you get caught? What if someone from the hotel finds you in the room?" A cold fist clutched at his heart. "What if Golding or a member of his security team shows up?"

A server approached and set their food on the table. As soon as he walked away, she leaned forward. "That's why you'll be keeping watch."

She winked and smeared butter on her pancakes. She seemed almost...delighted, not to mention ravenous, by the thought of danger. "I know you're worried, and I appreciate it, but if there's any chance we can stop whatever this is that Golding has planned, we need to take it."

Angie doused her breakfast with syrup. "Sometimes the reward is worth the risk."

He scoffed. "What motivational calendar did you get that off of?"

"That's what my dad said to me when I was learning to ride a bike." Her face sobered for a moment, and Nate wondered briefly why she so rarely mentioned her family.

"This is more dangerous than taking off your training wheels, Angie." How could she even put what they were about to do on the same level as that?

"Yes, thank you. I'm aware."

He didn't respond. Rationalizing with her wouldn't work. The more he tried to talk her out of this, the more determined she'd be to prove she could.

The server returned with the plate of hash browns that came with Nate's breakfast. He ignored it. His stomach twisted into a knot. Most of his childhood had been endless worry. Worry that Elise and Jack were in danger. Worry that the bad guys who were after his mom would find her. Worry that he'd make a mistake and someone would get hurt. And now, here he was again, worrying about someone whose life was in his hands.

He couldn't bear to lose her. Not now.

Not ever.

His trepidation must have shown because she laid a warm hand over his. "It's going to be okay. I promise."

He closed his eyes and nodded. "Tell me again what you want me to do."

Half an hour later, he knew the summit was scheduled to begin at eleven in the Blue Mountain room. He also knew that Mr. Golding occupied the presidential suite. Located at the end of the first floor, the room had a private infinity pool, a deck and ocean access. He'd followed Angie's directions and couldn't believe how easy it was to get the desk clerk to give up the information.

Despite his instincts screaming they were about to make a huge mistake, he was going to have to trust that she knew what she was doing.

Back in the suite she was still paying for, Angie rifled through her bag and wished Nate would stop wringing his hands. He'd eaten only a couple of bites of his breakfast, pushing his eggs and potatoes around until they formed a ketchup-covered pyramid of goo. He'd voiced concern over the plan but hadn't told her not to do it.

Somehow, that made her feel worse.

She removed her gun and extra magazine from her bag and placed them on the coffee table beside her lock-picking kit. If only she'd thought to bring a bug. "It's going to be okay. Really."

His right eyebrow went up.

"It's not like I'll be defenseless, and you're going to be keeping an eye on Golding. It'll be fine. I promise."

"You're saying that a lot."

"Because I mean it." She climbed onto his lap and pressed her mouth against his. Strong arms wrapped around her back and pulled her close. "Besides, you've given me more incentive to be careful than I've ever had before."

He rested his forehead against her own. "I hope that's true."

"Never meant anything more." She kissed him on the cheek and stood to pack her supplies into her bag. "You ready?"

His almost imperceptible nod didn't offer a lot of reassurance. "It's just—" He tilted her chin and stared into her eyes. "I don't want you to get hurt."

"I don't want that either." She clasped his hand, squeezed, and held his gaze. "I've trained for scenarios just like this. I'm good at adapting. Staying calm under pressure. Moving quickly and quietly. I've got this."

He attempted a shaky smile. "You don't think we're rushing into this? Shouldn't we do some reconnaissance first? At least come up with some sort of disguise or cover story?"

"Yes, yes, and yes." She saw no reason to lie. But that didn't mean she couldn't at least try to put his mind at ease. "In a perfect situation, that is exactly what we'd do, but right now we have an opportunity we may never get again. I don't think we can pass it up." Nor did she want to. Not to mention, if this were some sort of terror plot, there could be thousands of lives at stake. "If something happens, don't you want to be able to say we did everything we could?"

For a moment, he looked like he wanted to say more, but then he rolled his neck and stood. "Let's do this."

In the elevator, she went over the plan again. "We'll hang out in the lobby and make sure Golding goes into the meeting. Then you stay there to keep an eye out while I get to his room and sneak inside."

"That doesn't sound too difficult."

He was coming around. She squeezed his arm. "It's not. I'll be in and out of his room in less than five minutes."

"What do you think you're going to find?"

She shrugged. "Hopefully something to explain why Golding needs all those weapons."

They arrived in the lobby and sat in two cushioned chairs with a view of the conference room.

Nate craned his neck to see inside the banquet hall. "Should we check to be sure he's in there?"

"Let's give it a minute. If he's there, the organizer will want to thank him for hosting. If he's not there yet, he'll be here soon."

Nate drew on her bare leg with a fingernail. Her muscles loosened, and she longed to stay beside him, savoring every single touch. Now that she knew how it felt to have another person in her life, she never wanted to go back to being alone.

"What are you doing?"

He gave her a furtive glance. "Writing my name."

"Is this your way of saying I'm yours?" She was perfectly happy to let him claim her.

Whoa. Time to take a breath. They'd had sex two times—okay, maybe three counting the night in Miami—and she was ready to pick out China patterns? She needed to slow down. If she got ahead of herself, she'd only end up disappointed.

She glanced up in time to see a handsome man with a small entourage strolling across the lobby. Golding.

"Let's talk after..." Golding's voice was deep, gravelly, and accented.

She gripped Nate's thigh and studied the man who pulled so many of the strings in this small island country. A natural charmer, he had a friendly smile.

The group of men entered the conference room, and the doors shut behind them.

Angie picked up her bag and pressed a quick kiss to Nate's lips. "Stay here. I'll be right back."

She followed the hallway off the lobby to the end of the building. Staring at the paisley patterned carpet, she fast-walked to the end, made a right turn and came upon a closed door with an infuriating sign.

Suites 16-20. Concierge access only.

Damn. Not ideal, but also not a crisis. Her plan had always been to sneak through the back door, but she'd wanted to get as close to the room as possible. Improvisation was part of the job. So was adaptability. She backtracked to the main hall and exited the building onto a path lined with thick, lush vegetation.

After a few hundred yards, the path continued to the right, but she went straight over mulch and grass. A short iron fence stretched from the side of the building to the ocean. Low enough she could climb over, but the villas between her and the one she needed to reach all had privacy walls that would be much more difficult to climb.

Time for a swim.

———ell———

Nate stared at the conference room door. Still shut. No one had been in or out. He scanned the lobby, looking for the guy who'd followed them yesterday and the guys from the cave.

Angie left about fifteen minutes ago. He'd expected her back by now. Maybe it took longer to get into the room than she'd expected. She said she knew how to pick a lock. Hell, she'd packed an entire kit for it.

Or maybe something happened.

He couldn't let his brain go there. Angie could protect herself. Besides, the sedentary security guard still lounged behind his desk near the lobby doors. Surely if something had gone down, he'd have given up the sloth impression.

Nate's eyes flitted from the hallway he'd watched Angie disappear down to the conference room. He rubbed a hand on the back of his neck. How long did these meetings last?

His phone rang.

He said a quick prayer that Angie wasn't in trouble and flipped the phone over to see the display.

Elise. Again.

Good grief. He'd waked this morning to five missed calls from his sister. Looking for gossip, no doubt. Since settling down with Eric, she'd turned into a real romantic and had been beside herself when he called to say he'd stayed to help Angie with the investigation.

Answering questions about his love life didn't need to happen right this minute. Elise would probably hound him for Angie's number, and once she had that, there'd be no stopping whatever new scheme she devised.

He declined the call.

It rang again almost immediately. *Not good.* Those old feelings of worry crashed into him. What if something happened?

His hand shook as he swiped the icon to answer the call and lifted the phone to his face.

"Hello?" Even to his own ear, his voice sounded hollow. He swallowed the lump rising in his throat.

"You don't call me back and then you send me to voicemail?"

This didn't sound like an emergency. He tapped his foot and glanced at the door. "What's so urgent?"

"How's Angie?" There was a lightness in her voice.

He scrubbed a hand against the side of his face. "Everything is fine. What is so important that you keep calling and not leaving a message? What's going on?"

"Well…" Her voice pitched into a singsong timbre. Whatever she wanted to tell him, she planned to drag it out.

"Spit it out or I'm going to hang up."

She huffed. He didn't need to see her to know she was pouting. Picturing it almost made him smile.

"Fine. Eric and I are getting married. He proposed three nights ago."

"What?"

"You heard me. He took me out for dinner in Key West. Afterward, we walked along the pier to watch the sunset. Then he proposed." She squealed.

"When?" He knew he wasn't giving her the reaction she wanted, but he couldn't help it.

"Christmas Day. You'd better be back by then."

He frowned. The news wasn't completely unexpected. He knew it would happen sooner or later. He'd been thinking later.

"Why so soon?"

"Eric's mom is going to be in town. We're thinking of doing it in Key West. Ceremony on the beach, party on Duvall."

He stared at the ground. "That's only two weeks away."

"I'm aware." Her voice was hard.

"Are you sure you don't want to wait a little longer?"

She snorted into the phone. "This is happening, Nate. I don't know what your problem is, but I'm not putting my life on hold because you're lonely and miserable."

The silence hung heavy.

He heard a deep inhale over the line. "I shouldn't have said that."

A dull throb started between his eyes. "Look, I'm sorry. It's just a surprise. I'm happy for you. And Eric too."

"Uh, huh." She didn't sound convinced. Then her voice softened. "Anyway, I have things to do. I hope you're having a good time."

They disconnected. What was wrong with him? The only thing he'd ever wanted was for her to be safe and happy. It all came down to his guilt about how Elise and Eric met. If he hadn't been a hardheaded ass, she never would have run off, never would have been kidnapped.

Of course, now that he had Angie, he realized the circumstances of how they met didn't change his feelings. So why did he doubt his sister? Because her relationship was a never-ending reminder that he couldn't be trusted to look out for the people he cared about. He pinched the bridge of his nose and took a deep breath.

Conversation rumbled from the conference room. He glanced up. The doors were open. Conference goers streamed out of the room. *Shit*. He jumped to his feet. Where was Golding? He peered into the room.

Then, he glanced down the hallway and saw a dark head and a cream suit walking toward the suites.

Fuck fuckity fuck fuck.

CHAPTER 27

Angie crept up the wooden deck to the glass door at the back of Golding's suite. Prior to her ocean plunge, she'd tucked her sandals and bag beneath the branches of a red-leafed shrub. The bag contained her Sig, which she could only pray would stay hidden, and her new mobile phone.

Not having a phone presented many problems. First, she had no way of contacting Nate and telling him she'd made it, though now that she thought about it, she probably should have sent him a text before diving into the ocean.

Another problem was that no phone meant no camera. Anything she found would have to be committed to memory. Most concerning of all, she had no way of knowing if Golding had headed back to his room. And now she was wet. *Crap*. Perhaps she'd gotten a little too into the improvisation part of the plan.

Too late to turn back now. Not that she wanted to.

She twisted her tank top into a knot to squeeze out as much water as possible, then did the same with her heavy shorts. *Shoot*. That wasn't going to do it. A quick scan of the spa-like deck revealed a pile of towels stacked between the hot rocks and the fruit water. Bikini it is. She slipped out of her shorts and shirt and pulled a towel off the stack. She rubbed it up and down her legs. The towels in the honeymoon suite were nice, but these were next level. Soft and fluffy. Decadent. After drying her torso, she took care to rub the bottoms of her feet, then tossed the towel into the bin.

She picked up her shorts, cupping the pockets. Dammit. Her lock-picking kit must not have survived the ocean detour. Well, maybe she'd get lucky and the door would be unlocked. She gripped the handle and pulled. Of course not. That would've been too easy.

Stepping back, she considered her options. Sliding glass doors were notoriously easy to break into. Not that she'd ever done it herself, but she understood the mechanics—assuming the door lacked basic protection.

She examined the upper frame. No clips or screws. No security bar either. Theoretically, she should be able to lift the door off the track and pull it out. The question was, was she strong enough to do it? She took a deep breath. One way to find out.

Gripping the frame with one hand and pressing her other palm flat against the glass, Angie crouched slightly and tried to lift. The door didn't budge. She adjusted her stance and tried again. This time, the door rose just a hair. But then her fingers slipped on the metal frame. *Shit*. This was more difficult than she'd expected. Resetting her grip, she strained as the heavy door inched above the bottom track. She tilted the bottom edge outward, nearly losing control.

"Come on," she muttered to herself, arms burning.

With a heave, she pulled the door free of the frame and leaned it against the side of the building.

Triumph shot through her, but her satisfaction was temporary. What were the chances she could get this thing put back in place when she left? She'd worry about that later.

A blast of frigid air greeted her the moment her feet made contact with the cool tile floor.

Floor-to-ceiling windows lined the two exterior walls. The neutral color scheme set off the blue of the sky and the green of the ocean. Her entire apartment could fit into this one cavernous room.

Moving deliberately, she opened stiff drawers and musty cabinets. Nothing. The high she'd felt when she first gained access dropped from her chest to the pit of her stomach.

She entered the bedroom. The faint scent of expensive cologne lingered, and her eyes zeroed in on a briefcase tucked between a chair and a nightstand. She crept over and picked up the case. Setting it on the desk, she lifted the lid. Bingo.

Her hands moved quickly through a stack of papers. Building permits, some handwritten notes she'd never decipher, and something regarding the purchase of a new cigarette boat.

If only she had her phone. Shuffling some more loose documents, a stack of papers secured with a binder clip. *No.* This can't be.

An eagle. A compass rose. A shield. She knew that watermark like she knew her own signature. What was a Jamaican drug lord doing with confidential CIA documents?

She flipped through the pages. Information about Caribbean heads of state, military personnel, and government officials. All of it familiar. Some of it very familiar.

Because she'd written it.

Every part of her wanted to reject the papers as fakes, but they weren't. Golding couldn't have gotten these on his own. He had help from the inside.

A glacial cold spread through her veins.

She dropped the papers on her lap and looked around the room. Not only had she lost track of time, but she was sitting on the bed. Bear Golding's bed. She jumped up as if it contained a deadly disease. The stack of papers fell to the floor. She scooped them into a pile, shoved them back into the briefcase, and closed the lid.

She'd have to process what she'd seen later. Right now, she needed to get out.

A murmur of voices drifted to her from the hallway, getting louder.

Fuck! Shaky legs carried her into the living room and through the off-track back door. She grabbed her clothes, stepped into her shorts, and pulled the soggy tank top over her head.

She pivoted, heart pounding. Fix it? Or get the hell out of here?

Gripping the outer edges of the door, she hauled it up, gritting her teeth and letting loose a guttural groan. She nearly toppled under the dead, unyielding weight, and a sharp ache shot from her lower back to her shoulders. The door wobbled violently in her grip, threatening to slip from her grasp completely. She staggered back a step, sweat trickling down her face, then bent her knees and jammed the bottom edge into the track. One last shove and the door slid into place. She backed away, hands raised, in case it came crashing down.

It didn't.

Voices. This time inside the suite.

Her instincts screamed at her to move. She bolted down the deck and dove into the cool water of the bay.

———ℓℓℓ———

Nate wiped sweat from his forehead with a shaky hand. He'd been following Golding for several minutes, thinking he was going back to his room. But then the man made a left turn off the main hallway and entered what Nate assumed was an office. A familiar voice—the desk clerk who'd checked them in four nights ago—filled him in on resort business. Full house. Bookings three months into the next year.

A vending machine a few yards down the hall would be Nate's cover. As soon as he saw the doorknob turn, he darted to the dispenser and started digging change out of his pocket for a soda. Golding exited the office. *Clunk.* The can dropped.

He grabbed the drink and stalked after the devil in a linen suit.

Back at the main hall, Golding turned left and moved deeper into the resort. Every alcove, every windowsill provided a false sense of security. Nate couldn't believe the man hadn't detected his presence. Finally, Golding stopped at a closed door. Nate looked around. This was the end of the line. Angie couldn't have gotten past that door. Could she? Golding waved a key-card, and the lock popped open.

Where would she have gone?

Think. If he were Angie and he came across a locked door, what would he do?

Go around the outside and look for another way in.

He hurried back to an exterior door and pushed through it, emerging onto a meandering path that ran between the building and the pool deck.

No Angie.

He sped along the building as if propelled by jet stream winds. Ragged breaths tore from him, dragging the moisture from his already-parched mouth until his tongue was as dry as a piece of sandpaper. At the end of the trail, he stopped and stared at the sea.

A small figure neared the shore and climbed onto the beach. *Surely not.* Nate's muscles tightened. She moved closer, her dripping form stomping up the sandy incline, moving as if nothing had happened, as though she hadn't deviated from their plan without a word. Relief and exasperation swirled into a funnel cloud inside him.

From somewhere in the bushes, she pulled her bag and sandals. She still hadn't seen him. Did she even care what her escapade would do to him? He stared as she dug through the bag, then pressed a hand to her heart. She slipped on her sandals and looked up.

"Nate." She seemed surprised to see him.

His heart ballooned at the sound of his name on her lips but deflated at the realization that, had she been caught, he might never hear it again. "You didn't answer your phone." It wasn't a question. His words were stilted, his voice shaky.

Her response was an infuriatingly nonchalant shrug, and his heart seized like a prop strike on a bad landing. What possible reason could she have for doing something so risky?

"I couldn't very well take it with me, especially not after losing the last one. But you'll never guess—"

He swept his arms wide and shook his head. "What is wrong with you?" His concern for her safety manifested as anger, but he couldn't help it.

"I had to improvise." She said the words like she was firing a flare.

A code red. Obviously, he should heed her warning and wait to talk about this once he'd cooled down.

"Are you fucking kidding?" The words burst out of him. "I've been trying to alert you that Golding was going back to his room. I called. I texted. You didn't answer."

Her nostrils flared. Her stony stare spoke volumes.

His hands twitched, and his fingers curled into fists. "What do you have to say for yourself?"

"I don't answer to you."

"You don't answer to anyone, apparently." He ran a shaky hand through his hair. If he didn't get a handle on his emotions, he was going to say something stupid. "Maybe before you decided to swim up to the hotel room of a crime lord, you could have given me a heads up." He blew out a frustrated breath. "I thought we were in this together."

"And I thought you'd understand that I would do whatever needed to be done." Her eye twitched. "But I guess we're different."

A knot tangled in his stomach, his breaths came short and shallow, and the heaviness in his shoulders rooted him into place. "You're right about that. I prefer to make decisions using rational thought, while you go with whatever idiotic whim hits you." So much for not saying something stupid.

Her eyes widened briefly, but then narrowed. She pushed her shoulders back, her expression seeming to harden before his eyes.

"Wow. What do you really think?" Her voice was low and steady. Too steady. "I did what I did because sitting back wasn't going to get us any closer to figuring out what Golding has planned."

She pushed wet hair from her face, tilted her nose up, and strode past him.

After a few steps, she turned, eyes locked on him. "You don't have to agree with what I did, but don't you dare call me selfish."

He wanted to call after her, explain his anger, but his throat closed around the words. Instead, he stood frozen in place.

Too late to take it back. Too pigheaded to go after her.

CHAPTER 28

A ngie stared at the ocean from the balcony of the suite. *Breathe.*

Nate was right. She should have told him when her plans to access Golding's room changed. But how had the argument escalated so quickly?

Because she was a dumbass who reacted first, paid the price later.

Not to mention, she'd been on her own for so long, she wasn't used to having anyone else to think about. Let alone a person who tangled her insides like one of those old, wall-mounted phone cords.

She groaned. As usual, she'd screwed up everything. The difference? This time she regretted it. What would she do if she couldn't make this right? Guilt constricted her chest, making it hard to breathe. She should find him, tell him she was sorry.

But first, she needed to call Gary. There were only a handful of people with access to the intel she'd seen in Golding's suite. An ache stabbed at her stomach. God, she hated not knowing who she could trust.

But she could trust Nate. He was squarely on her side, even when she acted like a jackass. She needed to go to him, hope she hadn't ruined everything.

But first things first. Phone call.

Gary would be furious, and she'd probably lose her job, but this was too big to keep to herself. She glanced at the time. The workday would be nearly over. Good chance he'd be in his office, wrapping up before heading home.

She dialed his cell.

"Angie!" His familiar, boisterous voice felt like a hug. "How's the time off treating you? Don't tell me you're ready to get back to work already."

She took a deep breath and pretended she wasn't about to flush her career down the toilet. "Well, I haven't actually stopped working."

Silence.

"I'm in Jamaica—"

A furious voice cut her off. "Please tell me you didn't."

"Umm...." Like a bandage. "I came to investigate Rick's death."

A fiery calm lanced his words. "You were told to leave it alone."

"I know." She tried to ignore the quiver in her voice. "But I needed to do something. To see if my suspicions were correct."

"What suspicions were those?"

"That he learned something, and it got him killed."

"Christ, Angie. What were you thinking? His death was ruled an accident."

"I know, but it doesn't make sense. His plane was sabotaged."

"You need to stop. As it is, I'm going to have to report this. You're probably looking at a suspension. Maybe worse."

"Don't you get it?" She dug her fingers into her thigh and squeezed, the self-inflicted pressure creating a sharp ache that compelled her to say the words. "He worked for me. And he died because of it."

Gary's voice softened. "He agreed to the job. He knew the risks."

"He agreed because we coerced him!" She couldn't control her volume. "He got in over his head, and it's our fault."

She heard a deep sigh and could imagine Gary leaned back in his chair, face tilted to the ceiling, head shaking. "I know you didn't call because of a guilty conscience. Have you found something?"

"Not about Rick, but I did uncover some other interesting activities." She quickly filled him in on the anti-terrorism measures, the guns on the boat, and the stockpile in the cave. She decided not to share the info about the CIA docs. Not yet. There was no such thing as being too careful when it came to dealing with a mole, and even though she trusted Gary, she couldn't expect him to keep it to himself.

"Let me look into this and see if any of the other departments or agencies know about the guns or the banking scheme." His voice trailed off in thought and then came back. "I'm going to have to tell Claudia what you've done."

"I understand."

Claudia Carter was one of the highest-ranking women in the CIA. She was tough, ambitious, and known for getting shit done. She was practically a legend, not to mention Angie's hero.

Getting assigned to work in Claudia's department had been an honor. Angie had hoped the older woman would see something in her, take her under her wing, but she'd been too star struck to get close to her. Claudia may not have noticed Angie before, but after the stunt she'd just pulled, it seemed unlikely she'd forget her again.

Gary disconnected. Angie covered her face with her hands.

What a mess. It would take time to clean it up. Might as well start with the one thing she could fix. Apologizing to Nate. He was right. Her actions had been inconsiderate. She shouldn't have made the decision to leave her phone without telling him what she was doing. She'd never worked in the field or had to consider someone else's feelings. Instead, she'd grown accustomed to doing what she wanted when she wanted. But if this thing with Nate had any future, she needed to get over that.

Heavy limbs had carried Nate to the poolside bar. His stomach twisted at the memory of Angie striding away, not looking back. He took a deep breath, a useless attempt to quiet the storm churning his insides.

They both needed to cool off. He'd indulge his hurt feelings in a pint of beer—maybe three, then find Angie to talk about what happened. Sitting under the thatched roof, the sweet, fruity scent of daiquiris mingled with the humid air as he watched happy couples suck down their drinks.

He tried to let the soothing rhythm of the music piping through the speakers ground him. But it was no use. Every pulse, every thrum, every tick echoed into his consciousness. A reminder of how badly he'd screwed things up.

Control. That was his crutch. He'd grown up hovering around his brother and sister, influencing their decisions and making sure they didn't get into trouble. His entire life, he'd felt like he had everything to lose. One misstep and *BOOM!* Game over.

He shook his head. With Elise safe and her kidnapper behind bars, he'd thought those days were behind him. And then he met Angie.

Now, he had a whole new list of worries. On the other hand, she was a grown-up—a CIA officer—who knew what she was doing. He believed in her. He trusted her.

He needed to tell her.

Leaving a tip on the bar, he gave the bartender a nod and made his way across the pool deck. He couldn't help but look up at the balcony of their former room, hoping she'd be looking down, waiting for him.

Nope. Empty.

The entire trip up the elevator, he prepped what he wanted to say. He'd spent the last hour telling himself some hard truths. Now it was time to be honest with her. He'd lay it on the line. Tell her how he felt.

His steps down the hallway to the room were lighter. It felt good to make a decision, to be in control. And God knows, where Angie was concerned, he felt like a plane in freefall.

He pushed open the door to their room and stepped into the suite. The bedroom doors were open, and she sat perched on the end of the bed, sitting on a towel in her wet clothes. She had her phone in her hand. She glanced up at him.

Time to get it out, tell her how scared he was when he couldn't get ahold of her.

"Can we talk about what happened back there? About why you put yourself in danger without the courtesy of a heads up?"

Something wild flared in her eyes. "I didn't realize I needed your permission to do my job."

This wasn't how he'd planned to start the conversation. "It's not about permission. It's about us being in this together. We're supposed to be partners, for fuck's sake!" Jesus. He'd never met anyone with the ability to so thoroughly tie him into knots. "Why are we even here? What if the guys from the boat are looking for us?"

"I had to adapt. Only one of us has any actual training. You know that, don't you?"

Oh boy. His anger flared, sharp and sudden. "There's a reason you have nothing but work and spend most of your time alone. You know that, right?"

She glared at him, her hands clenched into fists. "Oh, really?" Defiance seeped into her voice. "This is the conversation you want to have?" She hopped off the bed and stalked toward him. "The guy who spends more time obsessing over his sister's relationship than trying to have one of his own?"

"You act like you've got it all figured out, but inside you're scared. Scared of getting close. Scared of your emotions."

She leaned forward and glared up at him. "Go to hell."

That same scent that drove him almost mad that first night wafted over him like a drug. Then it hit him. That's what this was. His attraction to her was an addiction. Every little fix only made him want more.

This couldn't continue. His body sagged as hope drained from his muscles. His breath came out with hoarse, dry gurgles. It had to end. They weren't good for each other. Maybe they weren't good for anyone.

Seeming to sense the change, she raised her eyebrows and opened her mouth.

After a moment when she didn't speak, he gave a half-hearted shrug and turned to leave. "You're right. You don't need me. I'll leave for home tomorrow."

A strangled noise came from behind, almost as if she wanted to say something but stopped herself.

He stalked through the sitting room. "I'll be at the apartment if you need me—which I'm guessing you won't."

He stepped into the hallway and pulled the door shut. This time he'd be the one who didn't look back.

ele

Angie braced a hand on the arm of a chair to keep herself from crumbling to the floor. If she fell apart, there'd be no putting herself back together. No coming back from losing Nate. She couldn't focus on that.

Not now.

Not ever.

Keep going. It was what she'd always done and what she'd continue to do.

Work. Her refuge. She stepped into the bedroom and reached for her phone. Nate's distinct woodsy scent still lingered. *Oh God*. How could she be so selfish? So stupid?

Nate. The one good thing that had happened to her in...ever. Now that she knew how it felt to have a partner, she couldn't go back. She needed him.

Closing her eyes, she inhaled deeply and lifted her arms above her head. Pressing down with her hands, she exhaled. Her knees naturally fell into a relaxed bend. She pressed her feet into the ground. Breathe in. Breathe out. In. Out.

The memory slammed into her like a wave crashing against the shore. The backyard of the house where she grew up. Her mother laughing. Their daily qigong routine.

Cindy.

Angie's eyes flew open. She'd forgotten about the movement and meditation practices she'd done with her mother every day from the age of seven to fourteen. Had she blocked it out? Why?

Because she'd been a stupid kid who couldn't deal with her role in her sister's death.

After Cindy died, she never again joined her mother for Qigong. Her mother hadn't wanted her there. Sure, she'd never said it, but Angie knew. Her parents blamed her for Cindy's death.

Hadn't they?

All these years, she'd told herself her parents hated her. She'd been so focused on her own guilt and grief, she'd never stopped to question her assumptions, instead allowing herself to revel in their rejection, to content herself with the condemnation she knew she deserved.

But her parents hadn't created the distance between them. That had all been her doing.

Angie lowered herself onto the bed. She'd reacted to Cindy's death with recklessness, simultaneously craving their attention and daring them to stop her. Impulsivity became her fuel, and she'd barreled from one crusade to another until she finally found herself at the CIA. And while she'd tamped down some of her more outrageous impulses, she carried that same rashness into her work. It was the one thing her performance reviews had consistently said she needed to work on.

And now she'd thrust her thoughtless, careless actions onto Nate. When had she become such an asshole?

Would he forgive her? If not, she didn't know what she'd do. The thought of never seeing him again hollowed her out inside. The hole it left flooded with remorse and missed opportunities.

Once the first tear fell, there was no holding back the others. She collapsed in on herself, bent at the waist, her arms crossed over her abdomen. Before she knew it, she was crying harder than she'd ever cried in her life.

She cried for her little sister and for her relationship with her parents. But most of all, she cried for the one man who might have loved her and who she'd driven away with her stupid bullshit.

The tears were unending, and that was okay. For the first time in years, she let herself feel. Without excuses or rationalizations or regret.

The time had come to get it out.

CHAPTER 29

Nate's stomach rumbled, a hollow ache reminding him hours had passed since he'd eaten. Angie clearly had no plans of returning to the apartment. Time to stop feeling sorry for himself and find food. There was a cafe down the street that looked promising. Even if he'd be alone, standing out like a mismatched sock, he had to eat. Besides, it wouldn't be the first time he'd dined alone. Wouldn't be the last either.

The door swung open, and she stepped inside. He froze, his gaze riveted on her.

Her eyes were puffy. Her skin was blotchy and pale. When her lower lip trembled, it required all his willpower to resist the urge to gather her up and murmur soothing words. But what she did was wrong. Consoling her wouldn't change that. She needed to face the truth.

"Nate." She breathed his name like a whisper. And the two words that followed were also barely audible. "I'm sorry."

She slipped her hand into his and interlaced fingers. Her pleasant heat radiated up his arm and into his chest. He blinked and bit his lip, afraid to speak. Unsure of what he'd say.

"I'm sorry I told you to go to hell. And I'm sorry I didn't tell you when my plans changed for getting into Golding's room."

She dipped her chin, averting her gaze. "I got caught up in the moment and when I thought about it, I was already at the bungalow. I was wrong."

His resolve softened. Of course, he forgave her. He'd always forgive her. He resisted the urge to scoop her onto his lap and hold her tight.

She looked down and drew circles on the back of his hand with her index finger. "It's been only me for so long." She wrinkled her nose. "That's not an excuse."

He turned over her hand and, though smaller than his own, marveled at how well they fit together. "I shouldn't have yelled. Or said those things. I overreacted because I was scared."

"You're right, you know. I'm lonely, and that's always been my choice." She took a shaky breath. "Until now."

"I'm sure you had your reasons." He lifted her chin and pressed a gentle kiss onto her mouth, tasting the salt of her recent tears. This time, it wasn't about physical attraction. He wanted to soothe whatever turmoil churned inside her.

"Will you promise not to give up on me?" She pursed her lips. "Even if I try to push you away?"

He watched her for a moment. She didn't move or say anything more. "I promise."

"Thank you." Her voice was husky.

He leaned forward. "If you'll do the same for me."

She closed her eyes and nodded. "Are you still going to leave?"

"Do you want me to?" His pulse beat against his neck like a drum.

She shook her head. "I'd like you to stay, but only if that's what you want."

"Wherever you are is where I want to be."

"Good."

Something warm and soothing expanded in his chest. "I know we have things to talk about, but are you hungry?"

A stomach gurgle answered his question.

"Want to try the cafe up the block?"

She perked up. "Yes, please. I'm starving."

After a quick shower and a change of clothes, they entered the restaurant fingers joined, and Nate kept her hand in his, massaging her palm, even after they were tucked away at a table. The aroma of spices and fried plantains drifted from the kitchen. As soon as the server left, Angie leaned over. "We haven't talked about what I found in Golding's room."

She scooted closer. To everyone else, they probably looked like the typical over-the-moon vacationing couple. It would be so easy to forget that's not who they were.

"Tell me." He savored her nearness and fought the urge to nip her earlobe.

She cast a furtive glance around the room. There was no one within twenty feet, and still she lowered her voice. "CIA documents."

Fuck. His pulse raced. "What type of documents?"

"Information on some of the other nations. Mostly general stuff about heads of state from some of the nearby islands. Political affiliations, assets, things like that."

The tiny hairs on the back of his neck stood at attention. "Where would he have gotten that?"

"Well, I'm wondering if that's how Doc fits into all of this. Maybe he's working as a go-between. Someone in the department might be using him to funnel information to Golding."

"Do you think Doc knows what he's doing?"

She shrugged. "Maybe. But maybe not. For all we know, he thinks he's acting on behalf of the CIA."

Doc might not be dirty. Relief loosened the knot in Nate's chest. "What do you think it means? Why would Golding need this sort of information?"

"Intel for negotiations?" She twisted her hands together. "Blackmail?"

If he'd thought things were dangerous before, this new discovery wasn't helping. Nor did it sound relevant to what happened to his dad.

She took a deep breath. "And I called Gary."

He suspected she'd been in contact with her supervisor. "What did he say?"

"He wasn't happy. Said he'd have to tell Claudia—she's the department head. He also told me to back off until I hear from him."

He wanted to breathe a sigh of relief but resisted, not wanting Angie to know how glad he was all of this was over. Because if she couldn't investigate, she wouldn't be in danger. "Sounds like our job is done."

"And if we're officially off the clock—" She kissed him on the jaw. "We might as well enjoy ourselves."

Halfway back to the apartment, Nate spotted the guy leaning against the wall, a cigarette burning between his fingers. Same jean shorts. Different shirt.

If Angie noticed—and Nate knew she did—she didn't say a word.

Somehow, Nate resented this more than before. The short reprieve—thinking it was over and that they might get a chance to be normal—somehow made seeing their tail feel that much worse.

When they got back to the apartment, Angie opened her mouth, but Nate cut her off. There'd be time to talk about the guy following them later. First, he wanted to talk about the way Angie had looked when she'd arrived at the apartment. "You were upset when you returned from the resort."

Wariness pooled in her eyes.

"It wasn't all about me, was it?" God, he hoped not. He couldn't stand to think he'd caused anyone that much pain.

"No...Yes...I don't know." She pressed her mouth into a frown and shook her head.

"Will you tell me?"

She nodded, her eyes dazed, her expression sad and tired. "I've avoided thinking about it for so long."

He clasped her hand, pulled it onto his lap, and closed his other hand on top of it with a squeeze.

"When I was fourteen, one of those pop-up carnivals came to town. You know the ones that always seem to set up next to a church?"

He nodded, knowing happy stories didn't start with a pop-up carnival.

"My parents agreed to let me go, but I had to take Cindy with me." She swallowed audibly. "Some kids from school were there. We waited in line with them for the Ring of Fire ride, but when we got to the front, Cindy started crying and saying she didn't want to do it. Some of my friends called her a baby." She averted her gaze. "I did too."

He ran his thumb along the ridges of her knuckles.

Pressing her eyes shut, she shook her head. "She got upset and ran off."

Their first meeting came back to him. She'd said she was an only child—by default. His body went cold. He wasn't sure he wanted to hear the rest of the story, but knew it was an important part of who she was.

Angie rocked back and forth as if working up the momentum to continue. "I looked for her but didn't take it seriously at first. I thought she was hiding to make me worry." She gulped. "Then, when it got late, and I still hadn't found her, I told a security guard. The police came. And my parents. Everyone looked everywhere. For days. She was gone."

Not knowing what to say, he guided her to sit on the bed.

"They found her a week later in a ravine a few miles away. She'd been strangled. She was only eight." She brushed away tears. "It was my fault."

"Shhhhh" He pulled her to him and rubbed what he hoped were soothing circles on her back. "It's okay to cry."

"My relationship with my parents was never the same. My dad blamed me. My mom lost interest in everything—or at least that was what I thought. Now I'm not so sure." She shook her head. "Regardless, all our lives were changed. My parents are still married, but after I went to college they started living in separate cities. I don't remember the last time I spoke to either one of them."

Wow, and he'd thought he carried a burden. Angie had spent the last twenty years feeling responsible for her sister's death.

"No one was ever arrested. There were never even any suspects. The sheriff thought it must've been someone passing through town with the carnival." She looked away. "It's why I went into law enforcement."

"And what happened today reminded you of your sister?"

She sniffled and wiped her nose. "Kind of. I was selfish and hurt someone I care about."

"Thank you for telling me." He grasped her face in his hands.

She closed her eyes and let out a shaky breath. "Don't leave me. Please"

"As if I could."

Angie ran her hand along the stubble on Nate's jaw, then leaned forward. Soft and slow, she pressed her lips to his. She'd never considered herself a skilled seductress, but with him, everything seemed so natural. Breaking their kiss, she leaned away to gauge his reaction and found him staring back at her, his eyes dark with desire.

Her brain engaged the pause button, and she stopped to reflect on how drastically her life had changed. And in such a short amount of time. She'd told him about her sister. That alone was miraculous, but combined with her saying she cared about him, it was almost unbelievable. Those were words she'd never said to anyone. Words she guarded like a buried treasure. It felt strange, and she wasn't sure what to do with these newly heightened emotions. She kissed him again.

"Angie—" His voice was rough like gravel. "Maybe this isn't the time for this. I think you need—"

She cut him off with a kiss, this time teasing his mouth open with her tongue. "I don't want to think. I want to feel."

He responded with a soft, conflicted moan. He was a good man. She didn't deserve him, but there wasn't anyone or anything that could tear her away now. This was where she belonged.

She ran a hand through his hair and watched a slow smile spread across his face. There would be no more resisting. He skimmed his hands down her arms and lifted the bottom of her shirt, all the while searching her gaze.

His hands found her breasts. He grinned like he'd discovered the promised land, his thumbs flicking over her nipples while simultaneously squeezing her breasts. Pleasure coursed through her, racing to the delicate spot between her legs and culminating in a delicious ache of need.

She ran her fingers through his hair. Though short, she grabbed hold. He reacted with a ragged sigh, the bass in his moan rumbling against her ear. She went in for another kiss but dragged her teeth along his lower lip instead.

He pulled her to the edge of the bed and slid her shorts down her legs before falling to his knees. He pushed her legs apart, and the anticipation sent heat prickling across her skin. Her breaths grew faster. Louder.

She dug her hands into his hair at the same moment his lips pressed a slow kiss against her inner thigh. A moan wrenched from her lips.

He kissed her again, this time closer to her sex, but still only on her thigh.

Her body bucked, and she found herself drawing her knees up and pushing herself closer. His breath feathered against her wet flesh, and her desire grew tenfold with each passing moment. She let out a groan of frustration.

And then at last, his tongue began its assault on her most sensitive place, flicking, taunting, sucking. The stubble of his beard scraped against her thigh, and when she was almost on the precipice, he pulled away to slide a finger inside her. "How's this?"

She could barely answer but managed to gasp an affirmation between pants.

His tongue got back to work with rhythmic, vertical strokes. And then, a long slow sweep. Her back curled off the bed, and he wedged a hand under her backside. Her entire being concentrated in that one little spot between her legs. And then he dragged a finger across her anus and pressed inside just the tiniest bit. Her climax broke, the pleasure flowing through her. She trembled and writhed against his mouth, the sensation consuming her entire world.

Her chest heaved. He stood and removed his shirt and shorts, then lifted her further onto the bed. She felt like a rag doll. Kneeling between her legs, he reached over her to the nightstand for a condom. She grabbed his cock, smearing a drop of cum over the tip with her thumb.

His hair was a mess, like someone who just rolled out of bed, except his eyes were heavy not with exhaustion but desire. A mischievous smile spread across his face. He raised her legs and wrapped them around his waist.

Instinctively, she lifted her hips to meet him.

"Fuck. You feel amazing." He pushed in, then slid out slowly. His lidded gaze focused on her.

Desire rose, coiling her insides. Their bodies moved in rhythm, but there was more to it than physical attraction. That wasn't just sex. It was surrender.

CHAPTER 30

Angie stirred against the steady rise and fall of Nate's chest. They'd gone to sleep nestled together like two spoons in a cutlery tray. She woke curled into him, his arm wrapped around her back and pulling her close.

Closing her eyes, she inhaled his woodsy scent. With lazy fingers, she swirled the swath of hair that spread across his chest, savoring the moment. Her heart felt full, her limbs light.

But comfort could hold off reality for only so long. The problem—the denim-short-wearing shadow watching their every move—wasn't going away. If Golding thought they were snooping into his business, they needed to do something about it.

Nate blinked awake, his features softening when he found her face. "How's my little cat burglar this morning?"

Last night, she'd gone into more detail about breaking into Golding's suite. Nate had been fascinated and impressed when she described how she'd removed—and replaced—the sliding glass door.

Angie brushed her fingers through his hair. God, how she wanted to pretend the danger wasn't real, to lose herself in the moment. But denial wasn't the answer.

"I've got an idea—"

"Uh oh," Nate joked, but his expression sobered the moment his gaze met hers. He propped himself on his elbow. "What's wrong?"

"I've been thinking about the guy following us."

"And?"

"Golding knows we're sniffing around." She took a breath. "I think we need to give him a reason—something to explain what we're doing."

"You want to go to him and tell him we think he had something to do with my dad's death?" Nate's eyes narrowed as if trying to make sense of her words. "Please tell me you're not serious."

"Hear me out." She held up her hand. "We don't need to tell him the truth, but as long as he thinks we're up to something, we're in trouble. We need to give him something that sounds plausible."

"A cover story?"

"Yes. A bluff to explain why we've been poking around his resort."

"Like what?"

"Well, maybe we pretend to be property developers. We can say we are looking to invest in the area and have been touring local properties trying to get an idea of infrastructure, security, guest expectations, things like that."

Nate frowned. "I don't like it. Do you think Golding would welcome investors snooping around his resort where illegal activities are happening?"

"Okay..." She chewed on her lip. "I could say I'm a security specialist sent by an American investment firm to conduct a risk assessment of local power dynamics before investing in the region. You can be a representative from the company."

She'd like to see Nate try to find fault with that one. A cover as a security specialist played into all of her strengths.

"How is that any better?" He shook his head. "No, I don't want you to put yourself at risk."

"Fine. Then why don't you march in there and tell him you're a pilot looking to make some money?"

The corner of Nate's mouth twisted into a slight smile. His gaze drifted to something across the room. "Actually..."

Wait what? She'd said that last one in jest. She sat up, holding the sheet against her bare chest. "That wasn't a serious suggestion. I didn't actually mean for you to consider—"

But the look on his face told her everything she needed to know. Something tight and heavy gripped her chest. Panic surged upward into her throat, spilling out with the rush of a river rapid. "You're not actually thinking about this, are you?"

He didn't answer, just kept staring into the distance like he was analyzing the idea.

Finally, he spoke. "No, not that, but what if I tell Golding who my grandfather is? I could say Papi is looking for a partner to help expand his business."

Her eyes popped open. Surely he was joking. This might actually be worse than the pilot idea. "But you never even talk about your grandfather."

"I know. I've spent my whole life protecting the family secret, trying to keep everyone safe. But there's no reason to hide it anymore—not since Elise's kidnapping. The truth is out. I'm the only one acting like it isn't."

"Can we slow down and think about this for a minute?"

"I've spent my whole life pretending things are different from what they are, but this is part of who I am. I need to stop being ashamed of it." He took her hand and gave a reassuring squeeze. "Wouldn't it be nice if the family name actually did something good for a change? If it could keep us safe and get us closer to finding out what happened to my dad?"

Her mind raced. Nate's idea was reckless, but also the quickest way inside. "I don't want you to put yourself in danger."

"For once, I think the Koslov name is what's going to keep me safe. And after Golding calls off the tail, we can confront Doc." He tucked a strand of hair behind her ear, his touch barely a feather. "So, what do you think?"

Angie traced a slow line down the center of Nate's chest with her finger. Telling Golding the truth was out of the question, and flat-out lying was a bad idea. They needed a story that was convincing and enticing, but also verifiable.

The thought of Nate putting himself in danger made her stomach twist, but it really was the fastest way to get them close to Golding.

Dread coiled in her stomach. Meetings like this could easily go sideways. Walking into a criminal's lair with only a name for protection was a calculated risk that felt anything but. She let out a soft sigh. If this was the best option, they needed to take it. "Let's go see Wayne. Maybe he can get us an introduction."

CHAPTER 31

The automatic doors to the casino swished opened. Slot machines whistled and clanged with never-ending noise. A combination of perfume and aftershave hit Nate as they entered the club that night. They were back at the resort—hopefully for good.

Earlier in the day, they'd found Wayne working his shift at the rental shack. He'd been guarded at first—and who could blame him after the nonsense with the paddleboat? But the moment Nate dropped the name Koslov, the other man's demeanor shifted. "Golding should be at the casino tonight," he'd said, then offered to make an introduction.

And now, here they were.

Nate looked at Angie. She was wearing a cotton sleeveless dress that looked like someone had cut up a huge t-shirt and sewed it back together into a skimpy little gown. His gaze consumed her shapely contours, the soft fabric clinging just enough to stir memories of what was beneath. A familiar feeling of heat spread through him. His fingers itched to peel the dress from her bronzed skin. To hold her against him. To remind himself she was real.

God, she was beautiful.

From her shapely legs, to the curve of her hips, to that sassy little smirk. The button nose and arched eyebrows. All of it topped with that sexy mane that fell onto her shoulders with messy perfection. And to think, she was his. He couldn't believe it. They hadn't said those exact words, but he knew it was true. There was no going back.

"What do you want to play?" He laid his hand on the small of her back, blatantly making sure every man in this place knew where she belonged.

"Video poker?"

"Sure." He guided her to a bank of machines.

The stiff vinyl on the stool squeaked when she sat. He took the stool next to her. The machine swallowed her twenty with a greedy whirr, and she pressed the button for Jacks or Better.

"Are you going to play?" She touched the ace of diamonds and the queen of hearts, then hit Deal.

He shook his head. "Maybe later. For now, I'm fine just observing."

She winked, but didn't look away from the game. He liked watching her, and the longer he sat beside her thinking of how right it felt to be here, the happier he became.

After several minutes, a waitress approached. Nate ordered two vodka tonics.

When she returned with the drinks, Angie cashed out. "What do you want to do now?"

He shrugged. Machines weren't really his thing. "Doesn't matter. I'm just happy being here with you."

She sipped her drink through the little black straw. "Should we go back to the room?"

After the discussion with Wayne, they'd gone back to the apartment, packed their things and moved back to the suite. Assuming they didn't end the night in worse shape than they started it, they hoped to be back at the resort to stay.

"We haven't been here very long. Should we wait a little longer?" Even though Angie had agreed to him dropping his grandfather's name, she'd not fully warmed to the idea, and he suspected she was hoping to avoid a meeting with Golding altogether.

She cast a teasing glance and slid the hem of her dress up, revealing her toned thigh.

The anticipation of sliding into bed beside her and feeling her warm body curled against his made him want to break into a sprint.

They were almost at the door when a familiar face caught his eye. Wayne waved at them, his voice cutting over the electronic clatter. "Hey, wait up!"

He ignored Angie and focused his attention on Nate, clearly believing him to be the more important half of their duo. Little did he know. "I told Mr. Golding about you. He wants to invite you to a card game."

"He's here?" Nate glanced around the casino, heart pounding. Then it hit him. Golding wouldn't be in the main casino. He had a private room. A room without witnesses.

Wayne rocked back on his heels as though he'd just scored the game-winning goal. "Some people wait months to get an audience with the boss. You're lucky to get this chance."

Nate put an arm around Angie and pulled her close. "Sure. As long as my wife can come. She's quite the card player."

Wayne's grin faltered. "Sorry, no guests." His eyes flicked between them.

"In that case, I think I'll pass." Despite being the grandson of a mobster, Nate didn't know the rules for interacting with criminals and wasn't eager to go in there alone.

Angie tugged on his arm. Nate put up his hand and turned to Wayne. "Give us a minute?"

Angie waited until Wayne was several feet away and talking to the bartender before lowering her voice to speak. "You should go even if I can't."

"I want to, but I wish you could come too."

"I don't think there's any other choice. You either go alone, or you don't go." She wet her lips.

He took a deep breath, fingers tightening around her hand. "Like you said, this might be our best chance to find out what happened to my dad and get the stalker off our backs." He grasped her face and kissed her hard. "Besides, maybe I can do something worthwhile with my family connections for once."

"Don't do this for me." She twisted her hands together.

"I'm not." He tilted her chin. "I'm doing it for us. And Dad."

"I don't know what I was thinking with this stupid idea. It's too dangerous." She gripped his arm and squeezed. "What if it's a trap?"

"This is what we came up with to get in front of Bear Golding, and it worked." Whether that was a good thing, he didn't know, but he intended to see it through. "I'm not turning back now."

She bit the inside of her cheek. "Be careful."

"Don't worry. I'm a Koslov. They won't touch me." He forced a smile, but looking into her eyes, could see she saw right through it. "It'll be fine. Promise."

"I apologize for every time I said those words." She gave him a strained smile and shook her head.

He cupped her face in his hands and gave her a long, soft kiss on the mouth. "This won't take long."

God, he hoped he was right.

CHAPTER 32

Standing at the blue felt poker table in Golding's private room, Nate inhaled the scent of expensive cigars. A handful of men were already seated, and a dealer stood at the far end. Wayne motioned for him to have a seat.

Nate nodded but didn't sit right away, instead letting his gaze land briefly on each player before settling on Golding. He didn't detect any malice or hostility, but Nate wasn't an expert in reading expressions or body language.

"What are we playing?"

"Five Card Draw." Bear Golding's voice carried that same Jamaican cadence Nate had heard all week. But with Golding, the soft island lilt was a sharp contrast to the calculating gleam in his eyes.

This version of poker was a classic, but it had been a long time since Nate had played it, and he'd need to think about his strategy. Also, he'd never played cards with criminals before. If only he'd thought to ask Angie for some advice on the expectation regarding winning or losing. "What are the stakes?" He only had a couple hundred dollars in his pocket.

Golding nodded at the dealer, who slid a stack of chips to Nate's position.

"Five-thousand-dollar makeup, then a fifty-fifty split."

This was a test. If he accepted, he'd automatically be in debt to a drug lord, and once he'd made up the debt—assuming he even could—he'd only get to keep fifty percent of anything he earned.

Nate suppressed a cartoon-like gulp, but his internal siren blared. First of all, this was high-stakes poker. Second of all, he had to win at least some of the hands or he'd owe big. He assessed the man across the table. Just going by size and demeanor, Bear seemed an entirely appropriate moniker. This was not a man to whom he wanted to be indebted.

"Five grand just to sit at the table?" Nate whistled. He didn't like the setup, but he was here and didn't see that he had a choice. "I'm in."

He was a good player—better than most—but starting off hot would be a mistake. Play well, but not too well. At the same time, he didn't want to stay in the red too long.

Great. No pressure.

The first hand was dealt. Nate ran his thumb along the hard outer edge of a chip and watched the other players throw bets into the pot. He flicked in a couple of chips. Golding discarded two cards. Nate discarded three. They tabled their hands. Golding won with three of a kind.

The dealer scooped up the cards and pushed the chips to Golding.

He watched Nate while stacking his winnings. "Wayne says yuh have some connections we might be interested in."

The dealer threw down another hand.

"Maybe." Nate picked up his cards, trying to appear unconcerned. He saw no reason to rush into a conversation about his grandfather. Despite everything, he didn't feel threatened. Who would be crazy enough to harm a Koslov? Even if they didn't believe he was who he said he was, they wouldn't do anything until they knew for sure.

Golding looked at his cards. "Been trying to reach out to the Koslov family for a good while now, but I've not had much luck."

For some reason, Nate found gratification in the idea that even his gangster of a grandfather had standards that kept him from doing business with the likes of Bear Golding. "I want to be upfront with you. I'm not involved in the business."

Wayne swiveled his head between Nate and Golding, clearly worried the introduction wouldn't come to anything.

Nate flipped up the edge of his cards. "Although it would be easy enough to get involved. Grandfather would be thrilled."

"Grandfather?" Golding shook his head and let out a surprised laugh. "Papi is well respected 'round here."

Nate gritted his teeth. It bothered him to hear people talk about his grandfather like he was someone to admire. True, he wasn't as ruthless as some, but he'd had his hands in illegal dealings since he'd first set foot in the United States. How he managed to convince everyone he was a good guy was something Nate had never understood.

"What sort of alliance are you looking for?" Nate tossed a few more chips into the pot.

Golding leaned back and studied him. "I have two main goals." He held up a finger. "First thing, expand distribution in the States. Papi's backing opens doors up and down the East Coast."

Nate nodded. How far would he have to take this fake introduction? He didn't want to be responsible for more drugs making their way to the U.S.

"Two." Golding held up a second finger. "I'm looking to forge new partnerships and step away from my current one, y'know?"

"I could reach out to my cousin." Maybe if he explained the situation, Sergei could come up with a way for Golding to feel he was being heard, but without negotiating any actual business.

Wayne nodded like a lapdog.

Golding's enthusiasm was much more restrained. "Sergei Koslov. I know 'bout him, mon. Word is he's ready to step outta the family business."

Was that true? Last year, Sergei helped Elise escape the family compound—something that had undoubtedly landed him in heaps of trouble with their grandfather.

Golding pushed a stack of chips toward the betting area. "An alliance between my side and the Koslov family might just set that in motion."

Nate owed his cousin big time. Who knew where Elise would be now if Sergei hadn't risked his own safety for her?

"It's been a while since I've spoken to Sergei, but I have no reason to think he won't take my call."

They played a few more rounds. Nate was up for a bit. Then he was down. When he'd finally broken even, he decided to call it quits.

"I think that's it for me." Nate threw down his cards. "I've only been married a couple of weeks. I'd like to keep it that way."

The men laughed.

"Ahh, that sweet honeymoon time." Golding extended his hand. "We'll be in touch."

As soon as Nate walked out of the room, Angie was on her feet and hurrying toward him. "How did it go?"

"Let's talk about it on our way upstairs."

They left the casino, crossed the lobby, and got into the elevator.

The moment the door closed, she peppered him with questions. "Who else was there?"

"Golding and Wayne..." He paused and tilted his head in thought. "Three other guys who didn't say much. Gary, Clifton...Joe?"

"Who did most of the talking?"

"Golding. Wayne made a few comments."

"Do they know you're related to Rick? Or that you're a pilot?" Rick had been careful to guard his real identity.

He shook his head. "Didn't come up, but I don't think so."

Angie let herself exhale. Good. If they knew who Nate's dad was, they might figure out what Nate was up to. Hopefully, they wouldn't pry too deeply into his background.

"Golding is hoping I'll facilitate an introduction with Papi. I told him I'm not involved in the family business, but that if

I expressed an interest, I was confident I'd be brought into the fold."

The elevator stopped with a soft bounce. Angie reached for Nate's hand as the door opened and another couple stepped inside.

Everyone rode in silence. Angie and Nate exited onto their floor.

They pushed into the room. Nate leaned against the counter. "Here's something that might be important. Golding said he was looking for a new partnership so he could get out of his current one."

"Huh." That was interesting. "Must be the big backer everyone is talking about. If this partner is so powerful, getting out from under him could be tricky."

"Dangerous?"

"Maybe. Why, what are you thinking?"

Nate scrubbed at his jaw. "The guns. What if it's not terrorism? What if he's amassing weapons because he's expecting some sort of war?"

She cocked her head, considering. "Anything else?"

"I mentioned Sergei, and Golding said he'd heard Sergei wanted out. He suggested that an alliance between his organization and the Koslovs might be what Sergei needed to leave."

"Sounds like he's thinking of a true merger. Do you think Papi would go for that?"

"I doubt it. Nothing matters more to my grandfather than family. He's not going to let someone into his inner circle he doesn't trust."

Angie squeezed his hand.

"Should I call Sergei? We aren't close. There's no guarantee he'll help. He might even be angry I used his name."

"Let's give it a couple of days and see how things play out."

Nate tugged her against him and kissed her like a man famished.

She could barely keep her hands off him. "I was so worried," she said between kisses. "Not knowing what was happening was torture."

"I wished you were there, but everything was—"

"Don't say it." She kissed the word *fine* from his mouth. Never again would she allow him to put himself in danger.

Her fingers went to work unbuttoning his shirt as she urged him toward the bed. "I never should have pushed you into this. I don't know what I'd do if something happened to you."

They fell onto the bed. She climbed on top of him and unbuttoned his pants, but then the blue flashing light on the top corner of her phone caught her attention. "I think I have a message."

"Do you want to check?"

She bit her lip. Want to? No. But should she? Probably.

"I'm sure it's nothing, but better safe than sorry." She picked up her phone, pressed the voicemail button, and heard a shaky voice. It was the MP they met earlier.

"Ms. Liu, it's Andrew Morgan. I think I have an idea of who that big fish might be, but it's not something I can talk about on the phone. Meet me at the cafe across the street from my hotel in the morning."

CHAPTER 33

After breakfast the next morning, Angie and Nate walked along the cobbled path that meandered beside the main road on their way to Andrew Morgan's resort. Every time she looked at Nate, it was like a star exploded in her chest, the warmth radiating from her core. Maybe she really was falling in love.

But that was something to ponder another time. Right now, she had a mysterious meeting to think about.

Nate nudged her in the shoulder. "You busy solving advanced calculus equations, or is something else on your mind?"

"Just trying to solve the mystery of how someone this handsome—" She motioned her hand at Nate. "Can be this annoying."

He hit her with that grin—the one that made her knees go weak. "Practice."

"And here I thought it came naturally," she teased, kicking a rock off the path and watching it roll into the grass. "Actually, I'm thinking about the meeting. Now that we know someone in the CIA is connected to Golding, I'm nervous to hear what the MP has to say."

"Well, whatever it is, I'll be there too. You won't have to face it alone."

That should have made her feel better, and in a lot of ways, it did. But having someone on her side also meant having someone to lose.

She hadn't slept much after hearing the message from Andrew Morgan. Not with her ricocheting thoughts—first about the meeting, and second imagining everything that could have gone wrong when Nate disappeared to play cards with Bear Golding.

She dug her hands into her pockets and scrunched her shoulders. Nothing like watching someone you care about disappear into a private room with a drug lord to make your feelings clear.

But, like Nate said, he'd never been in any real danger. At least not this time. You'd have to be pretty stupid to do something to someone connected to Aleksander Koslov. Families like that didn't take kindly to disrespect or violence against one of their own, and not many people would be foolish enough to claim affiliation if they couldn't deliver.

The cafe was directly across the street from the resort where they'd met Mr. Morgan the other day. The road curved to the south, and when they rounded the bend, his hotel came into view. So did a slew of flashing blue police lights. Angie's heart stopped beating for a moment, then resumed a slow, heavy thump. At least half a dozen police vehicles blocked the entrance to the hotel. Two officers hung yellow tape across the driveway.

She looked at Nate, noting the way his jaw pulsed.

He shielded his eyes and stared at the scene. "That's not good."

She swallowed the panic that threatened to bubble up from her gut. "Let's check the cafe and see if he's there." He wouldn't be. She felt it in the ache of her bones and the tingle of her skin.

They crossed the street and entered the small shop. Cracked stucco walls painted green and a linoleum tile floor. Men playing dominoes and patrons reading the paper filled the tiny space. She scanned the room. No Morgan.

"He's not here." Nate tugged on her arm.

With leaden steps, she followed him back to the cordoned-off resort. An officer stood on the grass next to the circular drive speaking with a woman in a bathing suit and robe. She had her hand over her mouth and kept shaking her head.

They walked up the steps to the front entrance. A young officer held up his hand. "What's your business?"

"We're meeting a friend for coffee." Pretending to look for him, she craned her neck to survey the scene. The hotel doors swooshed open, and an officer exited carrying evidence bags.

The constable spoke as if reciting a line from a play. "Entrance to the premises is off limits for now." He glanced at his clipboard, his official tone slipping away. "Is your friend a guest?"

Angie nodded.

"Name?"

Nate's voice came out deep and commanding. "Andrew Morgan."

The officer stopped flipping pages. "Stay here." He tucked his clipboard under his arm and disappeared through the automatic doors into the lobby.

She bit her bottom lip and glanced at Nate. Neither of them spoke. She wanted to avoid admitting the inevitable as long as possible.

The officer returned with another man. "Detective Sergeant Robinson." He extended his hand to Angie, then Nate. "What's your business with the MP?"

"I'm a journalist. I was working on a story about the banking regulation proposal. We met yesterday, and he called last night saying he'd like to meet again today." Angie pulled out her phone and tilted it toward the detective. "Do you mind if I record this?"

"Yes, I do mind." The detective took down her fake name and information about where they were staying. Not telling him her real identity was a risk, but she couldn't take the chance he might be on Golding's payroll.

"Can we see Mr. Morgan? Is he okay?" She didn't expect a straight answer but had to ask.

"There's been an accident. I can't go into any more detail than that."

"Has he been hurt?"

The detective turned without answering and walked away.

"What now?" Nate asked.

"We need to see Fitzroy."

―――⌒⌒―――

Nate sat in one of the hard plastic police station chairs while Angie approached the officer at the desk.

"Is Officer Fitzroy Brady available?"

"I'll check."

The clerk disappeared through a door, and rather than sit, Angie launched into an agitated patrol of the room.

The door buzzed open. Fitzroy stepped into the lobby, his face drawn, his eyes droopy and red. He appeared to have aged ten years in the three days since they last saw him. There was no smile, no hello. Instead, he went straight for Angie and gripped her by the elbow. She shot Nate a wary glance as the officer pulled her to the far side of the room.

Their whispered conversation lasted a couple of minutes. Fitzroy's hands gestured this way and that. His face was hard, his brow furrowed. Based on Angie's crossed arms and rigid posture, she appeared to be playing defense. Finally, they both straightened.

Fitzroy stepped away to nod at the desk clerk, who buzzed him back into the secure part of the police station. Nate waited for Angie to do or say something, but she stood, her gaze locked on the door. After several minutes, the door opened just wide enough for Fitzroy's head. He gave Angie a chin tilt and disappeared again.

She motioned for Nate to follow outside. The desire to ask what was going on practically burned his tongue, but she didn't say anything, so he didn't either. Again, they walked to the restaurant catty corner to the police department and found a picnic table around the back.

Angie sat in the same spot as the other day. Nate went to the window to order three iced coffees and a half dozen beef patties. He'd just started to tear into the crispy orange crust of one when Fitzroy rounded the corner.

The officer sat on the bench, accepted the coffee, but pushed away the offer of food. A bead of sweat coated his forehead. He snuck a glance over his shoulder, then leaned forward and spoke in a quiet voice. "I saw the report. Morgan was found floating in the lobby pool early this morning. Security footage has been sabotaged. The guard claimed he was dealing with an altercation at the beach."

"In other words, there's no record of what went down." Angie squeezed her coffee so hard the lid popped off.

"Could it have been an accident?" Nate suspected he knew the answer but asked anyway.

The man stared at his hands and shook his head. "Ligature marks suggest strangulation."

"He called us last night and said he had something he wanted to tell us." Angie closed her eyes and shook her head. "Do you think the issue with the security footage was an inside job?"

Fitzroy nodded. "Almost certainly, but there's no way to know if the saboteur is also our murderer. Whoever did it initiated a hardware reset, which destroyed any hope we had of recovering the files."

"They don't back up to the cloud?" Nate had investigated security for his own business and knew this was industry standard.

Fitzroy shook his head. "The camera system is twenty years old."

"How many guards are on duty at one time?" Angie asked.

"One."

"That makes no sense. It's a huge resort."

Fitzroy glanced over his shoulder, then shrugged.

Angie chewed on her fingernail, obviously thinking something through. "Thank you, Fitz. I know you took a risk checking out that case file. I appreciate it." She reached her hand across the table. The old police officer took it and gave it a squeeze.

Nate couldn't miss the way the other man's eyes darted to the street and back to Angie.

"Best be gettin' back to the station." He leaned in and stared into Angie's eyes. "Be careful."

"We will."

They stood and walked back to the sidewalk. Fitzroy stopped to throw away his coffee cup.

Thup. Thup. The noise was unfamiliar, yet Nate identified it instantly. A red mist spurted from Fitzroy's chest. The policeman sank to his knees. When he fell forward, blood soaked the back of his shirt in two different spots.

Angie turned to go to the older man, but Nate grabbed her arm.

Thup.

A section of the stucco wall beside them exploded. He pulled her into an alcove.

With heavy, labored breaths, she struggled to get away. "Fitzroy. We have to help him."

He wrapped arms around her and held her tight against his chest. He pressed his face against her head. "You can't help him if you get shot."

She thrashed against him. "Let me go. I have to see if he's okay."

He tightened his grip, and eventually she stopped fighting and sagged into him.

"Do you think the shooter is gone?" Her voice shook.

"I don't know." He studied the roof of a building across the street but was afraid to stick his head too far out to look.

Sirens wailed in the distance. They came closer until finally a police car and ambulance arrived. Police exited their cars and fanned out through the neighborhood. Nate released Angie. She bolted away from him.

When he rounded the corner, she was kneeling at the man's side, anguish sketched across her tear-streaked face. He didn't know what to do, but it broke his heart. The medical personnel surrounded the slain officer and asked Angie to move.

"It's my fault." She collapsed against Nate and clung to him as though she were drowning.

He wrapped one arm around her and smoothed her hair with his other hand. "You had nothing to do with this."

"He warned me that accessing the case file was dangerous. I asked him to do it anyway." Angie's voice cracked and broke.

An investigator headed their way. Angie wiped her eyes and glanced at Nate. "If they split us up, don't say anything about Andrew Morgan. You can tell them Fitzroy was a friend of mine."

"Real names?"

"Same names we're using at the resort. I don't need my name showing up on a police report."

"What if they ask for identification?"

"It's in the room."

He didn't think that sounded plausible, but didn't say anything. "Should we pretend we didn't know Fitzroy?"

She sniffled and wiped her eyes. "We'll be on camera at the police station and they'll question the coffee vendor, so we need to admit to speaking with him." She took a deep breath. "Let's go with the same story. I'm a journalist. You're here with me on vacation."

He grasped her hand and squeezed. The officer approached, pocket notebook ready.

***

Their hotel room faced west. Angie sat in a balcony chair and sipped one of the beers Nate had bought in the sundries shop in the hotel lobby. She resisted the urge to fling it over the balcony just to watch something break.

Nate sat beside her, staring at the sunset. She bit her lip and averted her gaze. No doubt it was beautiful, but it didn't matter because all she could see was Fitzroy falling to the ground.

"I'm so sorry I got you into this. I had no idea."

He squeezed her fingers. She loved it when he did that, his rough palms warm and comforting.

"This trip has been one disaster after another." She rubbed her face. "Two people are dead—not counting your father, and it's my fault."

Nate leaned over. "You didn't do any of this."

"Are you sure?" What if she got him hurt too? God, how would she live with herself if something happened to Nate?

"You aren't responsible for anyone else's actions. Don't you dare blame yourself for any of this."

She heard what he was saying, but if she'd focused on Nate's father and kept her nose out of the rest of it, Andrew Morgan and Fitzroy would still be alive. If it wasn't her fault, then whose?

Hell, if she'd listened to Gary and taken a real vacation, none of this would have happened. But if she'd done that, she wouldn't have Nate. She swallowed down the hard lump climbing up her throat.

Fitzroy was a good cop. He wasn't involved in any of this until she asked him to help her out. *Shit*. With everything else, she'd totally forgotten Fitzroy's email. She was on her feet and running for her laptop.

Nate followed into the bedroom. "What's going on?"

"Remember when Fitzroy came into the lobby and then went back to his office?"

He nodded. "He went to read the report."

"True, but I also asked him to send me what he could on the Morgan murder investigation." She opened her email and whooped triumphantly. The name Fitzroy Brady was at the top of her inbox. And there was an attachment. Her entire body suddenly came alive. Then went cold.

What if this last act of help was what got him killed?

She right-clicked on the attached file and extracted the contents. A little gray box appeared. "The compressed folder is invalid or corrupted."

"No, no, no!" She closed the message and tried again. Same thing. "Damn it!"

Nate sat on the bed beside her and took the laptop. He clicked through different screens and typed terms into a search engine. A few minutes later, he spoke. "I think it can be saved, but we might need to download some software."

She groaned and lay back on the bed.

He started a download, then put the computer aside. "Maybe we should eat. It's been hours since breakfast."

She nodded numbly. She didn't care about food, but respected Nate's need to feel like he was doing something. "Can we order to the room?"

He went into the main room and dialed the phone. He didn't ask what she wanted, and she didn't care. She just appreciated that he seemed to know what to do. When he came back to the bedroom, he propped the pillows against the headboard, turned on the television and found an old comedy show.

"Come here." He patted the bed, and she climbed up to nestle against him. It had been a horrible twenty-four hours, and yet, there was nowhere else she'd rather be.

Next thing she knew, there was a knock on the door. She startled, and Nate kissed her on the forehead. He got up and returned with a tray of food. An avocado BLT for her. A burger for himself.

"Avocados?" She couldn't help but smile. She loved avocados. The fact that he'd noticed left her speechless.

He gave her a shy, lopsided grin. "They're your favorite, aren't they?"

Her stomach did a flip. When was the last time anyone noticed or cared what she liked? A sob gathered in her chest. She crammed the sandwich in her mouth.

They finished eating. He took the dishes and put them on the counter by the front door. When he returned, she snuggled against him, and despite all the horrible things that had happened, she felt more secure with him than she had in years.

Her cell phone rang. It was Gary. She stepped off the bed and answered.

"I hear you were mixed up in a shooting." His voice was brusque but laced with concern.

She didn't know how he'd found out, but figured there was no point denying it. "I was there, but I wasn't hurt. A Kingston police officer was killed. I worked with him when I was here investigating that lottery scam." She choked on the words. She didn't want Gary to know how upset she was. It would only make things worse. "We don't know who the target was."

"We?"

Fuck. Though something in the tone of his voice suggested he knew exactly who *we* was. Of course, he would have tracked her travel to Miami and figured it out. For all she knew, he'd gone to Key Largo. Nate's brother or sister may have spilled everything.

"You need to lie low." His voice was stern. "Don't leave the hotel."

"But you know about the MP? He said he had information for me. Now he's dead. We need to find out what's going on."

Gary's voice shook with suppressed rage. "What you need to do is follow my orders at least one damned time."

"But—"

"Drop it, Liu. I mean it. Claudia is on her way to the airport. She'll be there tonight and wants to see you in the morning. And

Angie, when Claudia comes in person, it's never for a friendly chat."

CHAPTER 34

The next morning, Nate woke with Angie in his arms, her head on his chest, her raven-colored hair fanned across the pillow. He stared at the ceiling and inhaled the rightness of the moment. And that made him feel terrible. Two men he'd met had died within hours of one another. One of the deaths he'd witnessed, and still he couldn't shake the feeling he was where he was supposed to be.

Instinctively, he tightened his hold and pulled her close. The bedsprings creaked. She let out a soft moan, and he realized it was a sound he wanted to hear for the rest of his life. He froze, simultaneously startled and unsurprised by the thought. For years, he'd pictured himself alone. This was the first time he'd ever imagined a future with another person. And it made everything seem so much more significant.

Angie's job. The criminals. The danger.

He couldn't let anything happen to her. He would kill to keep her safe.

It was a feeling he'd had before, though never for anyone other than his brother and sister. The realization floored him.

She stirred and murmured his name. Her fingers brushed absentmindedly against his chest. He grasped her hand and brought it to his mouth, kissing a knuckle on every finger.

Other than the hum of the air conditioner and the distant lapping of waves, quiet settled over the room. A sort of peace Nate was rarely fortunate enough to enjoy.

He stroked her hair from her face. "My sister is getting married on Christmas Day." He didn't know why, but right now, it felt important for her to be there. With him.

Maybe because securing her agreement meant she saw a future for them too.

"Hey, that's great." Angie sat up and searched his eyes. "Are you happy about it?"

He suppressed the shrug he so wanted to give, knowing it was time he stopped acting like a controlling big brother. "I think so. I've not been overly kind to Eric, but I realize now that was more about him being the one to keep her safe while I was the person who drove her into danger."

She rubbed her finger across her bottom lip, gaze unfocused. "That's only two weeks away. Small wedding?"

He nodded and tightened his hold around her waist. "Will you come with me?"

"Is that what you want?"

How could she even ask? He didn't want to spend another family event or celebrate a milestone without her. But he couldn't say that. Not yet. "More than you know."

Angie hung up the room phone. "She's on her way up."

The Director of Transnational Organized Crime was coming to Angie's hotel room. Her stomach clenched, and her breath hitched. She thought she might puke.

Nate had dressed in slacks and a button-down. Angie's brain snagged for a moment. He looked good, and considering he purchased clothes after they got here and had worn nothing but swim trunks and cargo shorts, she was surprised to see the change in attire. Between his muscles and the preppy getup, he looked like a badass Ken doll. She couldn't help but notice the way the pants hugged his ass and invited a squeeze. Grabbing his backside, she pressed herself against him. "Can we pretend we're not home?"

He shook his head. "This is your job. You need to find out what she has to say."

She blew out a puff of air. He was right, of course, but she didn't like it. She swept her gaze up his body again, feeling like a slob in comparison. She hadn't brought anything professional-looking, only sundresses, swimsuits, and casual wear. So instead, she'd slipped into a pair of jeans and a V-neck t-shirt with three-quarter length sleeves.

Knock. Knock.

Angie jumped. God, she hated being on edge. But Nate was right. She needed to answer for her behavior. She pushed her shoulders down, willing her muscles to relax, then peeked at him one more time.

The look on his face told her that whatever happened, he'd be there. She wasn't alone. Somehow, that made all the difference.

He gestured to the door with his chin. "Open it."

She took a deep breath, smoothed her shirt, and pulled it open.

Claudia.

In black slacks with a coordinating blouse and pumps, the senior officer looked ready to get down to business. In her left hand, she carried an attaché case. Probably where she kept the termination paperwork.

Angie gulped. She'd been in board meetings with the department chief and had responded to her memos, but never had stood so close to the woman. She certainly never thought she'd see Claudia standing at the door to her hotel room.

She beckoned Claudia into the room. The woman stepped inside, spotted Nate, and smiled. "You must be Nate Hughes. It's a pleasure to meet you."

He shook her hand. "Likewise."

Claudia's shoulder-length blond hair was stylish and sophisticated. Her makeup was sleek and subtle and complemented expressive eyes that sparkled with shrewd intelligence. Her entire bearing exuded confidence, along with a graceful, mature beauty.

Angie caught herself in the mirror. Hair in a ponytail. No makeup. Casual clothing.

"Well, Angie." Claudia looked around the room. "I must confess, I never would have expected this from you. I knew you sometimes acted on emotion, but for the most part, I'd pegged you as a rule follower."

"I'm sorry, ma'am. Letting you down was never my intention."

"What do you have to drink?"

Angie looked at Nate helplessly.

His voice shot through the quiet room like a cannonball. "Beer and water."

"I'll take a beer, please." She walked to the couch, leaned her attaché case against the coffee table, and sat.

Nate popped the top off a bottle of beer, poured it into a glass, and handed it to Claudia.

Claudia looked at Angie over her shoulder. "Why don't you come over here so you can tell me what you've been up to."

She felt like she was walking on marshmallows—her steps light and unsteady—as she made her way to the couch. She tried to hide her nerves, but was sure Nate could sense every tremble and extra heartbeat.

An internal investigation to determine disciplinary action was the most likely outcome, but Angie couldn't rule out termination or the possibility that the agency would press charges.

She didn't speak. What was there to say?

Claudia waved a perfectly manicured hand. "Let's get this out of the way. You're not in trouble."

Angie blinked. That couldn't be right. She should be fired. She couldn't even count how many policies she'd violated.

"Don't get me wrong, all of this is a serious breach of protocol. Some directors might even yank your security clearance given that you've shared information with a civilian."

Angie felt the warm prickle of Nate's worried stare but didn't let herself look at him. They both knew that losing her security clearance would be the end of her career.

Claudia continued. "What you've done—depending on who you've interacted with—may very well have harmed U.S. interests. We just don't know the extent of the damage yet. And then there's the loss of trust. As you know, trust is especially important. Not just the trust of your colleagues, but also the credibility of the agency."

Everything Claudia said was true. Angie had been thinking about wanting to get justice for Rick and hadn't bothered to consider all the other consequences.

"It goes without saying, you've been more than a little dis-obedient, but that doesn't mean I'm not impressed by your in-genuity." Claudia leaned over as if sharing a secret. "This might surprise you, but I've conducted my share of unauthorized in-vestigations."

"Umm...Thank you." Angie's gaze found Nate. His eyes were wide, his mouth opened slightly.

"I'm proud of what you've accomplished here on your own without resources or backup." Claudia reached out and squeezed Angie's hand. "It's admirable, and to be honest, I see a bit of myself in you."

Emotions flooded Angie, and for a moment she thought she might drown. Here she was, with the person she most idolized, being told that her instincts had been right all along.

It was almost impossible to believe.

Dumbstruck by the words of encouragement, Angie mumbled a thank you. She still couldn't comprehend that the woman had come to Jamaica because of her. Dare she hope they might actually get Bear Golding? Maybe even find out who killed Nate's dad?

Claudia rifled through her attaché case and pulled out a notebook and a stack of files. A couple of the folders fell to the floor. Angie bent to pick them up.

"I got it," Claudia said. She straightened the papers in the folders and slid them to the bottom of the stack. "Tell me what you've learned. Then we can start planning our strategy."

Angie wanted to pinch herself. "We know Golding has a stake in the outcome of the banking regulation vote. I'm also pretty sure he's got some sort of arms deal going on out of this hotel."

"Interesting." Claudia nodded and scribbled on her pad. "Anything else?"

Angie opened her mouth but shut it again. She wasn't sure why, but she didn't feel ready to fess up to breaking into Golding's room. Obviously, telling Claudia about the documents she found was the right thing to do, but instinct had gotten her here. Maybe she should listen to it this time too. Besides, before she made any accusations, she wanted to get an idea of who might be involved. Only a handful of people had access to those papers, and as of now, she didn't have an inkling of who might have done it.

"That's pretty much it, I think."

She glanced at Nate, who raised an eyebrow, but didn't say anything.

Claudia stuffed the files into her case. "We suspected Golding would have a stake in the economic summit but hadn't pinned down the what yet." She leveled her gaze at Angie and gave a crisp nod. "Good work, Liu."

Angie couldn't stop smiling. She'd expected to have her ass chewed out, but instead had been lauded for her ambition, determination, and tenacity. It was a dream come true. Although she had a hard time believing Gary would see it the same way. Hopefully, she hadn't created any tension between her superiors.

Claudia stood. "I should get going. I'm renting a place on the beach." She lifted the bag to her shoulder. "Angie, would you mind walking me out?"

Always the consummate gentleman, Nate got to his feet.

Angie hurried to do the same. "Of course. I'd be happy to."

Nate stepped forward and offered his hand. "It was a pleasure to meet you."

"Keep an eye on this one." Claudia winked at him. "She's a handful."

"You're not kidding." Nate stuck his hands in his pockets as Claudia stepped into the hallway.

When Angie and Claudia got to the elevator, Angie pushed the down button.

Claudia turned to face her. "I assume it was Nate who got you into the country?" Her voice carried an edge of disapproval.

Angie swallowed. Neither she nor Nate had mentioned the connection. "How did you know?"

"For one thing, I recognized the name." She pursed her lips. "For another, I had your name checked against passenger manifests. I figured you'd either used an alias or you'd gotten someone to fly you in on a private plane. I never would have guessed you'd go to the Hughes family."

Angie nodded. What could she say?

Ding. They stepped into the elevator. Angie selected the button for the lobby.

"How long have you known Nate?"

"We met when I approached to ask for a ride." She wasn't about to go into their real first meeting.

"And now you're sharing a hotel room?" The question dripped with disapproval.

Angie needed her boss to know that she'd never intended to fall for Nate. "That wasn't—"

Claudia held up her hand. "You've obviously told him who you are. Should I assume you also told him how you are connected to his father?"

She bit her lip and nodded.

"Do his siblings know?"

"Yes." She felt about three inches tall.

The elevator stopped with a cushioned bounce. *Ding.*

"That was careless."

The door opened. Claudia stepped out, but Angie stayed where she was.

"I have a driver waiting for me. Walk with me to the front door."

Angie followed, too chastised to speak. Claudia said nothing until they arrived at the front entryway.

"I can see you care for this man."

Was she that obvious? "I do."

Claudia nodded. "If that's the case, I'm going to give you some advice. Our job is dangerous, and he's not one of us. Do him a favor and keep him out of this." Sympathy rushed in and out of Claudia's eyes so fast, Angie wondered if she'd imagined it.

She stepped through the door but turned back again. "I'm not going to do anything official right now, but when we get back to Washington, you will be reassigned. Something that has nothing to do with the Caribbean."

Angie watched Claudia's graceful figure walk down the steps and get into a black Mercedes, unsure how the woman managed to make her feel both grateful and devastated.

Claudia had made one thing clear. Angie couldn't continue to involve Nate in the investigation. She'd endangered him enough. It was past time to put some distance between him and her job.

CHAPTER 35

"Is everything okay?" Nate hadn't thought seeing Claudia off would have taken so long.

Angie stood in the middle of the room, brow furrowed. "I finally got that verbal smack down."

"Does she want you to go home?"

"Surprisingly, no." Her gaze darted around the room, looking at everything but him. "She wanted to know how I got into the country. Said I'd been careless."

He'd bet his stack Claudia had more to say than that.

Angie stood frozen in the middle of the room, posture stooped, staring at nothing in particular. He stepped closer and rubbed her arms before drawing her in. "At least she didn't tell you to stop investigating. That's something."

She sighed. "She told me once this is over, I'm going to be reassigned."

"To another department?"

She shook her head. "To another region. Somewhere far away from Jamaica."

"I'm sorry." He squeezed her against him.

"I hate this," she mumbled against his shoulder. "Having no control over what comes next."

"So, don't think about what's next. Think about now."

A smile flickered across her face as she tilted her head to look at him. "I like that idea."

She took his hand and tugged him toward the couch. He sank into a cushion, and she curled up beside him, her head resting in the crook of his shoulder.

But she didn't melt into him like she usually did. Something was wrong. Her body was tense, her breaths shallow.

"You sure you're okay?"

"Tired and worn out, I think."

He didn't buy it. Something Claudia said had gotten to her. She seemed guarded, distant. Distracted.

A dull ache settled beneath his ribcage. She was shutting him out. Again.

Why did this keep happening? Every time they started operating like a team, she retreated into her one-woman task force. Sneaking onto the boat. Exploring the cave. Swimming over to Golding's room without telling him. Always charging forward, keeping him half informed.

He wanted to press her, to demand the truth. But pushing would only drive her further away. The last thing he wanted was to widen the space between them.

Instead, he kept his voice low and steady. "Whatever it is, you can tell me. You know that, right?"

Her hand slid into his and squeezed. A confession of sorts. It wasn't much, but it would have to do. For now.

He'd let her be, but if there was any future for them, eventually they needed to break the pattern.

She shifted, angling herself to meet his eyes. A flash of vulnerability flickered in her gaze. "Can we forget about everything else for a little while? Pretend it's just you and me?"

How could he say no to that? He brought his hand to her cheek and brushed his thumb across her skin.

Cradling her face in his hand, he pressed his lips to hers, allowing himself to forget everything other than the pure pleasure of kissing the woman he loved. This time, he let the word wash over him. *Love.* After only eleven short days, it seemed impossible, but the realization he loved her might be more of a turn on than anything they'd done so far. He needed more, *yearned* for more. His brain knew it wasn't the time, but his body cared only about the primal need to claim her.

His gaze fell to her beautiful mouth. He kissed her again, and when he drew back, noticed something sticking out from under the couch. "Huh." He reached for it and pulled out a folder.

Angie sat up to get a better look. "This must've fallen out of Claudia's bag." She took the folder and opened it slowly, flipping through a few pages before sucking in a breath. There was a look of surprise on her face when she looked up at him. "It's information about Bear Golding and his organization."

CHAPTER 36

"You're up early." Nate's voice sounded rough, tired.

Angie was already awake when the coffee maker clicked on. She lay next to Nate's warm body until the earthy aroma beckoned her to the living room. After pouring herself a cup, she couldn't resist the file folder Claudia had dropped when she visited yesterday.

It included an address, as well as dates and times Golding and his associates entered and left the premises. Doing a quick internet search indicated the building used by the gangster had once been a rum distillery. The satellite images she found on the internet indicated a large, barn-like structure located several miles from Kingston, in the middle of nowhere and at the end of a dirt road.

The perfect place for a hideout.

She smiled. Nate looked adorable in his boxer briefs and with his ruffled hair and morning beard. The normal long-day fatigue hadn't hit her last night, and she'd become consumed with researching the information in the folder. Nate had started yawning long before her enthusiasm died down and headed to bed without her. It was more than two hours later when she'd crawled in beside him.

He glanced at the open folder. "What are your plans for the day?"

"I need to get this back to Claudia." She took a sip of coffee.

"She said she had a villa on the coast. Why don't we rent a car, make a day out of it?" Nate leaned against the counter, a hopeful glint in his eyes.

Claudia's warning played in her head. *Keep him out of this. He could get hurt.* The all-too-familiar tightness returned to her chest. Of course, she wanted to spend the day with him—she wanted to spend every day with him, but she had to keep him safe. She certainly didn't want him in harm's way when she checked out the distillery. "You know what? There are some things I need to talk to her about. I'm not sure how she'll react if you come along. It might be better for me to just go on my own."

He turned to pour himself a cup of coffee, but not before she saw his lips press into a hard line. "If that's what you think is best."

She forced a laugh. "Besides, if it's business, maybe I can get the agency to pay for the rental car."

Nate hummed with bogus indifference.

"What will you do while I'm gone?"

He shrugged and moved to the sliding glass door. "Don't know. Maybe just hang out here."

Well, shoot. He'd perfected the puppy-dog eyes thing. It was almost enough to make her forget the hideout or going to see Claudia. "You should see about renting a Jet Ski or find a snorkeling tour or something."

"Snorkeling? Maybe. Jet Ski? No way."

"Really? I thought you'd enjoy riding full speed over the waves."

"I would, but I'd rather not run into Wayne again."

Right. Wayne. The arms dealer who rented out watercraft. "I forgot about that. Sorry."

"It's fine." He waved his hand and turned back to look out the window. "I'll stay here until you get back."

Moving to his side, she grasped his hand. She didn't want to leave him. Maybe she should just call Claudia, tell her she had the file and go straight to her place to return it. But then she'd never get to see the hideout for herself. No, she'd stick to the original plan but be quick about it. No reason she couldn't do both. Drive to the distillery, check it out, then turn the file over to Claudia and return to spend the afternoon with Nate.

Satisfied with her decision, she drew in a deep breath. Should she tell him? He'd been so upset when she'd deviated from the plan to get into Golding's room. How would he react if he found out she'd gone off on her own to explore a criminal hideout? Probably not well. Besides, like Claudia said, she needed to keep him out of it.

Nate leaned against the kitchen counter and took a long sip of coffee. Man, it didn't hurt knowing she had something to come back to, someone waiting for her.

She gave him a peck on the cheek and then headed to the bedroom to shower and change. Twenty minutes later, she stood in front of the bedroom mirror trying to decide if her loose T-shirt did a good enough job concealing the gun and holster on her waistband. She twisted this way and that. It would have to do.

When she emerged from the bedroom with her purse, Nate was on the balcony. She leaned over to give him a kiss.

"I don't plan to be gone long."

He pushed himself to his feet and dragged her against him, his hand grazing her hip. Right beside her weapon.

"Any particular reason you need this to drop off a file?"

Considering she'd taken her firearm with her pretty much everywhere they went, it shouldn't be a big deal. It *wasn't* a big deal. The big deal was that she was lying to him. She gulped down the desire to confess everything. It might make her feel better, but it would make him feel worse.

"Just habit, I guess." She shrugged, feigning nonchalance.

Nate's face registered disbelief—downturned mouth, narrowed gaze, pursed lips—but he didn't say anything, simply bent to give her a kiss. "Be careful."

Emotions clogged her throat. She spoke through them. "I'll call you when I'm headed back."

After driving forty-five minutes east of Kingston, past green forests, run-down shacks, and fields of marijuana, Angie finally arrived at the distillery. Not wanting to get too close to the structure, she parked the rental car on a nearby gravel road and decided to go the rest of the way on foot.

She felt for the grip of her Sig on her belt, stuffed the car keys in her pocket, and grabbed her phone and the small flashlight she carried in her purse. *Damn.* Service was weak. Maybe if she were lucky, the hideout would have a tower. She put on sunglasses and began her trek. Staying off the road meant tramping through a knee-high pasture of weeds.

She had at least a mile to walk, and while she tried to focus on the task at hand, she couldn't stop thinking about Nate. In ways she couldn't explain and which defied logic, he made her feel safer than a handgun or rifle ever could. But Claudia was right. He wasn't one of them. She didn't know what she'd do if something happened to him. And that begged the question. What were her feelings for Nate?

Was she in love? The word had crept into her consciousness a few times now, but how could she know? She had nothing to compare it to, and it wasn't like her parents had been great role models. Stable relationships were something she'd only seen from afar, and she'd been okay with that, preferring to keep others at a distance.

Until now.

She tried to sigh away her anxiety. Her feelings for Nate were far more complicated than anything she'd felt before. One thing she knew for certain, she wasn't going to figure it out today. Still, she had to keep him safe. For both their sakes.

A thicket of bushes and trees blocked her view of the distillery. Coming up on an outbuilding, she removed her gun and unlocked the safety. Gripping it with both hands and with her trigger finger resting against the barrel, she pointed it ahead and down while side-stepping toward the small structure. She approached from the corner, then slid along the outer wall until she was adjacent to a window. Stretching her neck, she peeked inside.

Empty.

Moving past the window, she peered around the other corner of the building. From here, she got a clear view of the distillery.

Other than a couple of smokestacks and an inclined conveyor, it looked like a run-down barn.

No sign of life.

She pulled out her phone and snapped a picture.

She wanted to go closer but hesitated. No one knew where she was. The dirt road and driveway showed no signs of tire tracks. No indication anyone had been here anytime recently. Could Claudia's intel have been wrong?

Only one way to find out.

She took a deep breath and ran across the open yard to the building.

—ele—

Nate flipped off the television for the third time. He'd watched some classic comedies, part of a Hitchcock movie and the second quarter of a football game. He'd even walked to the bar and ordered a beer—just for something to do.

His piddling around led him to one inescapable conclusion. He was bored. And he missed Angie.

Turned out, Nate didn't know what to do with himself with her gone. He walked to the balcony and gazed over the courtyard and beach, trying to shake the idea she was going to get herself in trouble. Surely, she wouldn't have gone off to investigate that building without telling him. After everything they'd been through, he wanted to believe she wouldn't do anything rash.

But that wasn't Angie's M.O. Claudia had said something that upset her. Something she was keeping to herself. He scrubbed a hand over his face, disbelief edging into frustration.

Somehow, in such a short amount of time, he felt like he knew her better than he knew himself. He laced his fingers behind his head and paced the room. Hard to believe they'd been here only eight days. Time with Angie blurred past while somehow leaving the impression they'd been together forever.

That familiar, useless feeling started in his gut and multiplied until it seemed to pulse through his veins. He'd spent his whole life looking after his brother and sister, telling himself he was the only thing keeping them safe.

Angie wasn't like Elise or Jack. She was strong and capable in her own right. She didn't need him to protect her. Hell, he couldn't keep her out of trouble if he wanted to. Of course, Elise and Jack were never helpless either. That was a fantasy he'd constructed to give his life meaning.

Should he call home? Tell them things were okay? He'd not spoken to either sibling since Elise told him about the upcoming nuptials. Eric was a good man. He took care of Elise and treated her well. Nate needed to tell his sister he was happy for her.

She'd found something he hadn't even known he wanted. He'd treated Eric as an interloper because he hadn't understood.

Now he did.

He'd call her. Right now. Tell her he'd be home for the wedding and was bringing a guest. Knowing Elise, that would be what she'd want to talk about. Not the wedding that was happening in less than two weeks, but the new woman in her brother's life.

He picked up the phone and took a deep breath to prepare for the onslaught of nosy-sister questions.

But then the hotel phone rang. He put down his cell to answer.

"Nathan?" A strong female voice came through the line.

Hairs on the back of his neck prickled to attention. "Speaking. Who's this?"

"Darling, it's Claudia." The woman's southern drawl was warm and friendly. "Angie and I finished our business. I invited her to stay for lunch and wanted to extend the invitation to you as well."

Angie really had gone to see Claudia. A gush of air slipped from his lips, releasing the tension he held in his chest. "That's very kind of you, but you don't need to go to any trouble."

"You don't know me well enough to know this, but I never do anything just to be nice."

That sounded ominous.

"It's nothing bad. Just an opportunity I want to talk to Angie about, and I think your presence might prove persuasive."

He wasn't sure he had that much sway over Angie or why he'd have anything to say about an employment opportunity, but he liked being included. "Okay. I'll rent a car."

"Nonsense. Angie has a car. I'll send a driver to get you. Then you and she can ride back together."

"Sure. That would be great." He'd been hoping to spend the afternoon with Angie, maybe order room service, and then get in bed early. This lunch sounded like it could turn into an all-day affair.

"Excellent. Can you be in the lobby in half an hour? My driver's name is Carson. He'll meet you there."

CHAPTER 37

Angie stepped inside the distillery. Abandoned machinery, fifty-gallon drums, and trash covered the concrete floor. There had to be an office in here somewhere. Even if the intel was old and they'd abandoned this place for a new hideout, surely they'd have left something behind.

Moving further into the structure, her certainty began to wane. The place appeared to have been ransacked, probably by the brewery's employees looking to get their hands on anything valuable after the business went belly up.

Nothing in the file indicated the intel was unverified. There had to be something to it. Otherwise, why would Claudia have had it?

The beam from Angie's flashlight swept across the space, though it wasn't needed. Busted out windows located high above the ground let in natural light. An elevated balcony, probably to access the long-gone fermenters, crossed the length of the structure. There was nothing here. A total dead end. Not only had she wasted her time, but she'd lied to Nate for no good reason. She'd still take the file back to Claudia but wouldn't disclose her side trip. Not when she had nothing to show for it.

She made her way back to where she entered but stopped and craned her neck when she detected a soft rumble. The noise grew louder, nearer. Tires crunched over gravel. She pressed herself against the wall, gripped her gun and peeked around the frame of the door. The car wasn't visible from her location. Dammit. She hadn't gotten far enough into the structure to identify additional escape routes. She'd left her rental on the edge of a ditch a few hundred yards down a side street. If they were looking for uninvited guests, it wouldn't be hard to spot.

She sucked in a hard, sharp breath. How could she have been so stupid? She'd known coming here was risky and did it anyway. Not to mention, no one knew where she was. Not Claudia and not Nate. *Oh God.* Her heart clenched. She had to find another way out of here.

Voices. Male. Getting closer.

She couldn't make out the words, but it sounded like there were at least three of them. Pointing her gun at the ground, she took a quiet step to the side. Then another.

A shadow moved in front of the door. She took off, darting through a maze of broken-down machinery and ducking between tubes and pipes until she finally found a tall set of double doors at the back of the building. She pushed through one of them.

Pop.

She jumped and scanned the countryside. An open field surrounded by hills and trees. The shooter could be anywhere. *Pop.* The metal siding of the structure dinged. Crouching low, she darted to the door and retreated inside the building. She peered through a crack, hoping to spot the sniper. She didn't see anyone or anything. *Shit.* That could mean only one thing. A long-range rifle. They could be as close as a few hundred yards, or as far away as a mile.

How the hell was she going to get out of this?

She looked up. The second-floor balcony. Staying in the shadows and stepping heel-to-toe, she made as little noise as possible until she arrived at the stairs.

Voices echoed against the walls. The men were inside, and they weren't trying to be quiet. Probably because they planned to kill her.

She gripped the handrail. The metal creaked. *Shit.* That wasn't going to work. Instead of going up the stairs, she moved around the side and positioned herself underneath them.

"She's not 'ere."

She held her breath and prayed she could wait them out. Coming here had been stupid.

"Of course she's here. You heard the long gun. Fan out and search."

The stairs rattled beneath the weight of one of the men. She drew her knees up and made herself as tiny as possible, praying he'd look around the balcony level and then move on. Footsteps banged from above and then descended and crossed the room.

She mouthed a silent thank you.

The voices were back. "Waste of time. She done gone. Must've found a way out."

"Then you go tell the boss."

"That fool not the boss."

"Who cares? If things go how they supposed to, we won't be working for that maniac much longer."

Angie strained to hear. These men were talking about Golding's partner. If only they'd give away something more specific.

There was a deep chuckle. "Let's see how tough they are when the bullets start flying."

The door to the warehouse banged open, then closed.

She waited until she heard the car engine start, then moved back to the front of the warehouse. After watching the car and a cloud of dust disappear down the road, she crept back to her little sedan.

ele

The car ride took longer than Nate expected. For most of the trip, they traveled along the coast with spectacular views of the sea. Finally, Carson turned onto a palm-lined drive and pulled up to a posh estate. *Villa, my ass.* This place was a mansion.

The driver parked just past the front entrance. Nate didn't see any other cars. Nothing that looked like a rental. Where was Angie?

He climbed out of the car and approached an entryway flanked by two Doberman statues. The door stood open.

He glanced at Carson, who motioned for him to proceed. "Go on in."

The hair on the back of Nate's neck stood on end. Something about this didn't feel right.

He stepped into a marble-tiled foyer, and his eyes were immediately drawn to the guards, both dressed in black suits. Both holding short-barreled rifles. The man closest to Nate was lean and dark and had short-cropped hair. The other looked like a comic book villain—big and burly, with a mop of blond hair.

"Keep going." Carson nudged him further into the home.

The short hallway opened into a poshly decorated sitting room. Claudia stood, dressed in an expensive-looking white pantsuit, on the edge of a beige rug. In her hand, she held a tumbler filled with amber liquid.

"Welcome to my home." She spread her arms wide and motioned toward a large half-circle couch. "Please make yourself comfortable."

Nate stood in place, taking in the luxurious room, which seemed more than a little beyond the means of a civil servant. The ornate glass chandelier alone probably cost as much as his Key Largo condo.

"What can I get you to drink? I hear you're a Scotch man," she said in her smooth Southern twang.

A vortex opened in his stomach, swirling apprehension and anger into a ball. "How do you know I like scotch?"

"I have my ways." She winked, lowered herself to the sofa and crossed her legs primly. She patted the cushion. "Please sit down. Let's get to know each other."

He didn't sit. His voice was hard. "Where's Angie?"

"She'll be along soon. She had an errand to run."

Movement outside the window drew his attention. More men with guns. He turned to Claudia. "Who are you?"

"All in good time. For now, I want to get to know you, see why Angie likes you so much."

The phone rang. Claudia picked it up, looked at the display, then answered. "How'd it go?" There was a long pause. "I see." Another pause. Then a nod. "Keep an eye out."

She disconnected and took a sip of her drink. "You're not going to stand there all day, are you?" Her voice was sweet. She lifted the glass to her mouth and raised an eyebrow at one of the guards. "Sam?"

The lean man came forward. "The lady would like you to sit." His words carried the lilt of the islands.

"No, thanks. I'm good."

"Take a seat." The tone of his voice told Nate he had a choice. Sit of his own volition or Sam would do it for him.

He sat on the edge of the couch, his muscles tense, ready to spring.

"Was that so hard?" Claudia smiled again.

"What the hell is going on here? Where's Angie?"

"You sure are nice to look at," Claudia drawled. "Maybe not the sharpest knife in the drawer, but that's easy to overlook in a piece of eye candy like you."

A prickle crawled up his spine, but he resisted the urge to shudder. Whatever was happening here, he didn't like it.

The phone rang again. Claudia glanced at the display and smiled. "Sam? Desmond? Please escort Mr. Hughes to the car."

The two men came forward. Sam pointed a rifle at Nate while Desmond tightened zip ties around his wrists and shoved a rag into his mouth. The blonde giant pulled him to his feet and pushed him to the front door.

Claudia picked up the ringing phone and shot Nate a sleazy smile. "Oh look, it's Angie."

The cotton cloth in Nate's mouth soaked up his saliva and strangled his words. He tried to yell, to warn her it was a trap, but a garbled wail was all that came out.

He was a big guy, but he didn't stand a chance against these two, not with his hands tied. Even if he could fight back, they'd probably just clobber him and carry him to the car unconscious. Better to be lucid, to see where they were taking him and to know what was going on. Maybe then he could do something about it.

One thing was clear. Claudia Carter had chosen her side—and it wasn't theirs.

CHAPTER 38

A ngie yanked open the car door and fumbled with her phone. *Slow down*. She took a deep breath and closed her eyes.

The guys from the distillery hadn't followed her, but that didn't make her feel any better. Because if they weren't looking for her, where did they go? And who shot at her? Where the bullet hit was several feet to her right. Had they missed on purpose? The further away the shooter, the greater chance they'd miss, but any sniper worth his salt wouldn't have been that far off. Was it a warning? Meant to drive her back inside the distillery?

She should have taken the folder back to Claudia and been done with it. Considering what just happened, now she needed to confess her stupidity to her superior. Claudia would probably give her hell for it. And she'd deserve it.

Her heart beat like a blown speaker—hard, loud, and rough. She placed one hand on her chest, hoping to corral the out-of-control organ and scrolled through her contacts with the other. She called the number Claudia had given her.

"Hello?" The sound of Claudia's Mississippi twang calmed her almost immediately.

Angie steadied her voice. "It's me."

An audible sigh resonated through the line. "Thank God. I've been trying to get ahold of you."

She had? There'd been no missed calls, but also no signal in the middle of nowhere.

"What's happened?" Angie couldn't keep the alarm from her voice.

"I think Golding has Nate."

"What?" Angie's knuckles turned white gripping the steering wheel. It didn't make any sense, especially considering Golding hoped to use Nate for an introduction to his grandfather. She shook her head as if that would ward off the significance of what Claudia had just said. "You're wrong. Nate's at the hotel." But so was Bear Golding. "He said he wasn't going anywhere."

"Oh, sweetie. I'm sorry, but I'm not wrong. I didn't tell you, but I stationed a lookout in the hotel lobby as a precaution. He checked in about an hour ago to tell me Golding had entered the hotel. He called back later and reported seeing Golding and Nate leaving."

Like the sun going behind a cloud, Angie's vision darkened. This couldn't be right. Nate wouldn't leave with the crime lord. He knew better than that. Unless the mobster figured out who he was—and who his father was. "He must've been under duress."

Once again, this was her fault. Golding wanted a partnership with the Koslovs and thought Nate was his ticket in.

She slammed the heel of her hand against the steering wheel. "We have to get him away from that monster."

There was a moment of silence. "My lookout also reported seeing you leave in a rental car this morning. Were you going to tell me what that was about?"

Angie wanted to scream. None of that mattered if Bear Golding had Nate. She tried to keep her voice low. She wanted to convey calmness. Hysteria wouldn't do her any favors.

"A folder fell out of your bag when you were in our room yesterday. It had information about a hideout. I planned to return the folder, but not until I had a chance to investigate the location for myself."

There was another long pause. Somehow, Claudia's disapproval reached through the phone. "And?"

"And what?"

"What else happened?"

"The place looked abandoned, but then a car pulled up and men got out—I think there were three. I tried to escape, but someone shot at me so I hid. They gave up before they found me."

"Did they say anything of interest?"

"No, not really. Mostly they were arguing over who was going to tell the boss they lost me." She chewed on her lip.

Claudia's response was sharp. "Your behavior was stupid, but we'll talk about that later. Right now, we need to find Nate."

"What do you want me to do?"

"Take the highway east along the coast. A few miles past the last gas station, there's a turnout on the right. Look for the scenic overlook sign. Pull in and wait for me to get there."

The scent of the warehouse assaulted Nate. The smell of iron mixed with bleach made him wince. Rows of meat hooks and dark stains on the floor told him exactly what this place had been. Maybe still was.

He grimaced. How fitting.

One of Claudia's goons pushed him into the space while the other held his rifle nestled against his shoulder, the barrel pointed at Nate. Thug number one—the blonde Cro-Magnon—raised Nate's arms and slipped the zip tie binding his wrists around a giant meat hook. Nate's arms stretched toward the hook, and his heels lifted off the ground. There'd be no lifting his hands high enough to detach himself from the hanger. No using the sharp end to saw through the zip ties either.

When the goons moved, he was staring at Wayne. Also hung on a hook and gagged, but the other man had been battered. Dried blood dripped from his nose. His face and neck were covered with blotchy purple welts, and one of his eyes was swollen shut. Though only half conscious, Wayne stretched his toes, trying to find purchase on the ground.

Claudia strolled into the room, ignored Wayne, and stared at Nate. "Don't worry, my dear. You won't be stuck like that for long. Assuming Angie comes through and does what I want." She studied her manicure. "Dammit, Carson. I chipped a nail on the door handle. From now on, you will open my door."

"Yes, ma'am." The chauffeur nodded.

A door creaked, then slammed shut.

A deep, accented male voice boomed from behind. Nate twisted, trying to see.

"I come like yuh call. Wah yuh want?"

"Darling," Claudia cooed. "I'm so glad you could make it. You are the face of our enterprise, are you not?"

Nate heard a bitter snort, followed by a thick Jamaican accent. "Wah gwaan?"

"Come in and meet our guests." Even in the low light, Claudia's eyes shone.

A man stepped in front of Nate. Bear Golding. If Nate's hands hadn't been extended above his head, his shoulders would have sagged. Claudia was Golding's backer. If only they'd figured that out sooner.

Golding let out a growl as his gaze landed on Nate before shooting over to Wayne. The drug lord's face went from bored and unimpressed to confused and concerned in less than a second. His mouth dropped open, and he turned to gape at Claudia. "What the hell is this?"

"Teddy—" She used Golding's given name, presumably to mark him as her subordinate. "Meet Nate."

"A Koslov?" Golding rubbed his hand against the back of his head and growled.

"So, you know?" She eyed him suspiciously. "Did you know he's not the first person from the Koslov network I've introduced you to?"

"Come again?"

"His father. Rick Hughes." She watched him pointedly, as though waiting for the pieces to click into place.

Golding's eyes widened. "The pilot?"

"Yup." In a perverse display, the woman sauntered toward Wayne, using her high heels to accentuate the movement of her hips. She appeared completely at ease, her body relaxed as she placed a hand on Wayne's back. "The pilot that this idiot brought to the stash house."

Wayne's good eye was the size of one of the buoy markers lining the swim area at the resort.

"That pilot worked for the DEA. Then one of my overeager officers recruited him to gather intel on organized crime in the Caribbean."

Angie. The overeager officer was Angie. Is that what this was about? He wanted to yell at this asshole, but all that came out was a series of muffled grunts. He twisted and shook his hook.

"Calm down, cowboy." Claudia's mouth twisted into an amused smirk. "I let it go for a while, figuring where was the harm? I had direct access to all the information he shared with his handler, and I controlled whether the intel was used, filed away, or discarded."

Golding stood with a growl. "Yuh let somebody working for U.S. intelligence into my organization?"

Claudia waved her hand dismissively. "I had it under control until this one—" She pointed at Wayne. "Brought the pilot to the stash house on a day I happened to be there. And do you know what?" Her voice turned cold, angry. "He saw me."

"So, yuh orchestrated his death and never told me 'bout any of it?" Golding looked like he wanted to punch Claudia in the head. "And now yuh taken another person connected to the Koslovs? Yuh have a death wish?"

"Do I strike you as someone with a death wish? No, my life is way too good for that." She threw back her head to laugh but then pointed at Nate. "Don't worry. I have no plans to hurt this one."

The words *hurt this one* hit Nate like a punch to the gut. Claudia killed his dad. Had she gotten Doc to do it? His body braced as though preparing for a blow.

"He's only here to entice our friend into doing what I want. I have plans for her."

A chill crept beneath Nate's skin.

"I didn't sign on for this." Golding looked at Nate again, head shaking. "You're gonna get us killed."

Claudia tilted her chin and tapped a finger against her lips. "Well, probably not me. No one knows I'm involved in any of this."

Golding shook his head, turned away from the devious woman and moved to leave. "I want no part of whatever this is."

"I own you, Teddy." Her tone dripped with a sweetness that exposed the true meaning of her words. "Surely you haven't forgotten that?"

The man froze in place, then turned slowly. The cool-as-a-cucumber facade had lifted. His face contorted, his top lip curling up and his nostrils flaring. "Without me, yuh nothing. Do yuh understand that?"

One corner of Claudia's mouth kicked into a sneer. She lifted a gun Nate hadn't realized she had and pointed it at Wayne.

Bang!

The blast was loud and percussive, and a sharp, high-pitched whistle in Nate's ears made him wince. He opened his eyes and found himself staring at an unmoving Wayne, rag hanging from his open mouth, chin tilted down, a huge red stain coating his shirt.

"What the fuck?" Golding roared and rushed forward. Sam and Desmond moved quickly to wrench the big man's arms behind his back.

Through it all, Claudia's expression remained impassive. This woman was a fucking psycho. "A little reminder that just as I've given you wealth, prestige, and influence, I can also take those things away."

Golding shook the guards free. Hand over his mouth, he stalked away from Claudia, then lowered himself to sit atop a wooden crate. When he spoke, his voice contained a strange mix of reverence and disbelief. "Yuh outta control."

"Nothing like a drug lord getting a sudden bout of right-eousness." She tilted her head and looked down her nose at her partner in crime. "Personally, I've never seen the point."

"That's because you're a cold-hearted bitch."

"Really?" She smirked at him. "Is that all you've got? A de-meaning slur about my gender? And I thought so much better of you."

"At least my heart's not black like yours."

Claudia waved her hand dismissively. "I acknowledge your principled stand, but we both know you're going to do what I say." She spun on her stilettos as if daring him to prove her wrong. "Stay with him while I get his girlfriend."

The woman moved toward the door, waving for her guards to follow. "Desmond, watch the door. Sam, check the perimeter."

A few seconds later, the heavy metal door clanged. Nate twisted his body to get a look at Golding. The gangster had the posture of someone beaten down, the expression of a man defeated. He gave Nate a long, commiserating look. It was impossible to tear his gaze from Golding's dark, expressive eyes. Besides, he had no desire to stare at Wayne.

Golding shook his head in disbelief. "Whoever said women were the lesser sex never met that old witch. She'll cut yuh head off and gripe when yuh bleed on her shoes."

The words sunk in and Nate went to war to free himself, desperately sawing the zip tie against the metal hook. He had to get out of here. Angie was in danger, and she didn't even know it.

CHAPTER 39

Angie pulled off the highway and parked in a spot over-looking the bay. Claudia hadn't arrived yet. Unfortunately, the last thing she wanted was to be left alone with her thoughts. Nate had said it himself. His connection to Aleksander Koslov made him untouchable—to a point. Surely even Bear Golding wouldn't be crazy enough to harm one of Koslov's grandsons. That would be suicide.

She tapped her finger against the steering wheel. She should never have left Nate by himself. She'd worked with the Caribbean team for three years now, but everything had gone to hell once she'd been told to focus on Jamaica. First Rick. Now Nate.

A large tree obstructed her view of the sea. It didn't matter. She saw nothing anyway. Her brain was too focused on the man she loved and the likelihood he'd get hurt.

Please let him be okay.

Gravel crunched under tires. A dark sedan pulled up next to her. Claudia rolled down her window. "Get in."

Angie cut the engine, clipped her firearm onto her belt, jogged around the back of her rental, and practically flung her-self into Claudia's car.

The woman's face was grim, her mouth pressed into a thin slash.

She'd fucked up. Again.

But right now, disappointing Claudia was barely a blip on Angie's radar. There was only one thing that mattered. She needed confirmation that Nate was okay. "Do you know where Golding would have taken him?"

"I may have an idea." She didn't look at Angie as she turned onto the coastal highway.

Angie imagined the long, slow beep of her career flatlining. She'd forever be known as the idiot who elicited help from an unarmed civilian and then allowed him to get kidnapped by a crime lord. No one would ever want to work with her again. If she didn't lose her job completely, she'd probably be relegated to some bureaucratic division filled with wonks and drones. Her days as an analyst were over.

They drove along the seashore for several minutes. Angie fingered the file folder in her hand. "I'm sorry about not bringing this straight back to you."

"I didn't think you would."

Prickles, not unlike the sensation of watching a creepy horror movie, rippled up the back of her neck. "What do you mean?"

"I left the folder there to find out how you'd react." Claudia flashed a Cheshire Cat smile. "You did precisely what I thought you'd do."

Angie's mouth popped open. "It was a test?" She sank into her seat.

"Don't give me that look. Of course, it was a test. I needed to see what you would do with illicit intel." Claudia looked over the top of her sunglasses. "You did exactly what I would have done."

Angie's mind spun. The folder. The hideout. The sniper. "I don't understand. Why would you do that?"

"Isn't it obvious? I want you to join me. I've been looking for a partner."

Angie shook her head. This conversation made no sense. "You're a department head. You don't have partners."

"Don't be naïve. Think about it."

Angie's mind went blank.

"The CIA gives us access to information, but upward mobility is limited." Claudia huffed with the indignation of someone on the receiving end of a grave injustice. "Aren't you tired of working twice as hard as every man in the department? Of watching idiots get promoted because they drink the right type of whiskey or use the same escort service?"

Angie clasped her hands to still the tremble. She stared at the woman in the driver's seat—a woman whose career she'd wanted to emulate. "What are you saying?"

"Oh, come on, Angie. Aren't you sick of seeing intellectually inferior men climb the ranks? Receive awards and commendations they don't deserve? Based on the work of their subordinates, many of whom are women?"

She shook her head slowly. "I don't feel that way."

"Open your eyes. We're better than them. Smarter than them. But we're limited because of our gender. If we're tough, we're a bitch. If we're demure, we get steamrolled."

Angie couldn't bring herself to look at the career intelligence official in the driver's seat. She understood where Claudia was coming from and Angie agreed that a lot of men tended to put their female coworkers into one of two categories, but her mind couldn't wrap around Claudia's words. Angie didn't want to believe that this person she'd admired would behave this way.

"I, for one, am sick of it." Claudia gave her a sideways look. "I thought you were too."

Angie struggled to find words. To process what Claudia had just told her. "I know what you're saying, and I'm sure it's true in some instances, but I don't see it as a general rule. The CIA has already had a female director."

The other woman scoffed. "Political expediency."

How could she have been so wrong about this person? About everything?

"So, what are you doing about it?" Angie almost didn't want to know the answer, but she had to ask.

"I'm building the biggest criminal network in the Western Hemisphere." Pride filled Claudia's voice. "Bigger and more organized than the Colombian drug cartels of the 1980s."

She couldn't be serious. This woman had dedicated her life to protecting American interests and helping other countries root out crime. And now to learn she's the head of a drug syndicate?

The truth hit her hard, knocking a gasp from her lips. "You gave Golding those documents."

"Found those, did you?" Claudia cackled. "What'd you do? Sneak into his room during the conference?"

When Angie didn't respond, Claudia reached out and gave her shoulder a playful push. "That's exactly what I would have done. Told you—we're two of a kind."

Angie's heart pummeled against her chest like a fist hitting a punching bag. She was nothing like this woman.

"At the distillery, someone shot at me." Angie's voice rose as understanding dawned. "You ordered that?"

"Relax. You were never in danger. I needed you inside so my men could grab you." Her eyes clouded. Her voice was tight and bitter. "Lot of good that did."

"Fitzroy? Andrew Morgan? Did you have them killed?"

Claudia's tone was cold and menacing. "Your police officer friend should have known better than to go poking into things that didn't concern him. But also, I needed to make sure you understood the stakes."

"You killed him to teach me a lesson?" Nausea climbed up Angie's throat. "He was a good man."

Claudia didn't even flinch. "As for Morgan? Well, his sin was far greater. He had the nerve to get into my financial accounts." She glanced at Angie, eyebrow raised. "Where do you think he got that idea, hmm?"

Angie's breath hitched. "How'd you find out it was him?"

"When his forensics person connected to my account, I got pinged with his IP address. From there, it was a simple matter of following breadcrumbs."

Angie's breath caught in her throat. "How could you? You work for the CIA."

"That's the beauty of it all." A smile spread across Claudia's face. "Greatest intelligence agency in the world and they don't even know what's going on right under their nose."

Claudia turned off the highway. They bumped along a narrow road until they arrived at an old warehouse mostly obscured by overgrown vegetation.

A lot of what she said made sense in a demented sort of way. But one thing didn't. "Why Nate? What's he got to do with this? Do you plan to use him as leverage to gain his grandfather's cooperation?"

Claudia had the self-satisfied look of a Bond villain. "Go inside. Follow the hallway until it opens into a large room. I think you'll find your lover there."

Angie got out of the car and lifted her handbag to her shoulder. She couldn't get to Nate fast enough. She had to know he was okay, but didn't want Claudia to see how flustered she was. She squeezed that bag to her side in a way that allowed her hand to graze the grip of her Sig Sauer. Thank God she had a gun. The last thing she wanted to do was go inside unarmed.

She started for the door, but Claudia stepped around the back of the car and intercepted her. She held out her hand. "Leave the bag. And the firearm."

Spoke too soon. Angie stared for a moment, considering the most likely outcome of shoving the bag at Claudia and drawing her weapon. She'd already put Nate in danger. She wouldn't make this any worse for him. She handed the bag to her megalomaniac boss, then unclipped the holster from her waistband and laid it in Claudia's palm.

"Don't worry. You're perfectly safe."

Somehow, she didn't believe that. Angie stepped toward the door of the warehouse, but Claudia's next words nearly stopped her in her tracks.

"Assuming you choose correctly."

CHAPTER 40

Golding stared at Wayne's body for several minutes, then let out a loud sigh before removing a small knife from his pants pocket that he used to clean the underside of his fingernails. At the moment, it was hard for Nate to see anything other than a frustrated man looking for a way out. Maybe he'd listen to reason, consider striking a deal. Until the other night, he'd never used the Koslov name for anything. Maybe it was time for that to change.

Nate attempted to speak, but all that came out was, "Gm-mmph."

The mobster rose, stalked forward, and tugged the gag from Nate's mouth.

An immediate sense of relief overcame him. He moved his jaw up and down. Though sore, he couldn't hide his elation that the pressure of the rag forcing his mouth open was gone. He could finally breathe freely. "Thank you."

Golding waved and returned to his perch atop the crate.

"Do you think Claudia knows about our meeting the other night?"

Golding didn't look up from his switchblade manicure. "No, mon. Not that I know of. The casino and the resort are my territory. Even Claudia knows that."

Despite every effort to avoid looking at the body on the hook, Nate's gaze slid to Wayne. The man had seemed devoted to Golding. Had Claudia tortured him? The thought made him cringe.

Claudia was a monster. "Why do you work for her?"

This time, when the man looked up, his eyes were blazing. "I work *with* her, not *for* her." His features contorted, curling his upper lip and baring his teeth.

That apparently hit a nerve. How much further should Nate push it? "It seemed like she was telling you what to do. Does she have something on you?"

Two long strides, and Golding was standing in front of Nate, pointing a knife at his face. The other man's fist clenched around the handle. His hand shook with pent-up frustration. He folded up the knife and crammed it into his pocket.

Nate considered Golding's body language. This was a man desperate to get out of a bad situation. "Maybe you and I can help each other."

Hands on hips, Golding paced away, then back. "What yuh got in mind?"

"For starters, I could get you a conversation with my grandfather."

"Bah." He turned away. "I made my deal with the devil already."

"He's a powerful man. Help me, and I'm sure he'll help you in any way he can."

"Even he's not powerful enough to get me out of this mess. Yuh think I don't know she plans to kill me once she gets what she wants?" Golding returned to his perch on the crate. "If I'm going to get out of this, I'm going to have to do it on my own."

"How do you plan to do that?"

"With an army."

The guns. Golding was amassing weapons for a war with Claudia. "The weapons in the cave."

Golding's head snapped up, and Nate realized he'd spoken aloud.

"You know about that?" The mobster's voice had a hard edge.

Nate nodded and followed Golding's gaze to the body on the hook.

"I thought Wayne had more discretion than that."

"It wasn't Wayne. It was the guys on the boat."

Golding gave a slow nod.

Silence hung between them, dense and full, like the room holding its breath.

Nate had experienced enough sadness for a lifetime and thought the quiet might suffocate him. "Did you know my father?"

"The pilot? Yeah, mon."

"So, you know his plane crashed into the ocean. We came to Jamaica because we thought it was sabotaged."

Golding let out a light, steady exhale.

Studying the big man, Nate recalled what his dad had said to Doc. *Trust is a currency you have to spend wisely.* Dad had seen

Claudia at the stash house, and she killed him to keep him quiet. "You were our main suspect."

"I had no problems with your father. Didn't know 'e worked for the Feds until today." He gave an apologetic shrug. "Didn't know he was a Koslov either."

"He wasn't. It's my mother who's a Koslov." Nate shook his head, then thought better of his answer. "Though as far as my grandfather is concerned, that's pretty much the same thing."

Golding stood and paced with his hands on his waist while staring at the ceiling.

"Claudia come to me a few years ago to suggest an alliance. She wanted access to my organization. having a fed on my side seemed like a good business decision, but something 'bout the woman give me a bad vibe. I tell her no, not interested."

That obviously wasn't where the story ended. Nate waited for the other man to continue.

"She acted gracious at first, but then she reached out for another meeting. I couldn't say no. That was when she said I didn't understand what was at stake and suggested I reconsider playing games with her. Then she mentioned my mom. Asked if I wanted 'er to suffer."

Nate swallowed. His mouth, leeched of moisture from the gag, was suddenly wet with saliva. Golding hadn't wanted to work with Claudia. He'd been protecting a family member. A sentiment Nate could relate to all too well.

"I get it," he said seriously. "You didn't have a choice—"

The door clanged. Golding turned to Nate. "That'll be your girl."

Nate's stomach turned. Though desperate to see Angie and know she was okay, this wouldn't be a typical reunion. Claudia had a plan.

Nate listened for her voice, but the silence seemed to echo off the slaughterhouse walls. He closed his eyes and inhaled. *It'll be okay.* He didn't truly believe it but needed something to hold on to. He opened his eyes.

Angie took a hesitant step into the room. Her gaze went from Nate's face to where his hands were fettered above his head. Her eyes widened in alarm. "Are you hurt?"

He bit back the sarcastic comment that hovered on the tip of his tongue. "I've been better." He nodded his chin toward Wayne. "Could be worse."

Angie spun in the direction Nate indicated, gasping when she saw Wayne's body.

She turned to Golding, but not before Nate saw her lip curl into a sneer. "Get him down from there."

Golding stared back at her. "I don't take orders from you."

"But you do take orders from me." Claudia's voice boomed from the back of the room.

The man regarded her coolly, a vein in his neck pulsing an angry rhythm, but his face remained impassive, no doubt trying to hide his true feelings for the woman he'd taken on as a business partner.

Nate knew the truth. Any man could recognize that look on another man. It was the look of someone who'd been pushed to the edge and was going to fight with everything he had to keep from going over.

"I don't know why you even bother, Teddy. We both know in a pissing match which one of us would win." Claudia turned to Angie, as if expecting to find an ally. "He was barely holding his business together when I came along and bailed him out."

Golding got to his feet, his stance like a football player. "My business did just fine until yuh come along and muck it up."

"You're so dramatic." Claudia's Southern accent made her words sound incredibly condescending. "Now, let's get back to the matter at hand."

She turned to Angie. "Are you going to join me, or would you rather watch Nate die?"

_____ell_____

Angie gaped at the other woman. "Neither."

"Oh, come now. We can skip the theatrics. I'm offering you everything you could ever want. Money. Power." She gestured toward Nate. "That tight little ass."

Angie watched Claudia stalking through the dirty warehouse in her white pantsuit and perfectly styled hair. Something was very wrong with this woman.

"You can even keep your job at the agency. I did."

None of this made any sense. "Why are you doing this?"

Claudia exhaled dramatically. "I thought we covered this in the car." She strode toward Angie. "Men are the problem." She enunciated every word. "They work half as hard and get paid twice as much. Promotions, gold watches, country club memberships. You name it, it's theirs.

"The mansplaining, the undeserved kudos, the corner office. I'm sick of it." Her voice grew louder. She motioned toward Golding. "Their peanut-sized brains can't even comprehend that a woman might be better or smarter than them. The idea that they are at our mercy is incomprehensible to their caveman mentality."

"What happened to you?" Angie's voice came out barely louder than a whisper. She didn't think there was a woman alive who hadn't been demeaned or patronized by a man, but this level of righteous anger was psychotic.

The department chief ignored Angie's question and turned to Nate. "I'm pretty sure Mr. Hughes here would prefer for you to hurry up and make a decision."

Angie let out a slow, controlled sigh. When she spoke, her voice was sharp. "What exactly am I making a decision on?"

"I want you to be my second in command, my underboss, my consigliere."

She's a crime lord. Hearing Claudia list off roles in a mafia family certainly put things into perspective. Angie rubbed her forehead, then looked at Nate. Stretched out and pulled onto his toes, he shuffled his feet back and tried to adjust his weight distribution. She needed to get him out of here. Soon.

"Untie him. Then we'll talk."

Claudia looked at Nate, then at Golding. She nodded toward the prisoner. Her do-boy hopped up and sliced through the zip ties. The sudden release sent Nate to his knees. Angie ran to his side and helped him to his feet.

She spoke quietly, as if Claudia overhearing their conversation even mattered. "I'm so sorry. I never should have involved you."

He gave her a tired smile. "We can talk about all that later."

God, she hoped he was right.

"So, Angie, what's the answer?"

Geez, she was really pushing this. "Why me?" This was the question she'd been asking ever since Claudia had shown up at their hotel room.

"You're smart. You're determined. You don't get the credit you deserve."

Sure, there'd been times Angie felt she'd had to work harder than some of her colleagues, but she'd never held it against anyone. She'd certainly never resented them.

"I dedicated my life to the agency, and then one day I realized. No matter what I did, men would always have more opportunities. All those men who were given positions that should have been mine? I finally decided to do something about it. To show them I'm more powerful than all of them put together."

"We're supposed to protect people and make the world a better place."

Claudia's eyes glazed over. "I could have been so much more. Working for the government stifled me, held me down."

"But you're transporting weapons and drugs. That doesn't make you better."

"That's where you're wrong. Soon, I'll be the head of the largest criminal syndicate in the Western world. Do you know how long it took me to achieve that distinction?" She held up her fingers. "Three years. Three years to achieve all of this."

"That doesn't make you a hero."

"Maybe not." Her lips twitched into a smile. "But it does make me a queen."

"You're bat-shit crazy." The words left Angie's mouth before she had time to reconsider.

Claudia stilled. Her lips pressed into a thin line, and Angie no longer saw the strong and confident Southern belle. The woman's face flushed a dark red. Her nostrils flared. Her lip curled into a sneer.

She stepped toward Angie, slowly and deliberately. With each of Claudia's steps forward, Angie took a step back.

"I am not crazy." Her voice ended in a shrill crescendo. She unbuttoned her jacket, revealing a holster on her hip. She reached down, unfastened the thumb snap, and laid her hand on the grip of her gun. "Say it again."

Angie shook her head. This was it. She was going to die. Nate too. Claudia and Golding would continue with their schemes, while Claudia duped the CIA into thinking she was one of them.

After her sister's death, Angie had wished many times she'd been the one who'd been taken. Now, as she faced the last moments of her life, she realized she didn't want to die and never had. She closed her eyes. Mom and Dad. Cindy. Her graduation from the Academy. Riding her motorcycle on the Blue Ridge Parkway when the leaves were changing.

Nate.

God. Not even two full weeks yet. Such a short time, and so many memories. She should thank him. The days she spent with him were the best days of her life.

Pht.

The sound of a suppressed firearm.

She hadn't been hit. Unlikely Claudia would miss from this distance. She opened her eyes. Claudia stood before her, gun dangling at her side, while she stared at her other blood-drenched hand, her mouth forming a perfect *O*. If it weren't for the plume of red spreading across Claudia's torso, Angie would find the look comical.

Claudia looked from her hand to Angie, then fell to her knees and finally prone on the ground. Standing behind her, Bear Golding held a gun, its long barrel still smoking. Angie bent to feel her pulse. Nothing.

"Are you okay?" Nate stepped closer.

She nodded. "Are you?"

"Think so."

Bear Golding ejected the magazine and racked the slide to empty the chamber. He shoved the gun into the back of his pants. He tipped his chin at Nate. "Now we're both free."

Instinctively, Angie moved between Nate and the door. Protecting him was still her number one priority. "Claudia's guys will still be outside. What do we do about them?"

"Don't worry about it," Golding said. "They were my men before they were hers. Even her loyal followers will know they're outnumbered."

Angie recalled the guys at the distillery talking about the boss who wasn't really the boss, and she guessed Golding was right. She turned to the man who'd just saved her life. And Nate's. "Thank you."

The drug lord gave a terse nod, then turned, locking eyes with Nate. Something Angie didn't understand transpired between them. "We square?"

"You held up your end." Nate tipped his chin in a bizarre moment of male bonding.

The big man nodded to his men, who followed him out the door.

Angie was speechless. "What was that about?"

"Golding and I had a chance to talk while you were with Claudia. Turns out he's been looking for a way out of the arrangement they made."

She could believe that. "And?"

"I said I'd put in a word with Papi if he helped me out." He held up his hand before she could object. "He knows there's no guarantee."

A heavy silence fell between them, the gravity of what might have happened weighing down the moment. And then suddenly, she couldn't stand to be away from him a moment longer. She needed to touch him, to feel that he was real.

She ran into his waiting arms. He squeezed her hard and laid his cheek against the top of her head.

"Thank God. I was so worried." His words ruffled her hair. "You mean so much to me, I don't know what I'd do without you."

Angie looked up at him and said the three words she hadn't said since she was a girl. "I love you, Nate."

His grip on her tightened. And then his lips were on hers. He pulled away and spoke against her mouth. "I love you too."

CHAPTER 41

The next day, Nate sat next to Angie in the hotel lobby, awaiting the arrival of her supervisor. It hadn't even been twenty-four hours, but it felt like a lifetime had passed since Claudia set her plan in motion.

"How are you doing?" Angie watched him with concern in her eyes.

He gathered her in for a hug, hoping to ease the worry he saw in her gaze. "Stop worrying. I'm fine."

He'd seen a person die yesterday—two people, actually. And another a few days before that. Wayne and Fitzroy's deaths replayed in slow motion every time he closed his eyes. Claudia's death was there too, but despite watching the life leave her eyes, the anguish didn't come. The real trauma was seeing Claudia draw her firearm and point it at Angie.

The way Angie had held her breath, closed her eyes and squared her shoulders—prepared to die. *That* was the image he couldn't shake, the memory he suspected would haunt him for years to come.

Angie had been throwing him concerned glances since the police cruiser had returned them to the hotel yesterday evening. She'd tried to get him to open up about his feelings, but he wasn't ready. Maybe later, when they were back in the States, but right now, talking about it would mean having to acknowledge how close he'd come to losing her.

A thought he couldn't bear. Not after everything they'd shared. No, she was a part of him, for now and forever.

Maybe he was still in shock. Maybe later he would need to find a professional to talk to about what had happened. For now, he just wanted to be thankful they'd come out of it unscathed. They were alive.

He glanced over and squeezed her hand as if to confirm she was really there. The smile she gave in return wrapped around and embraced him like a hug. God, he loved this woman. So strong, so capable.

In an unhinged sort of way, he understood why Claudia wanted to recruit Angie. The woman had been depraved and contemptible, but she hadn't been stupid. Angie was good at what she did. She would be an asset to any team she joined.

What Claudia hadn't understood was that Angie was also honorable. She wasn't a traitor willing to sell out her country for wealth and power.

Things had moved quickly after Golding and his men fled the scene. When rescue arrived, they pronounced Claudia dead. When the police got there, Angie and Nate were questioned.

Given Golding's influence, he'd never be charged. Nate was okay with that. The man might be a criminal, but he'd saved their lives. Certainly Angie's. Most likely Nate's too.

In some ways, Golding was another of Claudia's victims, a pawn in her quest for world domination. Nate shook his head in disbelief. They'd met a real-life villain and lived to talk about it.

Some of Claudia's men were detained trying to leave the country. One of them had been a sniper in the Jamaica Defence Force. He was being held for questioning in connection with Fitzroy's death and the shots fired at the distillery. They still didn't know who had killed his dad.

A warm hand landed on Nate's leg and squeezed. "He's here." Angie sprang to her feet, then bounded to the front entrance where a tall, thin man had just stepped inside the lobby. Over his shoulder, he carried a leather duffel bag. He set it on the ground and curled Angie into him.

She'd spent much of last evening talking excitedly on the phone with Gary and had been practically giddy when she learned he planned to meet her in Jamaica. Though she'd given Nate no reason to think there had ever been anything between the two colleagues other than friendship, he couldn't help but feel unease surrounding the other man's arrival.

There was so much about Angie's life he didn't know. Gary was just one more uncertainty knotting into his gut. He pushed himself to his feet and made his way to their reunion.

Gary removed his sunglasses as Nate approached, but didn't take his arm from Angie's shoulder. He hung his glasses on the pocket of his sports coat and offered Nate his hand. "Well, this must be the man of the hour. It's a pleasure." His grip was firm, his accent thick and syrupy like Texas barbecue sauce.

"Great to meet you." Nate used the handshake as an opportunity to size the other man up. His brown hair was stylishly pushed back and away from his face. The tufts above his ears sported a fair amount of gray.

Angie appeared ready to burst. "I can't believe I get to have my two favorite men together."

Gary responded with a squeeze, and then finally released her to return to Nate's side. "Let me get checked in. Maybe then the three of us can get some lunch."

A groan crawled up Nate's throat. The last thing he wanted to do was spend time with this yahoo, but Angie clearly thought a lot of the man, so he might as well fall in line. Watching her fawn over another guy wouldn't be easy, but he needed to remember she didn't belong to him. He was going to need to learn to share.

"Ange, you want to hang with me for a few minutes while I get my room? We can get the shop talk out of the way, and we won't bore Nate senseless while we eat."

With that smooth Texas drawl, Nate imagined the man could talk almost anyone into doing anything. He started to protest, then thought better of it. Jealousy was his problem, not Angie's. "I'll get us a table in the dining room."

Angie led Gary to the reception desk, inhaling the familiar scent of his musky cologne. As soon as Nate was out of earshot, he flashed an amused grin. "He doesn't like me much."

"What makes you say that?" Angie whipped around just in time to see Nate enter the dining room.

"Call it male intuition."

"I didn't know there was such a thing." She tried to inject sarcasm into her voice but turned back to stare at the entrance to the restaurant. The last thing she needed was for Nate to get the wrong idea about her relationship with Gary.

"That man there" —Gary pointed across the lobby— "has it bad."

"What? No." She let out a shaky laugh. Had she told him she loved him? And had he said it back? Sure, but that was in the heat of the moment. Neither had said it since. "I mean, yeah, there's something there, but we haven't talked about what it means." Time to shut up. She scratched the back of her head and looked away.

Gary chuckled. "Clearly, he's not the only one."

She opened her mouth, realized she had nothing to say, and shut it again.

"I'm happy for you, Angie." His expression softened. He squeezed her shoulder. "You deserve to have someone in your life who knows how amazing you are."

She could do nothing but nod. Was she really that transparent? Gary had been here all of five minutes, and he'd already deduced her feelings for Nate.

Gary signed the receipt for the room and accepted his keys. "Claudia, huh? I didn't see that one coming."

Angie followed Gary to the elevator and stepped inside. "No one did. She always seemed above reproach, so dedicated to her work."

"Apparently not. We did some digging. She was passed up for promotions several times, and though she lost out to a man on each occasion, it had nothing to do with gender. Notes in the interview file stated that her references referred to her as difficult, arrogant, and inflexible. Among other things."

They got off on the fifth floor, checked the placard and headed to the left.

"Seriously? I came up hearing stories about how formidable she was, someone to be admired."

A heavy silence fell between them. Gary found his room and stepped inside. He motioned for Angie to follow. "As I'm sure you know, the insubordination is a problem. You were clearly told to disengage—several times, in fact—and still you decided to ignore direct orders."

Angie looked at her feet. She deserved Gary's scorn. And then some. "I was out of line."

He gave her a stern look. "Given the chance, would you do it again?"

What kind of question was that? So many things had happened—some of them good—that she couldn't imagine making a different choice. She opened her mouth to say as much but closed it without a word.

"I see." Gary looked down his nose at her. "The agency would be within its rights to press charges."

Wow. She'd expected to be disciplined, but she hadn't thought he'd go there. "I understand."

"Lucky for you, that's not a road I want to travel." He set his bag on the bed. "You will be suspended without pay pending an investigation, but given how you revealed Claudia's illegal activities and what that could have meant for the agency, I believe we can have things wrapped up before your leave of absence is over."

Angie stared in disbelief. Had she heard him correctly? "You're saying I'll face no consequences?"

"I said two weeks without pay, didn't I?" He stepped forward and gripped her by the shoulders. "If you hadn't come out here to investigate, we'd still have no idea what Claudia was up to. You averted what could have been a huge embarrassment."

She still couldn't believe it. She was coming out of this unscathed. And she didn't deserve it.

"Have you learned anything about who sabotaged Rick's plane?"

"Not yet. We looked into Doc, but we're confident it wasn't him. Claudia used him only to deliver information and documents. He thought it was part of a plan to set Golding up."

Well, that was something. At least Rick hadn't been betrayed by a friend.

"I've been asked to lead the department, and I've accepted. The job of Task Force Commander is yours if you want it."

The offer was generous. Especially considering how she'd gone rogue. She didn't know what to say. "That's incredible. Thank you."

"We'll have to have a discussion about following protocol, but you work harder than anyone else. You deserve it."

A promotion like this put her ahead of her career plan. It was everything she'd worked for. But things were different now. For the first time since college, she questioned whether giving her life to the agency, working her way up the ladder, and serving her country was still the life she wanted.

"I'm flattered. I don't know what to say."

"How about, 'How big is my raise?'" He laughed but must've seen something in her face that made him stop. "You're not coming back, are you?"

She fiddled with the collar of her shirt, trying to work out what she wanted to say. "Well, I thought I was, but now—" She looked up, realizing for the first time just how much everything had changed. "I'm not sure."

"Nate?"

"He's part of it. But also, I liked being in the field, investigating. If I stay in the department, I'll be a desk jockey for the rest of my career."

"You want to transfer to covert operations?"

Did she? "I don't know. This is the first I've really thought about it."

"You don't have to decide right now." Gary removed his jacket and tie and threw them on the bed. "You still have a couple more weeks of leave. Use it to relax and figure out what you want. We'll talk about it when it's over."

Gary moved to the door. "We shouldn't keep that man waiting too long. God knows what he'll do to me if he finds out you were in my hotel room."

CHAPTER 42

Most years, Christmas barely registered in Angie's life. Another glass of wine. Another takeout meal. Another day alone. But this year, she couldn't fathom a more perfect holiday. The mood was jubilant, the company irreplaceable, the setting incredible.

Scanning her surroundings, she inhaled the sweet scent of the plumeria that decorated the aisle and altar. To the west, the sun lowered to the horizon, casting the nearby pier in silhouette. Straight ahead, beyond the wedding arch, the sky reflected a raspberry glow across a smooth-as-glass ocean.

The wedding was small, with only about twelve guests in attendance, but it couldn't have been more beautiful. Elise was stunning in a tight, sleeveless white gown, while Eric had dressed in a beige suit. He'd ditched the jacket and rolled up his shirtsleeves before the ceremony, but it hardly mattered. That smile was all anyone could see. It emerged the moment Elise appeared at the end of the aisle and hadn't faltered once. Angie didn't think she'd ever seen a man more in love.

Beside her, Nate squeezed her hand, lifted it to his mouth, and pressed his lips to the back of her fingers with soft, reverent kisses. God, she loved this man. Not even a month of knowing him, and he'd already become a permanent fixture. For once, she actually had a person who was hers. A person for celebrating. A person to listen to her complain. A person for making love. In such a short time, he'd become the most important thing in her life, and she already knew without a doubt, she never wanted to be without him.

She'd been thinking about the conversation with Gary and how she'd told him she enjoyed being an investigator. The words had come out of her mouth without any thought, but she realized now she meant it, and she didn't need to work for the CIA to do that. The more time she spent with Nate, the more certain she was that staying in Florida and getting her private investigator license was what she wanted.

The officiant declared Eric and Elise "man and wife." Everyone stood, clapped, and offered hugs to the couple. Eric's mother dabbed at her eyes with a handkerchief, and when it came their turn, Nate kissed Elise on the cheek and pulled Eric in for a hug. Relinquishing responsibility for his little sister's safety hadn't been easy, but Nate finally conceded that Eric was a good man. Truthfully, Angie believed he'd known it all along.

Elise and Angie had become fast friends, and she couldn't have been more thankful for the siblings' willingness to welcome her into their lives, especially considering the role she'd played in Rick's death. She and Nate had returned from Jamaica just over a week ago. He'd been relieved to have some answers to share with his brother and sister regarding their dad.

Jack came up beside Angie. "It was a nice wedding."

"Beautiful." Angie liked Jack. When it came to the gene lottery, the Hughes siblings had all been winners. Jack had dark, wavy hair and light brown eyes. To hear Nate tell it, Jack had always had an easy charm. He liked to date and party and didn't take anything too seriously. But Angie thought there was more to him. Though he smiled and joked just like his siblings, she sensed a sadness lurking beneath Jack's affable surface.

"Eric isn't the guy I would have expected Elise to go for, but they really are perfect for each other."

Having spent a lot of time around the couple over the last several days, Angie had to agree. "They love each other very much."

"I'm glad she found someone." Jack's gaze drifted out to the sea. "And Nate too."

Angie blushed, trying to figure out what to share and how much to say, but before she got a chance, Jack's phone buzzed. His jaw ticked as he looked at the screen. "Sorry. I have to take this." He lifted the phone to his ear and moved away from the celebration.

The rest of the wedding guests made their way to the outdoor patio, where the small reception was being held. Angie and Nate stayed behind, taking their time and enjoying a moment alone. In one hand, she held her sandals. In the other, her fingers clutched Nate's.

He gave her hand a familiar squeeze. "I'm glad you were here."

She sensed he had more to say, so she didn't reply.

"Considering how we grew up, I never thought any of us would get married." Nate's voice was husky, threaded with emotion. "Although Elise always had the best chance at happiness."

There was something terribly endearing about the way Nate had made it his mission to give his youngest sibling a normal life. "She and Eric seem perfect for each other."

He nodded. "They both have pieces that are broken, but they mend each other's cracks."

"It's remarkable."

He stopped walking and turned suddenly. "I want that too. And I want it with you."

Her heart expanded, filling up with love and gratitude.

"I know your job is in Washington, and I'd never ask you to quit. I've been thinking about turning the business over to Elise and Jack." He paused, almost as if holding the words inside for fortification. "I know it's soon, Angie, but I love you, and I want to spend the rest of my life with you."

He reached into his pocket and pulled out a small jewelry box. She gasped and brought a shaky hand to her mouth. Tears spilled from her eyes, and for once she didn't try to stop them.

"Do you think you could love me for the rest of your life?" He opened the box, revealing an oval-cut diamond in a gold setting with diamond accents on the band. "I want you to be my wife. Please, say you'll marry me."

She threw her arms around his neck and kissed him. "There's nothing I want more."

Epilogue

One Month Later

The office felt smaller somehow, as though removing her presence had also drained it of significance. The bookshelf behind Angie's desk was packed into a moving box, along with her diploma, plaques, and framed commendations. She wrapped her 70.3 coffee mug in tissue paper—one of the few personal items she'd kept in the office—and placed it in the box on her desk.

She paused, her fingers resting on the edge of the cardboard flap. Hard to believe she'd worked here for over a decade and had acquired so little.

Nate stepped behind her, his arms circling her waist, his chin settling against the side of her head. "You doing okay?"

It was a question she'd been asking herself since they pulled into the parking lot an hour ago. She should feel more, shouldn't she? Sadness? Regret? Nostalgia?

But there was nothing other than certainty. She'd made the right choice. The only choice.

For years, this job had defined her. But now it was part of her past. And that was okay.

She twisted to face Nate, looping her arms around his neck and kissing him slowly. "Never better." And she meant it.

He reached past her for the bobblehead still on her desk and gave it a little shake. "You want this in tissue paper?"

"Yes, please."

He wrapped it gently and tucked it inside the box.

And that was it. Her time with the CIA—her old self—packed into two boxes. Six weeks ago, she thought a one-month leave was the end of her life. Now she was leaving for good, and it felt like her life was just beginning.

A rap on the door. Gary.

He shook Nate's hand, then turned to Angie. "Glad I caught you. Can I have a word?"

Nate lifted the boxes. "I'll put these in the car."

Gary leaned against the now-bare desk. "You sure about this? It's not too late to change your mind."

She smiled softly. "I'm not going to change my mind, but thank you for saying that."

"So...Florida?"

"Yep."

"To be a private investigator?"

"Correct."

"What will you do without bureaucratic red tape and day-long meetings?"

She laughed. "Guess I'll have to find a way to fight through it."

"You always do." His smile was warm, wistful, and sincere. "Seriously though, you'll be good at it."

Angie blushed. Even now, Gary's approval meant more than she would have guessed. "I have some coursework I need to take, and there's an exam, but I've got the experience requirement covered. I filed paperwork with the state last week to register my business. I hope to be up and running in the next few months."

"That's great, Angie. I'm happy for you." He leaned back against the desk and folded his arms. "Have you come up with a name?"

She had, and it was perfect. "Dragon Dance Investigations."

"Alliteration. Always a good choice." Gary cocked an eyebrow.

"I wanted something to remind me where I came from but also to honor my sister.

"And what will you do in the meantime?"

"Well..." She twisted the ring on her finger, a smile tugging on her lips. "I'm moving out of my apartment tomorrow. After that, we're headed to Vegas for a poker tournament and a wedding." The grin she'd been holding back broke free.

"Just the two of you and an Elvis impersonator?"

"Nate's brother and sister and his sister's husband are meeting us there." She took a deep breath. "My parents are coming too."

Gary tilted his head, his gaze assessing. "You know, I don't think I've ever heard you mention parents."

"It's been years since I've seen either of them. But it's time. And I want them to meet Nate."

"Speaking of Nate, there's something he should know. The DEA has officially exonerated Rick. His dad's name is finally clear."

She pressed a hand to her chest. "He and his siblings will be so relieved."

"I'm sorry we couldn't have gotten it done sooner."

She was, and she wasn't. If the investigations had continued as she'd wanted, she'd never have met Nate.

The man himself was suddenly at the door.

"Well, I'll let you two get on with it." Gary pushed himself off the desk and enveloped Angie in a hug. Pulling away, he leveled her with a steady stare. "Don't be a stranger." He turned to Nate. "Keep her out of trouble."

"No promises."

Gary clapped Nate on the shoulder and was gone.

Silence stretched for a beat after Gary left.

"Did he change your mind?"

She stepped forward and pressed her hands against his chest. "How could you ask that?"

He shrugged. "If you're having second thoughts, that's okay. I'll move to D.C. if that's what you want."

"I already have everything I want."

She pulled him toward her and pressed her lips against his. Just a brush, expecting him to pull away. Instead, he moaned softly, gathered her against him, and sucked her top lip into his mouth.

"Hey, you two, get a room!" The voice was light and teasing. Angie tore her lips from Nate's mouth. Henry leaned against the door frame, grinning.

"Did your girls like the candy canes?"

"Sure did. They got so much sugar I thought they might take the house down."

She chuckled, tugging Nate forward for an introduction.

"Nate, this is Henry. He's just been promoted to Task Force Commander." Henry was a perfect fit for Gary's former job. "He has two little girls who are absolutely adorable."

Henry shook Nate's hand and smiled with affection. "Oh, they're cute, but don't let that fool you. They're complete monsters." He hooked his thumb over his shoulder. "I stopped by to tell you everyone's in the break room. There's cake."

Angie squeezed Nate's hand and pulled him to the door. Maybe there were a few things she was going to miss about this place. "Come on. I want you to meet my friends."

About the author

Evie Jacobs is an award-winning author of romantic suspense who loves grumpy heroes, forced proximity, and a good sex scene. She lives in Colorado with her husband, two cats, and seven bicycles.

www.ingramcontent.com/pod-product-compliance
Lightning Source LLC
Chambersburg PA
CBHW020550120726
47903CB00001B/206